THE BEAR
AND
THE DRAGON

RISE OF A LEGEND

~~~~~~

JASON ROBERTS

Copyright © Jason Roberts 2024
This book is sold subject to the condition that it shall not, by way of
trade or otherwise, be lent, resold, hired out, or otherwise circulated
without the publisher's prior consent in any form of binding or cover other
than that in which it is published and without a similar condition including
this condition being imposed on the subsequent publisher.
The moral right of Jason Roberts has been asserted.
ISBN: 9798334030473

To my dad, who taught me 'all wot I know'!
And to my mum who had me reading from a young age and gave me a love of history and mythology.

CONTENTS

Chapter 1 1
Chapter 2 Leaving 5
Chapter 3 Rescue 13
Chapter 4 Friends 18
Chapter 5 The Bear's Claws 23
Chapter 6 Heroes 32
Chapter 7 Emrys 35
Chapter 8 Cavern 42
Chapter 9 Passage 50
Chapter 10 Clan and Kin 61
Chapter 11 Wolves of the North 67
Chapter 12 Uther 74
Chapter 13 Caught 85
Chapter 14 Razor's Edge 97
Chapter 15 Camelot 113
Chapter 16 Vengeance 132
Chapter 17 Escape and Alliances 146
Chapter 18 Pursuit 161
Chapter 19 Capture and Return 178
Chapter 20 Defeat 193
Chapter 21 Victory 204
EPILOGUE 224

ACKNOWLEDGMENTS

To my mum, who read my novel and gave great feedback, and to Mr 25% Steven A. McKay who told me to just write it. Also to the team who have helped me get this book from my head to the page, and last but by no means least, my long-suffering wife, Lisa, who just let me get on with it. A heartfelt thanks.

Chapter 1

Cambria (Wales) 350AD

Gaius Flavius Silvanus stared out at the rain from the open doorway of his quarters, watching as his breath steamed in the late autumn evening. Breathing in deeply and pulling his cloak around his shoulders he sipped from a cup of warmed wine, feeling its heat suffusing his chilled bones. 'Jupiter's eyes! I hate this country,' he muttered as he took another sip. As camp prefect, at the age of thirty-five he had been left as sole commander of this fort, ever since the legate and senior tribune had set off with the legion to join others in Gaul to quell a military uprising. 'Damn the Empire,' he said out loud, then looked about himself guiltily. He cursed the misfortune that had led him to this spot, and as he stood he gazed at the reflection staring back at him from his cup. Grey was threading its way through his once-black hair, and his muscular frame was starting to settle towards his middle. Cursing again, he slashed his wine to the sodden ground.

His mood not improving, he hunched into his cloak and strode into the rain, feeling his boots squelch in the mud. Slipping and slithering he made his evening rounds, although since the legions had left Britannia there didn't seem much point! The once glorious Roman Empire was shrivelling like a grape on the vine as bickering and in-fighting amongst power-mad generals stripped the farthest reaches of its fighting men to bolster claim and counterclaim to the title of Emperor. Britannia as a country was slipping back to barbarism, with attacks on local villages becoming more commonplace as once-serving troops took to banditry to subsidise their lack of food and pay. Discipline was harder to enforce at the fort and its surrounding area as men slipped away daily and capital punishment would only drive them off faster. Kicking out at the mud in frustration, he stopped at the base of one of the four towers marking the corners of the ramparts and started to climb.

Artos stared out at the vast forests watching the mist and rain wreath its way about the hills, when he heard the prefect approaching. Straightening up, he turned and opened the brazier, flooding the small space at the top of the tower with a burst of warmth.

'Well met, Artos,' greeted the commander as he entered the tower, and rubbing his chilled hands over the brazier he, too, surveyed the vast forest that seemed to press up against this fragile remnant of a dying past. 'A rotten night to be on guard duty, eh!'

'Mm,' Artos grunted in reply. 'We're so short of men that we all take turns now.'

Gaius looked sidelong and raised an eyebrow in query at his subordinate's reply. Artos was the decurion leading what remained of his auxiliary cavalry unit, now numbering only twenty-five men and maybe thirty horses. He was also built like a bear, which is where he got his nickname. His shaggy chestnut hair and beard surrounded a fierce countenance that frightened, Gaius admitted, even him.

'Something wrong?' he asked.

Artos turned to look at his commander. 'I'm not sure,' he replied. 'There's been a lot of tribal movement lately with rumours of invading forces from Hibernia.'

'I know,' said Gaius, pinching the bridge of his nose. 'Surely we should have heard something from our latest patrols by now.'

'They didn't return,' Artos replied. 'I think they might have decided they were better off just staying out there. Or maybe they were ambushed? The threat of imperial retribution doesn't seem to carry the same weight anymore,' he said with a bitter smile.

'You forget yourself, Decurion,' snapped Gaius, and then, after a few moments hung his head. 'But of course you are correct, my friend. Rome has abandoned us. We've heard nothing for two years.

Two years!' He beat his fist against the wet railing in anger. 'Why have they left us out here?' He swept his arm at the mist-shrouded hills. 'What do they expect us to do? We can't defend the border alone as we no longer have enough men, and many of the surrounding outposts have been abandoned already. Gods above, it'll be every man for himself soon, if we're not murdered in our sleep first!' Shaking his head he stared off into the distance, following the flight of a lone crow as it searched for somewhere to roost for the night. 'I think,' he said after a few silent minutes, 'that we need to make a decision, Artos.'

'A decision, sir?'

'Yes, Decurion, a decision. Do we stay and get picked off one by one, or do we leave and try to make it back home?'

'Home, sir?' Artos looked at his leader.

'Rome, Artos. Rome.' Gaius' eyes seemed to cloud over as he continued speaking in almost a whisper. 'Oh, how I miss my homeland. The heat of the summer sun. The food. The wine. God, the women. Yes, I want to go home, Artos. Back to my villa in the hills.' Starting to warm to his subject, Gaius continued, 'And the soil, my friend, the soil is as black as pitch and will grow anything – grapes, olives, grains, and cattle. I've herds of cattle and their milk, as sweet as honey. Yes, yes, I need to go home.'

'And what about the men, sir?' asked Artos.

'Well, I'll need an escort to the port at Caerleon.'

'And then?'

'Well, then I guess they're free to do whatever they want, aren't they? There is no Empire left here to release them of their service, so either they come with me and find their way home, or stay here in this Godforsaken place.'

'You can't abandon the men, sir,' said Artos, a look of amazement clear upon his face.

'Why not?' said Gaius petulantly. 'They're deserting their post on a daily basis.'

'They're not deserting you, sir. Many of them have families here. They've married into the tribes and need to provide; they've just not been paid in two years. You can't blame them for seeking their own way.'

'So, am I to forgive their transgressions and pretend nothing's happened?' snarled Gaius. 'And you, Artos, what will you do?'

'I...' Artos stumbled. 'I haven't given it much thought. The army is my life. I've known no other since I was small.'

'Small,' laughed Gaius, 'I can't believe you were ever small.' He slapped Artos on the back with genuine mirth in his eyes and turned for the ladder. 'I'm leaving, my friend. I can't stay in this shithole for one more day. Come daybreak I'm packing and heading for Caerleon. I suggest you join me.'

And with that, feeling lighter of heart than he had for many months, Gaius Flavius Silvanus climbed down the ladder and headed back to his quarters to start packing.

Chapter 2
Leaving

The morning dawned, a drab grey weighing down heavily over the hills, pregnant with the promise of more rain. Artos sat astride his horse, his oiled cloak drawn around his shoulders and his men arrayed behind him, plus the few dozen auxiliary soldiers who were left safeguarding the fort. Easing himself into his high-cantled saddle, the leather of his jerkin creaked beneath the weight of his mail shirt. His helm hung from the saddle wrapped in an oiled leather bag to keep it from tarnishing. His sword, the long-bladed spatha used by all imperial cavalry, hung from his side and he had set his lance to his stirrup. A bundle of smaller throwing spears lay tied across the rump of his horse. He looked every part the warrior he was.

He gazed around the palisaded structure one last time, remembering the years he'd spent serving the Empire here. A deep heaviness weighed on his heart at the thought of deserting this post for the promise he'd made to the Emperor to serve him faithfully wasn't a bond he wished to break. It had taken two days to organise the men and gather the supplies needed to make the trip to Caerleon. The prefect seemed content to wait in his quarters, drinking the last of the wine and railing against the failings of the imperial system, something that not too long ago would have seen him arrested and probably executed.

Many of the camp followers and slaves, upon hearing the news of the remaining men's imminent departure, had decided to leave over the previous two nights, stealing what they could before vanishing without trace, not that anyone went looking for them.

Artos turned to his second-in-command, a dark-skinned Syrian by the name of Barcus. 'Barcus, take command of the party. I'm going to see if our prefect is ready to join us yet!'

Barcus flashed a bright, toothy smile. 'Of course, Decurion, it will be my pleasure. Do not knock too loudly, though, for I fear the prefect may be feeling a little delicate this fine morning.'

Artos threw back his head and laughed, then turning his mount's head he trotted towards the camp commander's quarters.

'GO AWAY.' The insistent knocking continued. 'I SAID, GO AWAY!' Prefect Gaius Silvanus lay in his bed with the blanket drawn over his pounding head. *Why do the Gods mock me?* he thought as he lay there. He heard the door opening and risked opening one eye. Well, if the barbarians were here to kill him he wished they'd hurry up because his headache was getting worse.

'Sir.' Artos snapped off a smart salute and was greeted with a grunt as reply. He couldn't help but smile behind his beard at the comical figure Prefect Silvanus cut. 'With respect, sir, the men are ready to leave when you are.'

'Yes, yes, fine. Give me an hour, maybe two and I'll be ready.'

'Again, with respect, sir, the morning is well underway, and if we don't leave soon we'll lose the light before we've travelled any distance.'

Gaius looked over his blanket, his bloodshot eyes staring blearily across the room. 'In that case, Decurion, we'll leave tomorrow!' And with that, he rolled over in his bed and turned his back to the door.

Artos left, closing the door behind him and frustrated, mounted his horse and returned to his men.

Barcus looked to his commander. 'Well? Are we off, then?'

'Not today, it seems,' he replied. 'Tell the men to stand down 'til tomorrow.'

'God preserve us,' said Barcus, rubbing his hand across his face, smoothing his beard to a point. 'At this rate it'll be next summer before we leave!'

Suddenly, the harsh notes of a buccina sounded across the parade ground and from the rampart above, the cry of, 'Men approaching!' was bellowed by the guard as he pointed towards the western edge of the forest.

Artos jumped from his horse and ran up to the ladder leading to a watchtower. Climbing quickly, he looked to the west where at the edge of the clear ground two men supporting a third stumbled out of the treeline and stopped. The men waited as the gates swung open and a dozen heavily armed cavalry galloped towards them, fanning out into a broad line with lances dipped. Not waiting, they dropped their charge, turned, and fled back into the trees.

'Let them go!' bellowed Barcus as he reined his mount and jumped to the ground. 'He's one of ours!' he yelled. 'Form a defensive line. We've got to get him back to camp – he's injured!' The remaining cavalry formed up in front of the trees scanning for any sign of threat as their leader quickly checked the injured man's wounds and then gently placed him on the saddle of his own mount. Then gathering up the reins of his horse, he led it back to camp.

'How's he doing?' asked Artos later that afternoon as the surgeon finished up bandaging the injuries.

'He'll live,' said the medic. 'He's got a few nasty cuts and a bad stab wound to his side, but I'm more concerned about the knock he's taken to his head. Something large, probably a club, has put a nasty dent in his skull. His helmet stopped the worst of it and if he wakes up he'll have the mother of all headaches. Just like our prefect!' The surgeon winked at Artos and then turned to wash his hands in a basin of vinegar before drying them on a cloth handed to him by a helper.

'When will that be?' questioned Artos. 'Our prefect will want a full report on what happened as soon as this man wakes up.'

'Hmm.' The medic rubbed his bristly chin in thought. 'Maybe a couple of days if he's lucky, maybe longer. It's really hard to say with head injuries. He might never awaken; I've seen that before. Eventually, they starve to death.'

Artos shook his head sadly. 'I pray that's not his fate,' he stated earnestly. 'I'd rather meet my end at the point of a blade than just waste away unaware.'

'I think most men would,' said the surgeon. 'Come back in the morning and we'll see if there's any improvement.'

'Thank you,' replied Artos, leaving left the room and heading for the prefect's office.

'TWO DAYS? I'M NOT WAITING FOR TWO MORE DAYS!' bellowed Gaius, clutching his aching head. 'He might not even wake up. Isn't that what the surgeon said?'

'He said to go back tomorrow and see if there's any improvement,' Artos replied.

'No, no, no, I'm not waiting.' He raised a placating hand as Artos started to protest. 'I know I've held things up, but I was unwell,' he lied. 'Come tomorrow, I'm leaving and I'm not having some half-dead soldier hold me up. If he'd had any decency he'd have died on patrol with the rest of his squad.'

Artos held his tongue as he stood in front of his superior, watching him pace around his office.

'I think it best, Decurion,' the prefect began, 'if our mutual friend doesn't make it through the night.'

'You can't be serious, sir,' protested Artos. 'He might have important information about what's happening out there.' He swept his hand behind as if to show the prefect what he couldn't see. 'It may even help you get to Caerleon safely.' A risky gambit, he knew, but he wasn't above a little manipulation to get the prefect to see sense.

'Don't take me for a fool,' snapped Gaius. 'I know what you're up to. But I want this dealt with tonight and if you won't do it I'll find someone who will. Is that clear, Decurion?'

'Perfectly, sir.' Artos saluted his commander and left his office, frowning with frustration at the shortsightedness of his prefect.

'It could be a mercy, Decurion,' sighed the surgeon when Artos had finished telling him the prefect's order. 'He'd still need weeks of care for his wounds to heal properly anyway, and he certainly couldn't travel in his current condition!'

'I know, Daxios, it's just... well, if only we could find out what happened to the rest of the patrol we might just figure out what's happening in the wider world, and that could prove invaluable information.'

The camp surgeon sighed again, heavily, and slumped onto a nearby stool. His thinning grey hair, neatly swept back over his head, showed his fastidious nature. Everything in his hospital was neat and orderly and more importantly, clean. Finally he looked up into Artos' eyes and with a resigned look on his face, said, 'There is one thing I could try to rouse him, Decurion. It's risky and there's a good chance he'll die, but he should be awake enough to answer your questions. But, it's up to you. Do you want me to try?'

Artos paced the narrow space between the cots, his chin cradled in his hand as he thought. Abruptly he stopped and turned back to the surgeon. 'Do it, Daxios. This is our only chance to find out what's going on. It will work, won't it?' he questioned.

'Nothing is guaranteed in life but Death, Decurion,' was Daxios' reply as he turned and opened a small chest. Reaching inside he pulled out a small glass bottle with a waxed stopper. 'You won't have long,' he said as he cradled the patient's head and poured a pale yellow liquid down his throat. The pair of them sat there watching, waiting for the doctor's medicine to take effect. When nothing happened after a couple of minutes the doctor turned to Artos and said, 'Maybe this time it doesn't work.' He shrugged his bony shoulders with resignation. 'It doesn't always, you know.'

Suddenly the soldier's body shuddered and started to convulse on the bed.

'Hold him down!' shouted the doctor. 'We may get something after all.'

The man screamed. It was a blood-curdling sound of pure terror as he writhed in Artos' firm grip. His eyes snapped open and he stared about himself wildly.

'It's okay,' soothed Artos, 'you're safe now, back at the fort.' He smoothed the man's tousled hair and it seemed to calm him down as his body went limp and he slumped back onto the bed, but his eyes kept darting about the dim room as if he was looking for something.

'What happened out there?' queried Artos. 'Were you attacked?' The soldier's attention drifted back to Artos and he looked deep into his eyes and nodded. 'Can you tell me more?'

'Water…' gasped the soldier and an orderly handed him a cup, which he gulped down greedily.

'You don't have long, Decurion,' whispered the doctor. 'Best hurry.'

'Thank you, Daxios,' said Artos. 'Well, soldier?'

'We… We left camp,' he started and then broke into a gurgling cough that left him gasping. 'I don't know how long ago…'

'Four weeks,' answered Artos.

'Just four weeks? It seems a lifetime ago.' His head sagged in memory of his ordeal, but then he drew himself up. 'We were several miles from camp heading in a north-westerly direction as instructed, to see if the rumours of an invasion were true.' He took another sip of water. 'We'd passed through several friendly villages and none of them had heard anything of note so we pushed on. As we reached the furthest edge of our territory we met some refugees heading east. We questioned them about the Hibernians; they knew nothing, but they were frightened of something. So my optio took the leader to one side and demanded to know what they were fleeing from…' The soldier started to convulse.

'Quickly, man,' demanded Artos. 'What was said?'

The man writhed in pain, his fingers clawing at the sheet. '…Dragon,' he gasped. '…Gold.'

'What?'

The man seemed to gather himself, but his words were only a whisper.

'Not long now,' said Daxios.

'Tell me, soldier,' said Artos, holding the man by his shirt.

He whispered, 'The leader... He told us of the dragon... Dragon, sitting on a mountain of gold.' A crazed look filled his eyes. 'The optio said we must go and see for ourselves so we pushed on, I don't know how much farther.' His eyes rolled in his skull. 'We were attacked by warriors of the dragon. Most of us were killed, but the rest were captured and bound. We were told we'd be fed to the beast. And they laughed at us, and dragged us north.'

'Did you see a dragon?' asked the surgeon in wonder.

The soldier looked across to him. 'No, but I heard it, and saw the mountain where it lived.' His head fell back to the pillow.

'How did you escape?' asked Artos.

'Luck. They left us a small fire one night as it was freezing and they wanted us alive for the sacrifice.' He shuddered in memory. 'I was closest to the blaze and managed to burn through my bonds but I was seen and they pursued me.' His eyes welled with emotion. 'I couldn't save my friends,' he cried, fat tears sliding down his face. 'So I ran like a coward. But they followed me.' His face fell, then suddenly he grinned. 'Mercury gave my feet wings, for I ran like the wind all that night and they never caught up to me, though I could hear their cries in the darkness. But my luck ran out at dawn as I reached a ravine over a fast-flowing river that I couldn't cross. I could hear them closing in and just as they came into sight I turned and jumped off the cliff, choosing to die on my own terms and entrusting my soul to God. I don't remember much more until I woke up here.' He lay back and closed his eyes, his breath rattling in his chest.

'I think that's enough, Decurion, don't you?' said the surgeon.

'Yes, yes of course. Thank you, Daxios, for your help. What do you make of his tale?'

'Could just be the ramblings of a dying man.' Daxios shrugged. 'Or it could be the truth, who's to know? A fall from height into a rocky river would explain his injuries, I suppose. But as I said, who's to know?' He turned away.

Artos leant over the soldier and put his lips to his ear. 'I promise I'll find your men and avenge them. You have my word.' He placed his hand on the man's shoulder and gave it a gentle squeeze.

The man's eyes flickered open and he smiled. 'Thank you,' he whispered, and then his head lolled to the side.

'He's gone, Decurion,' said the surgeon as he pulled the sheet over the dead man's head.

Chapter 3
Rescue

'This all seems rather fanciful, Decurion, don't you think?' said Prefect Gaius. 'I mean a dragon, a real dragon sitting on a mountain of gold, preposterous!' He snorted and picked over the remains of his breakfast. The following day had dawned clear and Artos had made his report of the previous night's interrogation with the injured soldier. Gaius swirled his wine cup, and, taking a sip, he looked over the rim at the man standing to attention before him. 'And you want to hare off and rescue his comrades to boot – men who are probably already dead. No, I'm sorry, I can't let you go. You need to escort me to Caerleon. Today, you have your duty, Artos.'

'With respect, sir, my duty is the safety of this fort and the surrounding area, as is yours!'

Prefect Gaius Silvanus slapped his hand down on the table, scattering the remains of his breakfast. 'Damn you, Decurion!' he shouted. 'You overstep yourself. How dare you speak to me like that? I could have you arrested and flogged for this.'

Artos placed both fisted hands on the table and leant forward until his huge mass towered over the prefect. 'And who exactly is going to do that?' he hissed, the menace clear in his voice. 'The men know you're deserting them, fleeing back to Rome and leaving them to their fate.'

Gaius shrank back into his chair, fear sending icy tendrils up his spine. 'They're my men, not yours, Decurion. I'm in command here, not you!' he said, but he knew deep down that he was wrong, and cursing his cowardly soul, he also knew that Artos was doing the right thing.

'I'm going after our men, sir,' Artos said, 'with or without your permission. If you still wish to go to Caerleon I'm sure the remaining soldiers can escort you, but I'm taking my men with me. If you're still here when I return you can arrest me and charge me with desertion or mutiny if you desire. But I am leaving today, and whether or not those men are still alive I will have answers and someone will be held accountable.' With that, he saluted and turning on his heel strode out of the prefect's office into the bright autumn sunshine.

Prefect Silvanus sat in the gloom of his office, brooding on the ill luck that had left him with just a decurion, an auxiliary one at that, as second-in-command. Most of the senior and lower-ranking officers had left when the legions pulled back to Gaul. The few remaining centurions and lower ranks were the unwanted detritus the legions had dumped on him and most of them, seeing how things were going, had stolen the pay chest and disappeared at the earliest opportunity. Of those that remained, the bare handful, well, they'd either died of disease or been killed by the tribes in the many skirmishes that had marked his two-year command of this desolate fort in the arse end of nowhere. He reached for the wine jug only to find it empty. Bellowing for a servant to refill it, he then remembered they'd left a few nights ago, too. He hurled the jug against the wall where it smashed into fragments. He sat there with his head resting on his crossed arms, wracked in self-pity at the realisation that he, too, was surplus to the requirements of the legions, a disposable asset of no value. He started to cry, sobs shaking his shoulders.

Some time later, he sat up and wiped his eyes dry. Something had dawned on him as he wallowed in his misery. Jumping to his feet, he headed for the door. He needed to speak to the decurion before he left.

'Decurion... Decurion!' Gaius shouted. 'A word, please, before you go.'

Artos looked over at him as he tightened his horse's saddle girth. Stroking its neck, he said, 'I think we've said all we need to, Prefect.'

'Yes, I know. I shouldn't have lost my temper and I apologise for that.'

Barcus looked over at his commander and then at his decurion, wondering what was going on. The other men in Artos' cavalry unit couldn't believe their camp prefect was apologising to their decurion, even though he was the second-highest-ranking officer left and therefore acting second-in-command.

'What do you want, Prefect Silvanus? I think we've both said all we need to say to each other, haven't we?'

'Come over here in private, if you wouldn't mind, Decurion,' said Prefect Silvanus, beckoning him over to any empty barrack block. Artos followed, his huge frame dwarfing the Roman's. 'Listen, Artos,' whispered Gaius. 'I know we both said things we shouldn't have but we can't leave things as they are when we could turn this whole debacle into something that could further both our careers.'

'What do you mean?' queried Artos.

'Well, you mean to go out and look for these men no matter what, leaving this fort at the mercy of our many enemies.' He raised a placating hand as Artos started to protest. 'And I know I said I was leaving, but hear me out. I've been thinking, and if half of what that solider said was true, there's a sizeable amount of gold just sitting there waiting to be taken by—'

'Us?' interjected Artos.

'No, no,' Gaius fumbled. 'The Empire, of course. I'd never steal from the Empire; that would be suicide, as you well know. But the mines at Dolaucothi were closed centuries ago when the gold dried up. If there's more to be found, out there,' he waved his hand expansively towards the west, 'then why shouldn't we find and claim it in the name of the Emperor?'

'Whoever he is!' said Artos, clearly not liking where this conversation was going.

'Well yes, quite,' answered Gaius. 'But that's all semantics, really. If we discover this mountain of gold I can return to Rome in honour, don't you see?'

'I see it helping you. But what of your men? What of them?'

'Of course, I'll look after you all. When I'm back in Rome I'll get you all reposted somewhere far better. How about that? And I won't report your mutinous behaviour, which will surely see you hanged or crucified,' Gaius replied slyly.

'What's stopping me killing you now and taking all the gold for myself? My men would follow me to Hades and back if I asked them,' Artos threw back.

'Why, your sense of honour. You forget I know you, Artos. I've watched you over the years. I see how honourable you are. How the men love you because you treat them well. I know your honour wouldn't allow you to commit murder on an imperial prefect. You couldn't live with the guilt, and that's why you'll help me recover the gold.'

'If there really is any gold,' Artos said, knowing he couldn't go through with his threat. 'So what? You'll wait here until I get back and then take all the glory?'

'Our glory, Decurion. Our glory. Of course I'll wait here with the rest of the soldiers while you and your unit go off in search of the lost patrol. You'll move quicker that way, obviously, and as I've said I'll look after you when the time comes, and I will.' *I'll see you to the gallows along with your treacherous men,* he thought to himself. A faint smile curled the prefect's lip. 'Do we have an accord, Decurion?' Gaius thrust out his hand.

Artos stared at the proffered arm for a few heartbeats and then grudgingly grasped it and said, 'Aye. We have an agreement. Just make sure you keep your side of the bargain.' And with that he returned to his men and mounted his bay gelding.

He looked down at the remaining troops and said, 'You men remain here to guard the fort, and I'll take my horsemen and go look for our brothers.' The auxiliary troops visibly slumped in relief at not having to venture outside the safety of the fort. Artos spun his horse around, shouted for his men to follow, and kicking his heels into his mount he spurred forward through the gate followed closely by his twenty-five men, into the unknown wilderness of Cambria.

Chapter 4
Friends

Artos reined in his horse at the edge of the forest and turned in his saddle to look back at the fort. Men lining the wall watched in silence, waiting for the moment that the vast trees swallowed man and horse into their twilight embrace. Prefect Gaius stood there too, above the gatehouse, and Artos could have sworn he was smiling.

He addressed his troops. 'My friends, today we leave the safety of our home to search for our lost brothers. They may already be dead, but we must know for sure. If they are, then we shall avenge their restless spirits. If they live then we are bringing them back!' He said the last with a surety that bolstered any nerves that flickered and twitched in the souls of his men. 'I tell you this now for some of us may die on this journey. We shall go farther into unknown territory than any before us. But there lies glory, and deeds that shall be sung of for years to come. Men will tell their children of our valour and hang their heads in shame that they were not with us this day. But we are here now. It is the hour of reckoning. Are you with me?' He pumped his fist in the air and twenty-five throats roared back in affirmation. Kicking his mount forward he shouted back, 'We ride!' and then they vanished into the trees.

'Gods rot you,' spoke Prefect Silvanus from the gatehouse, raising a cup of wine in mock salute. 'May you fall from your horse and break your bloody neck.' He then giggled at his toast before draining his cup and throwing it into the ditch beyond the wall.

The forest seemed to close in on the riders as they made their way deeper into the trees. The tracks disappeared after only a few hundred metres, swallowed in a sea of ferns and briar. 'Keep close, men,' said Artos. 'These may be friendly lands so close to base, but that doesn't mean we can't expect trouble. There are plenty out here who'd relish taking a shot at us from the safety of the greenway.'

'Damn cowards,' muttered Lionides, a Greek who'd arrived three summers ago and had proved his mettle time and again. A tall, handsome blond man with blue eyes, olive skin, and a friendly spirit that made him popular amongst the men. He was countered by his best friend Alcaeus, also a Greek, who'd arrived at the same time. He was darker skinned with a mass of curly black hair and two dark, piercing brown eyes that stared out from a bushy black beard. A more powerful squat frame than his tall friend but totally loyal to Lionides.

'We'd cut 'em up for sure. Don't you worry, Lio,' countered Alcaeus. 'Why, the two of us could carve a path through this wood to the sea if we chose,' he laughed.

'Just as well,' Barcus retorted. 'You're both on point from here.'

Lionides threw his companion a look and Alcaeus just shrugged and laughing, spurred his horse forward to the front of the line.

'The men seem in good spirits, Barcus.' Artos leaned toward his number two and spoke in a low voice. 'How long do you think that will last?'

'Until we're truly in the wild, sir,' answered Barcus with a grin. His white teeth seemed to glow in the gloom of the forest.

'We're being tracked,' said Alcaeus in a whisper to his commander some time later. The forest paths had remained elusive and the warm, humid air under the trees had lulled them all into a monotonous rhythm. He'd slowed his mount so he could fall back in line.

'How long and how many?' queried Artos, all tiredness evaporating at the potential threat. He cursed himself for not being more vigilant, and vowed it wouldn't happen again.

'No more than two and probably for the last hour, sir,' he replied. 'I only caught glimpses of 'em amongst the trees. They're good at staying hidden, but I saw 'em both.'

'And you're sure there's only two?'

'Positive, sir,' said Alcaeus.

'Good work, soldier.' Artos nodded in thanks and Alcaeus beamed in pride, looking over at Lionides who raised his eyebrows in exasperation.

Turning to Barcus, Artos said, 'Tell the men we'll stop here to rest the horses and get something to eat.' Calling over Lionides and Alcaeus, he whispered, 'Circle back round behind our guests and ask them to join us, would you?' Both men nodded in understanding and slipped away into the undergrowth, daggers drawn.

A few minutes later there was the sound of scuffling from a few metres away. It soon stopped and Lionides and Alcaeus emerged from the bushes pushing two bound and dishevelled-looking men in front of them.

'They were a little shy, sir,' said Lionides.

'So we chivvied them along a bit like,' Alcaeus added with a grin.

Both men looked around wide eyed as they were forced to kneel in front of Artos. 'Why are you following us?' he asked. The pair looked at each other, obviously not understanding what had been said, so Artos switched to a local dialect and asked the same question, at which point both men started talking animatedly.

'My lord, we are sorry to come upon you in this manner,' they cried out, prostrating themselves in front of him even further. 'We are the men who found your wounded soldier and brought him back to your fortress. We're simple hunters and when we saw your men bearing down on us from the fort, we thought you believed we had killed your man and were coming to kill us.'

'We grew scared and ran,' said one of them. They both remained flat on the ground, shaking in fear. The other continued speaking. He looked up at Artos, who stared back. 'Our village is west of here and we thought you were coming to put us all to the sword for what we had done. But we only helped your man. Please don't punish our people. We offer ourselves to you now to take the sting from your vengeance,' he pleaded.

'If you truly helped our man—'

'We did, sire,' burst in one of the men.

'As I said, if you truly helped our man, why would we punish you or indeed your village?'

'Roman justice, sire,' they answered, 'it's always been that way.'

'Indeed it was,' answered Artos. 'But times have changed and we all need to look to a future where we can exist together. The legions have left, taking their brand of justice with them. So we must work as one and strive to treat all men as equals. Now get up and join us in something to eat, and afterwards you can take us to the place where you found our man.'

After a short repast they packed up their supplies and mounting their horses, followed the two hunters, who, happy now that their lives weren't forfeit, trotted alongside the riders like faithful hunting dogs.

The village was set in a wide, shallow valley dotted with enclosures and fields. Older children tended herds of cattle and sheep while the younger ones ran around laughing and playing while being chased by barking dogs. Older men worked amongst the crops of barley and wheat, as birds hopped and flew around them looking for worms or spilled grain. Smoke from the dozen or so thatched huts spiralled up into the late afternoon air and the sounds of wood being cut could be heard echoing from the surrounding forest. It was an idyllic scene and Artos couldn't help but marvel at the seemingly normal life that could exist in a world where violence and death were the norm. He knew they lived a hard, short life, but still he envied what these farmers had. Family, community, love. He shook off his melancholy and settled himself in his saddle. He was aware of the path life had chosen for him and had made peace with it long ago.

'Will your tribe welcome us?' he asked his new companions, whose names he'd learned were Gruffyd and Bryn. They had insisted on this detour to their village, saying that the spot where they'd found his man was a further two days north and west of there. Artos had agreed to spend the night in their village as honoured guests.

'Of course, Lord,' replied the two men, who as it turned out, were brothers. Short, dark-skinned and powerfully built with mops of curly black hair, they resembled most of the local tribesmen that Artos had seen while stationed in Cambria.

Gruffyd, the older of the two, produced a small horn from his tunic and, setting it to his lips, blew a long, sweet note that drifted across the valley, followed by three smaller, sharper notes. The sounds faded and Artos saw the villagers staring up at them; even the wood chopping had ceased.

Gruffyd looked up at the huge horseman and said, 'I'm just letting them know we have guests and not to run away.' He smiled with a hint of sadness.

'I understand,' he said. 'Your farmers are not warriors, and even your best hunters wouldn't be a match for armed men. There is no shame in avoiding battle when you're unprepared.' He smiled warmly at Gruffyd. 'You are a wise man, my friend.'

Chapter 5
The Bear's Claws

The night passed quietly in the village, and Artos' men spent it in the largest house drinking ale and relaxing while he and Barcus talked with the tribal leaders about what was happening beyond their western border. They were told of the invasion by the Hibernians, who, having learned of Rome's withdrawal of the legions, decided to take advantage of the power vacuum in Britannia by attempting to claim Cambria for their own.

They also asked about the rumour of a dragon to the north and were surprised when the tribesmen confirmed the tale, going on to tell them of raids on other villages and also clashes between the Hibernians and the dragon. The Hibernians were now avoiding that whole area because of their losses.

Artos couldn't quite believe what he was hearing. Could there really be a mythical beast roaming the wilds of Cambria? So he asked about the rumoured mountain of gold and wasn't surprised when the leaders said they'd heard of this too.

'Many of the wilder tribes have flocked to the north for protection from the invaders, and the promise of gold is a powerful weapon,' they said. 'And you have chosen a dangerous path, to go in search of your men. For they are surely dead by now and past caring if you come or not. But you are welcome to stay here with us. You and your men could defend this valley with ease, and we will feed you and tend your animals. All your needs will be met.'

'Thank you for your kind offer,' said Artos, 'but we must go on in the morning whether or not our men live. But if we should pass back this way...' He left the words hanging and the tribal leaders looked at each other before nodding in acceptance of his decision.

Early the next day, just before dawn broke a lone figure crawled his way through the dewy grass up to a moss-covered boulder overlooking the valley. He felt the moisture as it soaked through his jerkin, chilling his skin underneath. Conor MacDuid stared down into the village, watching as a line of horsemen rode off to the north following two men, who he guessed were their guides.

Having arrived from Hibernia two months earlier Conor was familiar with this land now. His well-planned and successful raids on other villages had raised his status in the clan so well that his chieftain gave him almost free rein to do as he pleased, something he relished, for he had a particularly cruel streak that had earned him the name of Red Conor, and that wasn't just for the colour of his hair, a coppery auburn.

Happy that the large party of warriors was leaving, he slithered his way back down towards his men gathered not far off in a dip amongst the trees. As he entered camp his men looked up expectantly. 'Well,' said Fionn, his second-in-command, a wiry, fair-haired warrior with a white scar running through his left eyebrow and down his cheek.

'They're leaving,' he replied with a grin. They'd been watching this village for over a day to see who came and went and were surprised when the horsemen arrived the previous afternoon. Hoping they'd leave, they'd taken it in turn to watch the comings and goings. If the warriors stayed, there was no way they could attack this rich target.

'We'll give them an hour to get clear,' said Conor, 'and then when they're safely away, you, Fionn,' he pointed to his second-in-command, 'shall take a handful of the men and work your way to the upper part of the valley. When you're in position I want you to charge on the village screaming like all the banshees in hell and drive them into my wall of warriors, who'll be waiting below.' He grinned with a wicked look and his men smiled back wolfishly, knowing today they'd get to kill again and take what they wanted. These Cambrians had grown soft under Rome's boot, but Conor would show them the meaning of fear this day. 'Pick your men and go now,' he said, and suddenly the camp burst into life.

Rhys ap Bryn walked along with the small herd of sheep he tended daily. At ten years old he was just a little too young to go off into the deep forest with the hunters, tracking stag and boar. He still carried a small spear. More of a sharpened stick, really, with a fire-hardened tip that he periodically jabbed into imaginary targets as his feet crunched through the first light frost of autumn. Coupled with a low, swirling mist, it gave the early morning an eerie, still feeling.

As he climbed the gentle slope of his home valley the air warmed slightly, touched by the first rays of the morning sun and the frost and mist magically cleared, revealing a Brutish-looking man standing in his way. He went to shout out a warning, but a coarse hand clamped over his mouth, stifling his scream. He felt a sharp blade at his throat and in pure instinct he thrust his spear down into his assailant's foot. The man let out a shout of pain and let go of the boy as he hopped on one foot. Needing no other encouragement, Rhys spun away and ran off, dodging the hands that reached out to grab him.

'Let him go!' shouted Fionn as the others started after him. 'He won't get back in time to warn the others.' He looked over at Darragh, the man who'd been stabbed. 'How's the foot?'

'Painful, but it won't slow me down too much,' he said as he wrapped some cloth around the puncture wound. It looked messy. But if Darragh said he was okay, that was fine with Fionn. The man was as hard as they come.

'Well keep up, and if we catch that little bastard I'll let you gut him slow, okay?'

'Fine by me, boss,' said Darragh, licking his own blood from his fingers.

A roaring war cry echoed down the valley as a band of men burst from the treeline and charged towards the village, hacking down any who stood in their way. The women and children screamed in fear as they tried to flee in the opposite direction, only to encounter even more men in front of them who, laughing, bundled them together in a group under the watchful eyes of a half-dozen guards.

The village men grabbed at weapons and prepared to defend themselves and their families but they were no match for these heavily armed raiders who attacked with savage brutality, cutting them down mercilessly with axe and sword. Soon they were driven into the centre of the village in a tight knot, surrounded by grinning, leering beasts who advanced over the bodies of fallen family members. The remaining men stood in a circle around the women and children with spears thrust out in a protective circle.

A vicious-looking raider with red hair stepped forward and said, 'Who speaks for this village?' No one came forward. He pulled a long, thin dagger from his belt and with a swift movement threw it. The blade pierced the chest of a young boy of no more than six, who dropped to the ground, lifeless. His mother cried out in horror at what had just happened.

'I won't ask again,' he said. 'Who speaks for this village?'

'I do.' A man stepped forward. He was broad-shouldered and handsome, with a neat beard and dark hair braided down his back. He held his spear levelled at the red-haired warrior.

'Good, now we're getting somewhere.' He raised his arms, turned round and looked at his men, smiling. They laughed back. Then with a quickness that defied belief, he turned, drew his sword and thrust it into the stomach of the village leader, tearing it upward in a fluid motion and ripping out his guts. The man's eyes widened in surprise as he turned them towards his wound, watching his entrails spill out of him. His legs suddenly buckled and with a groan he dropped to his knees and toppled sideways as his eyes rolled up into his skull in death. Women started to scream as Conor stepped forward, shouting, 'Kill the men and take the rest as slaves. The village is ours!' His men roared in triumph and leapt forward.

A battle horn blared stridently from above the village as an armed host surged from the trees with lances levelled. Conor spun to face this new threat and saw the horsemen who'd left the village returning, at full tilt, towards him and his men. 'Form a shield wall!' he bellowed, but the villagers, seeing that the tables had turned, were attacking with a renewed lust for vengeance born of a desperate hope to survive, hacking and stabbing any who got close enough.

'Fionn, you and your men kill those fucking villagers. The rest of you, with me.' He raced off to face this new threat. He knew he couldn't stand against a cavalry charge on open ground so he ordered his men to stay amongst the huts, which would slow the forward momentum and force the riders to split up amongst the buildings, making them easier to kill.

He watched and waited as the horsemen thundered towards him, his men strung out between the buildings, spears ready. A great bear of a man led the charge, his hair flying behind him like a banner, chainmail armour glinting in the morning sun. The hot misted breath of the horses blew like dragons' breath as they got closer. All this he saw while time slowed around him. Then at the last second, just as he thought the horses would crash into the buildings, they broke left and right at some unseen command, and each rider threw a short javelin as they passed, with unerring accuracy, spitting his men where they stood. And then suddenly they were gone. Conor quickly dashed out from among the buildings but there was no sign of the horsemen.

A shout from behind forced him to turn around. They'd reformed on the other side of the village and were now riding amongst the huts, slashing left and right with long-bladed swords, killing his men with practised ease.

Above the head of the leader Conor spied two ravens circling in the sky, and he knew in his soul that this man was touched by the Gods themselves. But it didn't stop the rage he felt igniting in his guts as he watched his men being slaughtered. What should have been an easy kill was turning into a rout as his battle-hardened men tried to flee in fear of these mounted warriors.

'Fight me!' he roared in defiance, racing towards the melee, slashing out at riders as they streamed past.

Artos and his company had left Dyffren village and headed north, led again by Gruffyd and Bryn, who'd promised the day before to show the company where they'd found the wounded soldier. About half an hour later one of Artos' men's mounts had thrown her rider, spooked by a game bird that suddenly flew up into its face as they passed through some tall brush. The other men laughed as Gavain, a slim, wiry man from somewhere deep in Gaul, sat on his backside with a comical expression on his face.

'Come on, man,' said Lionides as he sat looking down at his comrade. 'Now's not the time for a rest, although I can understand why you're tired. We all saw you chasing after that pretty dark-haired lass last night!' The other men roared with laughter at their fellow's red-faced discomfort.

Giving a rude hand gesture, Gavain stood and checked over his horse, which had wandered off a few metres and was now cropping contentedly on some late-season grass. 'Made me look daft there didn't you, girl?' he said as he fed her an apple he'd been given by the villagers. She whickered and crunched the offered fruit as Gavain gave her neck a gentle caress with his hand and then remounted.

'All good now?' asked Barcus, checking his men were ready to move. They all nodded. 'Good then,' he said, and turning to Artos, he stopped what he was about to say. 'Are you alright, sir?' he asked.

'Do you hear that?'

Barcus hushed the men and listened. In the distance a crashing sound could be heard. Suddenly alert, the men pulled their mounts around to face the threat. The crashing steadily grew louder and they nervously fingered their weapons in anticipation.

'Let us go and see what it is, Lord,' said Gruffyd, indicating his brother. 'We move quietly and can report back quickly.'

'Go then,' said Artos, 'but hurry back with any news.' The two men disappeared into the trees and minutes later returned, carrying a small boy with them.

'That's your son, isn't it?' said Artos, looking at Bryn as the two men stopped in front of him. 'What's he doing here?'

'The village is under attack,' said Bryn, holding his son in his arms. 'He escaped and came to find us. We must hurry back and help.'

'Of course.' Artos shouted for his men to ride as fast as possible back to the village. 'We'll go ahead. You catch up as soon as possible.' The brothers nodded and followed after the swiftly moving horsemen as they retraced their path.

The sudden charge had caught the Hibernians off guard and several fell swiftly as the horsemen took advantage of the chaos. But too soon, small groups had gathered together to put up a fierce resistance against the attacking cavalry and spear-wielding villagers. Artos thundered towards two of the invaders who had separated a man from the rest of his friends. Sheathing his sword, he galloped up behind the two men and grabbing them both by the back of their tunics, he lifted them off their feet and with his horse's momentum threw them forward, where they both hit a hut's doorframe with a resounding crack, splitting both their skulls and killing them instantly. He had turned in the saddle to see his men making short work of the rest, when he heard the redhead warrior shout his challenge. Spurring his mount forward he charged, slashing down at a man with a blood-covered face who jumped in his way, swinging an axe at his leg. His sword bit deep into the attacker's neck and blood gushed as he wrenched the blade free.

Conor threw his spear and watched as the huge rider, who had just dispatched one of his men, leant sideways and let it whistle past his head to lodge in the thatch of a hut. Bracing himself, he drew his sword and prepared to cut the legs from under the horse. A cruel waste of a precious mount but Conor wasn't a man to worry about such things, he enjoyed inflicting pain.

Artos, reading his intentions reined in his horse and slipped from the saddle. Holding his sword lightly he stepped forward as the man suddenly charged.

They clashed in a fury of sparks then pulled apart. Conor feinted to the left, trying to draw his man in but Artos countered and narrowly missed, slicing cloth instead of flesh. Both men attacked and defended but were unable to strike a killing blow. Then Conor pulled a knife from his belt and threw it at Artos, who narrowly deflected it, but it was enough to allow his opponent in. Conor brought his sword down with all his fury and shattered Artos' blade at the hilt, leaving just a jagged shard no more than six inches long. Looking at his broken blade he threw it in Conor's face and then stepping in to his guard, threw a punch that knocked him onto his back. Reeling from the blow, Conor brought up his sword as Artos, roaring like a wounded bear, pounced upon the prone figure and threw blow after blow into his face. With lights bursting behind his eyes Conor smashed his sword hilt into the side of Artos' head, knocking him off and allowing him to roll away into a crouch while he gathered his wits.

Artos, dazed, scrabbled around for something to use as a weapon, but only found the hilt of his broken sword, which he clung on to in desperation. Both men looked battered but unbowed as they faced off again, while all around them the battle raged. Conor sought the advantage of his longer blade and swung hard at Artos' face, only to miss and receive a hard hit to his ribs. Sucking in air, he tried to backhand his enemy, but he wasn't there. Suddenly a huge hand wrapped around his right arm and he felt the vicelike grip crushing his bones. Artos stood there in his righteous anger. Breathing heavily and with all his might he brought his broken blade down on Conor's wrist, severing his hand in a gout of blood and white bone. As he let go of the now useless limb his enemy cried out, doubling over in pain clutching his ruined arm as blood rushed from the stump. After quickly wrapping it in his cloak he turned and ran off towards the safety of the trees. Artos let him go as he was too tired to give chase, and just like that, the skirmish was over. The remaining attackers, seeing their leader defeated, took to their heels and ran.

White-faced with blood loss, Conor reached the treeline and staggered up the slope until he found the abandoned camp and searched for something to staunch the blood. He fell to the ground, overcome with dizziness, and crawled to the fire pit. It was out, but no, a small ember glowed deep in the ash pile and he blew on it, feeding the small spark until it burst into flame. Adding twigs and small branches, he got the blaze going and when he deemed it was hot enough he thrust his ruined arm into the bright flames, howling in pain like a wounded animal as the smell of burning flesh assailed his nostrils. As he pulled the now-charred stump from the flames he saw that the wound had cauterised and slumping back against a tree, he passed out.

Chapter 6
Heroes

A sombre mood filled the valley as the villagers tended to their wounded and laid out their dead for burial. Of Artos' men, only two had been lightly wounded in the fight and the good villagers had tended to these wounds as well, showing great care and skill while dealing with their own grief. As the headman had been killed, a new leader was elected almost immediately. Gruffyd, being well respected as one of the senior hunters in the village, had been chosen and immediately set about putting things right. The following night, there was to be a feast to honour the dead and celebrate the men who'd saved them from certain destruction at the hands of the Hibernian raiders. As for the bodies of the fallen attackers, they were stripped of anything of value and then dragged away from the settlement to be burned on a large pyre later that evening. It amazed Artos yet again that these people could carry on living in such a hostile place, and he made a vow before God to always live with honour and protect those who couldn't protect themselves.

The next morning a slow procession wound its way up to the rim of the valley through a thin drizzle of rain, to a spot where they buried their dead – a row of mounds that had been used for centuries. Large stones were rolled away from the entrances and the bodies were placed reverently inside small niches, amongst the bones of their ancestors. Eight men, women, and children had died in the fighting. A lot for a small settlement to lose as the burden of work now fell upon the shoulders of those who were left.

After the burial ceremonies were completed they made their way back down to the village to prepare for the feast, which left Artos and his men with little to do but repair damage done to their mail shirts and polish the nicks and dents from blades and helmets. Artos held the broken pieces of his sword in his hand.

'Well that looks fucked!' laughed Barcus, slapping his commander on the back as he stared over his shoulder at the ruined blade.

'Aye, it is at that,' smiled Artos sadly. 'This belonged to my father and his before him. I guess the iron got brittle.' He hung his head sadly. 'Still, it had meaning for me, and I hate to see it broken when there is so much need for it.'

'Indeed, brother. But look,' he produced a roll of cloth, 'this belonged to that rat bastard whose hand you took yesterday.' He handed it to Artos who unwrapped it, revealing a sword shorter than his spatha but with a thicker blade tapering to a sharp point. The hilt was gold and studded with garnets that sparkled in the sunlight as he held it up, giving it a few gentle swings to feel the heft.

'Hmm, heavier than I'm used to, but not a bad blade. I think the handle belonged to a different sword once, probably one much finer than this one.' He re-wrapped it and thanked Barcus for his gift.

'Oh, it's not from me,' he said, 'it's from the people here, as a thank-you. They don't have much and they are too in awe of you to gift it personally. They're calling you Arthur now, you know.'

'Arthur? But that's not my name!'

'Neither is Artos, is it? But they heard us calling you that, and that means bear,' he said with a laugh. 'Arthur means, "strong as a bear",' said Barcus with a grin. 'I mean, you've always looked like a bear and you're bloody strong too. So...' He laughed and walked away towards the rest of the men.

Artos looked down at the wrapped sword and whispered to himself, 'Arthur.' He smiled. Maybe it was time for a name change. After all, Artos was only a nickname he'd been given as a child because he'd always been bigger than the other kids in camp. The Roman world was changing so why not his name too? *Why not indeed?* he thought.

The fire in the centre of the village blazed, fed by the fat dripping into the flames from the beef steer roasting over it. Ale mugs were drained and topped up from foaming jugs that the younger members of the village carried in their role as servers, as the survivors celebrated their loss and the victory of the previous day's conflict.

'A toast, my lord!' shouted Gruffyd, the newly elected headman, raising his mug in salute. 'To you and your knights and to the lives you saved from certain death, or a life of slavery and pain.'

The gathered locals cheered and raised their own mugs and voices, chanting, 'Arthur, Arthur!' over and over. Soon even his own men joined in and the salute echoed off the sides of the valley and rang throughout the forest.

High up in the valley sheltered in a dip, Conor shuddered awake, his arm a throbbing ball of pain that caused him to groan out loud. He looked around and saw that the fire was now truly out and the ash cold. How long had he been unconscious? He wasn't sure, but knew he had to leave before he was discovered and killed for the attack on the village.

He listened for any sound that could indicate someone was coming but all he could hear was a distant chanting, repeating itself over and over. He listened for a few minutes and could faintly make out the chant.

'Arthur,' he said. That must be the name of the big bastard who'd cut his hand off. He tried to push himself up and cried out in pain as he put weight on the injured arm without thinking. He'd make him pay, he swore, as he stumbled upright and headed west in search of his missing men. They'd be heading back to the clan chief's main camp and by all the Gods, he'd make them pay for abandoning him to his death.

Chapter 7
Emrys

The following morning, the newly named Arthur, followed by his twenty-five faithful knights, wound his way out of the friendly valley after showing the villagers how to build a quick protective palisade. At the lip, they looked back and could see people lined up to wave farewell, crying out his name, which was carried to him on the wind. He raised a hand in salute and then following only Bryn, set off north to find his lost men.

Two uneventful days later, they reached the point in the river where weeks ago, Bryn and Gruffyd had pulled a dying man from the water's icy embrace.

'It was here, my lord,' said Bryn, indicating a spot where the fast flow slowed and eddied into a pool of calm water. 'We found him amongst those reeds.' Arthur waded out into the cold water and examined the spot but could find no clue to help, not that he had expected to.

'My man said he jumped from a ravine into this river. Do you know how far away that is?'

'No, Lord,' said Bryn. 'We seldom come this close to the dragon's territory. But the land rises towards the high mountains in the north almost continuously from here.'

'Well then, my friend,' said Arthur, clambering out of the flow, 'I think this is where we shall part ways. You need to return to your family and farm, and we must pursue our quest to find our men.'

'But I could still be of help, my lord,' said Bryn. 'I can hunt and bring you food. I can fight!'

'I know you can, my brother, and I would welcome you into our party with an open heart. But what if raiders attacked your home again? What then? Who would defend your family? You might be the difference between victory and defeat.' Bryn's head sagged, knowing he spoke true. 'And that palisade won't build itself, you know,' chided Arthur with a warm smile. 'It'll help protect your people from future attack.'

They said their goodbyes, each man gripping the other's forearm in the martial salute of brotherhood, and they watched as Bryn walked back into the trees until he was lost to sight.

'What now, sir?' asked Alcaeus.

'We need to get across, if what Bryn said was true about the ground rising up further along,' said Arthur. 'Barcus, we don't have time to check for a ford further downstream. We'll have to try and swim the horses across here.'

'Sir,' Barcus said. Turning to the others he enquired, 'Gavain, Lionides, you're our best swimmers. Do you think you could cross here with a length of rope and tie it off to a tree on the other side?' He pointed at a large willow that hung over the bank, dragging its branches in the swift-flowing water. 'Maybe that one,' he said.

'I think we can make it. How about it, Gavain?' said Lionides with a grin. 'Fancy a swim?' he challenged.

'How about a wager?' laughed Gavain. 'A silver denarii to whoever gets across first?'

'You're on.' Lionides shook hands with Gavain and started to remove his armour. 'I'd opt for that one a few metres further back, sir,' he said, pointing to a huge ancient oak that looked as if it had been there since the dawn of time. He grabbed a coil of rope, tied it around his middle, and strode to the water's edge.

'That looks mighty cold, Lio,' barked Alcaeus, looking at the rusty brown water rushing by. 'You can't afford the shrinkage, mate!' he shouted. The men burst out laughing as his friend playfully splashed frigid water at him.

Gavain stood next to Lionides. 'Ready?'

They both leapt into the freezing river.

They struck out with powerful strokes, although weighed down by the rope around their waists. They reached the swift current and were dragged downstream as they struggled to stay in a straight line. Lionides suddenly disappeared beneath the roiling water as Gavain ploughed on, unaware of his friend's misfortune.

Alcaeus bellowed, and Gavain looked around but couldn't see him. 'Pull him back in!' he shouted, and Arthur and his men pulled on the rope line but it was slack and wound in too easily. Lionides wasn't on the other end.

'Quick!' shouted Arthur to his men. 'Check downstream and see if you can spot him.'

His knights ran to obey, shouting for Lionides over and over. Gavain dipped his head under the freezing water but couldn't see his comrade in the darkness beneath. He breached the surface, drawing in a gasping breath and then dove back under, disappearing for what to the others seemed an eternity. Then suddenly he resurfaced with Lionides clutched in one arm and strove bravely against the current and pulled him to the other bank. Dragging him up the other side, he rolled him onto his back and started to push the water from his lungs.

Coughing and spluttering, Lionides rolled onto his side and vomited a large amount of water onto the already damp grass. Wiping spittle from his chin, he cocked his head towards Gavain and said with a weak smile, 'I guess I owe you a silver denarius then.'

Gavain grinned back. 'I'm just glad you're still alive and able to pay up. I didn't fancy fishing about for your money at the bottom of that river!' With that, he slapped him on the back and rocking to his heels, stood up and went to tie off his end of the rope.

Arthur had watched the events unfold fretfully, pacing the bank until Lionides was pulled from the river. Seeing him okay was a great relief and when Gavain signalled the rope was secure he made sure his men crossed safely before he attempted it himself. On reaching the far bank he checked Lionides, who was shivering with cold crouched on the ground with his knees drawn up under his chin. Alcaeus fussed round him like a mother hen. 'We need to warm him up,' he said. 'I've seen men succumb to this before. Someone get a fire going!'

Gavain stood nearby with a blanket wrapped round his shoulders, looking outwards into the surrounding trees. 'Sir,' he whispered through chattering teeth. 'Do you see that?' He pointed at something amongst the brush. Arthur stepped forward and drawing his sword, gently pushed aside the undergrowth and stepped through into a clearing, at the centre of which stood a large stone carved with intricate whorls and patterns and dominating all, a large dragon motif reared up, appearing to rake the sky with its claws.

'Well, I guess we've left the Empire now,' he said, stepping forward to examine the stone. As he got closer he saw that the dragon carving was a different colour than the rest. He reached out a finger and gently brushed it against the brownish stain on the rock; it flaked off like dust and as he rubbed it between finger and thumb he realised it was dried blood. Brushing his hands clean on his breeches, he walked around examining the rest of the clearing. Spotting a fresh earthen mound at the far side, he poked his blade into the soft soil and as he pushed the dirt aside a human hand appeared, its pale green pallor showing it had been in the ground for a while.

Swallowing, he moved more earth aside, dreading the possibility that this could be the last resting place of the lost patrol. But as he dug he soon realised that the hand belonged to a dead Hibernian raider, his plaid tunic, dirty and blood-stained, wrapped around the skeletal body. Arthur sagged in relief and covered the corpse again, saying a small prayer for the man's soul. No one deserved an end like this.

With the men and horses safely on the far bank they made their way upstream until they came to the rocky ravine the soldier had told them of. In his tale he told them he had run all night. But from which direction? Arthur sat on his horse in thought, trying to work out their next step.

'Sir,' spoke Alcaeus, 'with respect, we're losing the light. We can't travel much further today and in the dark it's too risky. We ought to find a place to camp that we can defend if need arises.'

'You're right, Alcaeus. We can pick up the trail again tomorrow with fresh eyes.'

Decision made, they started to look for a likely campsite but were forced to continue along the river as it wound its way up from the treeline until it reached the low hills surrounding the mountains. There, it plunged into a narrow gully that twisted through the landscape like a serpent.

'Let's try farther into the gully,' said Barcus.

The failing light threw deep pools of shadow in the narrow space between the rocky cleft. Their tired mounts pushed on until they came to a narrow gravel beach.

'This'll have to do,' said Arthur. 'We can go no farther in this light. Get a fire lit as soon as possible. We'll eat and then rest. Stay alert. We're in enemy territory now and anyone could be watching us so post guard, and we'll take it in turns. We're all equal here from now on.'

Arthur walked a little way along the beach until it curved around a rocky outcrop. There he stopped and sat on a boulder listening to the sounds of early evening. High above, on the clifftop birds sang their evensong and they echoed down in a beautiful cascading melody. A couple of bats hunted just above the river surface, skimming bugs out of the air with balletic grace. *A man could grow old in a place like this and never need anything more,* he thought. *Couldn't we all be at peace one day? Is it in man's nature to always fight for more than he needs?* He rested his chin on his fist and watched as the light faded into darkness, brooding on the future as he followed the flight of the bats until he could see them no more.

After their meal the men settled in for the night, talking low or playing dice. Guards in groups of two patrolled the narrow entrance to the gully, alert for any approaching danger.

Arthur took his turn at guard duty and was relieved by Alcaeus and a now fully recovered Lionides. He wished them a good night and made his way to where he'd laid his blanket out. He lay there in the darkness but felt a sense of restlessness as sleep eluded him until, with a sigh of resignation, he threw off his blanket and went upstream looking for solitude. After passing through clumps of damp ferns and splashing through shallow pools, he finally came upon a place of soul-quieting tranquillity. Moss-covered rocks surrounded a deep pool of reflected starlight. He sat and idly tossed small pebbles into the water, watching as the tiny ripples spread out to encompass the whole pond.

'There are few alive whose ripples touch the world like that,' said a voice from the darkness.

Arthur jumped up in shock, unable to believe someone had crept up on him in such a quiet place.

'Who goes there?' he challenged, drawing his dagger from its sheath and dropping into a defensive crouch.

'Fear me not,' said the voice. 'I mean you no harm.' An old man stepped into the dim light cast by the moon. He looked ancient with long, thinning grey hair bound by a strip of leather in a ponytail. His lean body hung loosely with faded clothes torn and repaired many times over. In all, he looked like one of the many dishevelled beggars who would hang around a military camp asking for scraps of food.

Arthur put away his knife with a small smile. 'I don't fear you, old man.'

'Well you should,' snapped the grey hair. 'Any man out at this most ungodly hour must be up to no good, hmm?' he questioned.

'And are you?' said Arthur.

'Am I what?'

'Up to no good?'

'Well, are you?' the old man replied with a knowing grin.

'Me? No, I just couldn't sleep. How about you?'

The old man considered his answer carefully, scratching his

wispy chin in thought. 'I was looking for a man,' he finally replied. 'Maybe you've heard of him. His name's Arthur, or so that's what the folk of Cambria are calling him. Apparently he killed a hundred men with his bare hands and used their skulls as drinking vessels for his mighty host, who thunder through the hills like avenging demons killing the Outland invaders.' He cackled.

Arthur looked dumbfounded, and then he burst out laughing in genuine mirth. 'You mock me, sir,' he said. 'For I am the one they call Arthur, and as you see, I am no avenging demon, nor some wild man-killer that takes skulls as totems.'

The old man sat across from him and laying his staff across his lap, said, 'Yes, you are a little underwhelming.' He winked.

Arthur laughed again and wiping the tears from his eyes, continued. 'Who told you this tale of my deeds? And anyway, who are you, and why are you looking for me?'

The old man smiled and settled a little more comfortably on the rock. 'As to who told me. I am a teller of tales, a spreader of myth. I heard of your deeds a few days past from some local hunters and it interested me. As to my name, I have many, but you may call me Emrys. For that is how I'm known in these lands. As to why I looked for you? That is yet to be known. But I am here and would beg your indulgence for a few days if I may, to learn more about you and your heroic knights.' He made a small bow and then looked at Arthur with bright, sparkling eyes that seemed almost to glow in the darkness.

'Well then,' said Arthur, 'you are most welcome to travel with my men and me. But I fear you'll be sorely disappointed with the reality of who we are,' and saying that, he stood and beckoned Emrys to follow him back to the camp.

'No,' said Emrys under his breath, 'I don't think I will be,' as he followed in Arthur's shadow.

Chapter 8
Cavern

The party wound its way up through the hills in search of any trace of where their comrades may have been taken. While this was happening Emrys, after refusing to share a horse showed incredible stamina by keeping up with and occasionally questioning members of Arthur's party about their leader.

'Are you not going to write any this down, old man?' said one of the men later that day, after Emrys had received a lengthy telling of his life story.

The old man smiled and tapped the side of his head. 'It's all safely up here,' he said.

'What if you get a knock?'

'Then I'll make something up,' laughed Emrys, which brought a merry chuckle from the men riding alongside.

The oak and ash of the deep forests slowly gave way to pine as the trail wound higher and higher through hills that soon became the foot of a mountain range topped with white peaks. Further up, the trees disappeared completely, leaving a barren scree-covered slope that would leave them exposed to any watchers amongst the surrounding crags. 'We'll have to stick to the edge of the forest to avoid being seen,' said Arthur as they took their midday meal.

'Seen by who?' inquired Emrys. 'Nobody lives this far up. This is a barren wilderness loved only by snow and ice, and the occasional wolf pack.' As the words left his mouth a distant howl echoed from the mountain, answered a few moments later by another. He waved his hands as if making a point. 'See!'

'And anyway,' said Gavain from where he sat, 'there's no sign that our men, or anybody, has passed this way. We should head back down and try to work our way around these mountains before our food runs out.' He took a bite of some stale bread, making a face as he chewed, and a few heads nodded in agreement.

'You're right,' Arthur replied. 'We've already wasted too much time up here. Finish up and we'll head back down and try to pick a more favourable route.'

'You won't make it, you know,' interjected the old man. 'These lands belong to the dragon, and you'll be spotted and taken long before you find your friends.'

'And how would you know?' said Alcaeus crossly. 'Have you been here before? Have you seen this famed dragon?'

'Yes, and yes,' Emrys stated flatly.

'What?' All heads turned towards the old man as he sat calmly eating his meal. He looked up in surprise at their reaction. 'Would it be so unbelievable,' he chided, 'that an old man like me has travelled these lands before and seen all the things of wonder it contains? I was young once too, you know. You young folk seem to forget that in your rush of youth.'

'So you've seen the actual dragon then?' Alcaeus said.

'Yes. Of course. And he was not as doubting as you.' He jabbed a bony finger into Alcaeus' chest for emphasis.

'He?'

Emrys turned to Arthur with a calculating look. 'You don't miss much, do you, boy?' he cackled. 'Yes. The dragon is a he. Did you think it would be some blonde-haired princess?' He laughed at his own joke.

'Does it have wings?'

'Is it covered in scales?'

'Does it breathe fire?'

The questions tumbled out of the men in a torrent. Emrys held up his hands to quiet them down. 'Please. Enough with these ridiculous questions,' he said. 'Are you under the impression that the dragon is some mythical beast?' He could tell from their faces that's exactly what they thought. *Gods, give me strength,* he thought as he pulled on his beard. 'The dragon is no mythic creature, you fools. He's a man, plain and simple, albeit a powerful one. He is Uther Pendragon, a great warlord with ambitions to become a king of these lands if he gets his way, and your lads from Rome clearing off back home has opened the door for men like him. This whole land will burn with civil war soon, unless someone steps up and stops it.' He looked over at Arthur with a penetrating stare.

Arthur squirmed under his gaze uncomfortably. 'Don't look at me,' he said. 'I'm just a lowly decurion trying to rescue a lost patrol and then I'm done with the armies of Rome. I just want to leave all this behind me and find somewhere I can call home. What part could I possibly play in great men's power games?'

'What part indeed!' said Emrys with a small smile. 'Great men are created, you know. They're not born that way, and you have the makings of greatness. I saw it in you the first time we met.'

'Then you are truly mistaken.' Arthur plucked a stalk of grass and slowly tore it to pieces, throwing each part with obvious anger. 'I can't even find my missing men. How could I be great when I can't even do that? Tell me!'

'Because you have a strong sense of right and wrong, and a good heart. A rare combination these days. Many would have given up by now and headed back to the safety of their own lands, but not you and your men, and they haven't even questioned your leadership. Have you asked yourself why?' Arthur shook his head. 'It's because you're a natural leader and your men love and respect you. It shines from you like a bright star. Only you refuse to see this yourself.'

Arthur felt himself blush. 'You are mistaken, old man. I fear age has addled your mind.'

'Maybe so. Yes, maybe so. But I'm not blind to who you could be. You just need purpose. Like that village you saved. You'd already left it behind, yet you returned at speed to save them. Why? They couldn't pay you, and you owed them nothing. They just gave you a dead man's sword that was yours already by right of conquest.'

'They needed our help,' said Arthur quietly.

'But you and your men could have been killed. Or worse!'

'I couldn't let them die. It wouldn't have been right!' Arthur said more forcefully.

'Exactly. It was the right thing to do. See. Greatness.' Emrys clapped his hands together in glee.

'He's mad,' Lionides muttered to Alcaeus out of the corner of his mouth.

Emrys' eyes locked on to Lionides. 'Mad, am I? Who's the madder? The one who leads or the one who follows?'

'I. Umm…' stammered Lionides.

'And what about the mountain of gold, then?' asked Alcaeus. 'Is that not what it appears to be as well?'

'No. The gold is real,' Emrys said, 'only you'll need to get through the dragon and his men to get it. So it's a moot point, really, isn't it!' He grinned at Alcaeus and winked.

'Enough of this foolishness,' barked Arthur. 'We've wasted enough time over this talk. Let's be on our way. The sooner we find our men, the sooner we leave.' He stood, brushing down his cloak as he stalked off to his horse.

'I think the old man's words struck a chord,' said Gavain to no one in particular. Emrys looked up and gave him a wink before struggling to his feet and heading off back down the hillside.

As dusk fell they were still no closer to finding a route off the mountains and the sound of wolves howling was becoming more persistent with each mile.

'We need to find shelter soon,' said Barcus, looking at the

darkening sky. 'I think it may snow tonight.'

'Well aren't you a ray of sunshine?' joked Kai, a handsome, well-muscled African who like the rest of Arthur's party seemed to have washed up on the shores of Britannia and ended up in his unit by chance. His deep voice rumbled as he laughed.

'Indeed I am,' agreed Barcus with a smile, 'but that cloud building up in the west could really fuck us up if we're caught out here exposed when it hits.'

'But this is Britannia. If it ain't raining, it's snowing. If it ain't snowing, it's foggy. And most of the time it's blowing a bloody gale.' Kai boomed his rumbling laugh again.

'Hush, man. I hear something.' Arthur slid from his horse and handing his reins to Barcus, slipped off into the bushes closely followed by Emrys, who moved like a wraith in the gloom.

Creeping through the undergrowth Arthur felt Emrys grip his arm and bring him to a halt. Up ahead, they saw the outline of a dozen or so men sitting around a small fire, talking and joking.

'It'll be a patrol of Uther's men, I guarantee you,' he whispered.

'How do you know?' said Arthur in a hushed tone.

'Animals make little or no sound in the woods, and only the Pendragon's men would dare to walk his lands so brazenly,' Emrys explained as if talking to a child.

'But we're here.'

'True. But we're a fool's company.' He winked. 'We'd best move.' They turned and crept back to where the men waited silently.

The wolf pack howled again, closer this time. 'Seems like we're stuck between a rock and a hard place,' said Barcus after Arthur told them of the patrol.

'Yes. We need to move away from both Uther's men and that damn wolf pack before either spot us out in the open,' said Arthur. 'We need somewhere to hole up for the night.' He looked at Emrys, who was looking about the upper forest. 'Any ideas?' he asked.

The old man turned his head and said, 'I think I remember there's a place not too far from here where we should be safe. It's somewhere I've not been in a very long time.' A look of sadness clouded his face. 'This way,' he said, and without another word set off westwards.

An hour later saw the tired party staring at a moon-washed granite rockface framed on each side by dense thorn bushes and gorse.

'Well this is a great improvement,' griped Alcaeus, pulling his cloak tighter as the first light flakes of snow started to swirl about them. 'A blank wall, fantastic. We should be nice and snug here. I'll break out the wine!'

'Not everything is as it seems, my doubtful friend,' said Emrys as he strode up to the rockface and walked straight through it.

'Impossible,' said Alcaeus, starring agog at what he'd just seen. 'He must be a wizard or worse, a demon!'

Arthur dismounted and walked up to where he'd last seen Emrys. Just as he thought he'd touch the rockface an opening appeared before him at such an oblique angle that it would easily be missed, even in daylight unless you were stood right next to it. He stepped inside and though the path wasn't wide it soon entered a much larger space that could easily house the men and their mounts comfortably. Emrys was busy in the middle, lighting some kindling in an old fire pit that still had a good supply of dry wood nestled up against one wall.

'Welcome to the wizards' cavern,' he said. 'Don't just stand there gawping, go bring in the rest of your men and the horses before they freeze to death!'

Arthur hurried back outside to see the men still waiting, although several had dismounted obviously preparing to come find him.

'It's a huge cave,' he said. 'It'll be a squeeze for the horses getting in, but there's room for all of us inside. Now come on.' He took his horse's bridle and walked her to the narrow opening. The animal, nostrils flaring, tossed her head in protest as he tried to guide her through into the cavern. Gently stroking her muzzle and whispering softly, he managed to coax her inside although rolling eyes showed the fear she felt. Soon after, the rest of the men found their way through and it wasn't long before they all sat around a merry blaze, warming chilled hands and feet. Only Kai refused to join them, instead choosing to sit at the entrance wrapped in his cloak with a short spear across his lap, watching as the snow fell in silence, blanketing the forest in white.

'Why don't you join the others?' asked Arthur, placing his hand on Kai's shoulder.

'Someone has to keep watch, sir,' he said by way of reply.

'But there's more to it than that, though, isn't there?'

Kai smiled up at his commander. 'You are a perceptive man, sir. In truth I don't like caves much. They remind me of something I'd prefer to forget.'

'Would you like to talk about it?' said Arthur, settling by Kai's side and offering him a bowl of warm porridge.

Sighing, Kai took the offered bowl and spooned a mouthful, chewing slowly as he gathered his thoughts. 'When I was a child, back in Africa,' he started, and then coughed in discomfort, 'the Romans came to my village. I was only very young, you understand, no more than three or four. Anyway, when they came our men resisted, fighting as hard as they could against the might of the Empire, and naturally they lost. But as punishment the Romans gathered up all the women and children and put us in a nearby cave, then blocked the entrance with brushwood and set fire to it. I still smell the smoke and hear the screams in my dreams.' He choked back a sob as the memories came flooding back. 'My mother, holding me in her arms, saw the smoke making its way up a narrow crack in the ceiling. She kissed me and said she loved me, and then she pushed me up into that crack and told me to climb and not stop until I was free. So I did. I was small, so I got through but another that followed got stuck and when I was free, I learned that they'd all choked to death, trapped in that small space.' He shuddered with the telling. 'A day or two later a Roman patrol picked me up wandering alone in the remains of my village. A centurion, Castos was his name. Well his wife couldn't have children so he sort of adopted me and raised me as his own and that's how I ended up here.'

'Is Castos still alive?' Arthur inquired.

'He was last time I saw him, but that was a long time ago now,' Kai said sadly.

'Maybe after this you can go find him?'

'Maybe.' He finished the porridge, and turning to his commander, said, 'Thank you for listening, sir. I've never told anyone my story before. I feel like a weight has been lifted from my shoulders.'

Arthur gave his shoulder another squeeze and promised to send someone to relieve him so he could get some rest.

Back in the cave everyone was settling in for the night. As he lay down he noticed the old man fast asleep on the far side of the fire, and wondering just exactly who he was, closed his eyes and drifted off to a dreamless sleep.

On the other side of the cave Emrys watched Arthur through slitted eyes, a smile of satisfaction playing on his lips.

Chapter 9
Passage

A great red dragon reared up on its hind legs, spraying liquid fire throughout the cave. Arthur's men cowered in the corner as the fire spread toward them, begging him for help even as the flames washed over them and turned their bodies to ash. From behind he heard Emrys calling his name, and turning, he saw the old man in robes of a dazzling blue, hands coruscating in blue flame as he battled the beast.

'This way!' he shouted. But Arthur's feet refused to move. 'If you don't move now you're doomed to fail like your men. Move, damn you, MOVE!' The old man's voice radiated power and Arthur's leaden feet obeyed.

Arthur shuddered awake, suddenly aware he was being shaken by someone unseen. 'Shh.' A hand pressed over his mouth to keep him quiet. 'Follow me,' came the whispered voice again and the hand was lifted from his face.

'Emrys? What are you up to?' he hissed.

'Just keep quiet, and follow me, and bring your sword. We'll need it,' replied the old man moving off to the back of the cave. As Arthur stood in the dim light cast by the glow of the fire pit, he noticed his men still deep in their slumber. The horses, too, seemed contented, occasionally shifting from hoof to hoof as they dozed in the warmth of the cave.

He followed the old man to the back of the large space and watched as he pulled aside some growth revealing another passage leading further into the hillside. 'Where are we going, Emrys?' he whispered.

'A quiet place. A sacred place. Somewhere we can talk. I need to show you something,' he said as he lit a small torch and bright light flooded the narrow space.

'What?'

'All in good time, Arthur. But for now, just trust me, and keep up. It wouldn't do to get lost here. These caves are truly ancient, expanded by the men of stone thousands of years ago in their search for... well, whatever they were searching for! No one really remembers anymore. But in their digging they discovered something truly spectacular, and now you need to see it for yourself.' The old man continued on and Arthur followed behind in silence.

After maybe half an hour of trudging through narrow, twisting passages the two men stopped before a seemingly solid wall. 'More tricks, Emrys?'

'No. Just a bit of a tight squeeze, especially for one of your size.' The old man knelt down to show Arthur a narrow gap, no more than a foot high.

'You must be joking.' Arthur's face paled as he stared at the small space Emrys expected him to crawl through. 'And how far is it?' he asked, his naked fear of the tiny gap showing in his voice.

'Only a few feet, you'll be fine. Just remember to breathe out a bit before you start or you might get stuck.' The old man crouched and indicated with the torch that he should go first.

'But I can't see anything. How will I know when I'm through?' His words shook as he said them. 'And what if this is some elaborate trap you concocted to kill me?'

'I've had ample opportunity over these past few days to kill you easily, least of all in your sleep. So why would I bother leading you here only to murder you when you could obviously overpower me in this tiny space? What possible purpose would that serve? But if it makes you feel any better and if it will stop you quaking in your boots, I'll go first.' And with that, Emrys ducked down quickly and wriggled under the tiny gap. Arthur watched as his boots vanished into the space and then waited, realisation dawning on him that he was now alone in the dark with no idea of how to get back to the cave and his men. Cursing himself for a fool he pounded his fist against the wall and then felt his way down to the lip of the gap. Scrabbling in the inky blackness, he felt panic rising in his chest threatening to unman him. Dipping his head below the gap, he could just discern the faint light of the torch, and then a voice floated back to him. 'Get a move on. We don't have all night.'

Cursing again, Arthur took a few deep gulps of air then remembered what Emrys had said, let most of his breath out, and squeezed himself into the space, hands grasping rocks and stones as he pulled himself towards the promise of light and safety.

He rolled out of the crushing gap, breathing heavily as the panic lifted from his racing heart. Emrys squatted a few feet away, the torch in his hand and a smile on his creased face.

'Not much fun, is it?' he said ruefully.

'Go fuck yourself,' cursed Arthur as he lay on his back, his chest heaving. 'That's the worst thing I've ever done.' He rolled onto his side and stared across the packed dirt floor at the grinning face.

'You should try it when it's flooded, now that's much more of a challenge.' He smirked at Arthur's discomfort.

'Well I'm here now. What is it you want to show me?'

'Right you are, then,' said Emrys, jumping nimbly to his feet, 'follow me,' and he set off again. Groaning, Arthur got up and stumbled after the crazy old man. After an eternity he stopped and handed the torch to Arthur. 'You must go first this time or you won't get the full impact of what I want you to see.'

'How much farther is it?' he queried.

'Just around that outcrop.' He pointed to a large glistening stone that half-blocked the way. As Arthur stepped forward he heard running water. It grew louder as he reached the stone, until turning the bend, he stepped into a mighty cavern.

Suddenly a bright light flared around him and he threw up his hand to shield his face from the glow. After a few seconds his eyes became accustomed to it and he realised it was the reflected light from his torch, thrown back from the myriad of crystals that seemed to cover every surface of the cave.

'This is incredible,' he said, the torch hanging forgotten in his hand. 'I've never seen anything like this in my life. It's. It's... wonderful.' He stood there in awe.

'This,' said Emrys, coming up behind him and making a sweeping gesture with his hand, 'is the crystal cavern. The spiritual heart of Cambria and its most sacred place. Known only to a handful over the millennia.'

'You being one of them,' said Arthur. 'Who are you? Really, this time, I need to know.'

'Fair enough,' said the old man. 'But first let me show you why you're here.'

They walked across the cavern until they came to a huge lake fed by a crystal-clear waterfall that cascaded from an opening near the ceiling. Arthur bent down and scooped up some of the clear water. It was icy cold and tasted like nothing he'd had before.

'The lake is sacred too,' said Emrys. 'Although it's alright to drink of its waters.' He smiled.

Arthur stood and looked about sheepishly, then noticing an island in the middle of the water he said, 'And what's over there?' indicating the dimly lit island with a nod of his head.

'Ahh. That is the holy isle of Avalon, and that is where we are headed now.' He started to walk around the southern shore, looking intently at the clear water as if searching for something. With a cry of delight, he waded into the cold waters and plunged his hands under its frigid surface, tugging and pulling at something held in its icy embrace. 'Some help, please!' he shouted over his shoulder as he tossed a large stone aside. Arthur waded to his side and saw a narrow canoe sunk beneath the surface filled with rocks. They emptied the vessel of its cargo, slowly bringing it to the surface. As it finally floated with only a few inches of water in the bottom Arthur could see it was completely coated in a resin-like substance similar to pitch, which had stopped it becoming waterlogged and protected the wood from rotting. '

How in God's name did that get here?' inquired Arthur, eyeing the boat, which was near seven feet long with a paddle wedged firmly inside. 'It certainly didn't arrive here the same way we did!'

'No, it didn't. I put it here many years past when the original entrance was still open.'

'What happened?'

'It's a long story, maybe better suited for another time. But for now, we must cross this lake to that island.' He clambered nimbly into the canoe followed by Arthur. It rocked alarmingly as Arthur sat down and he had to grasp both sides firmly to stop himself from falling out.

'I take it you're not used to canoes,' said Emrys simply as he effortlessly paddled out onto the water.

'You could say that,' gasped Arthur as the boat bobbed and threatened to capsize.

'Stop moving about,' the old man chided, 'you'll have us both out in a minute.'

The canoe moved more smoothly as Arthur finally relaxed, allowing Emrys to direct the craft to the rapidly approaching island. As he stared into the black water Arthur could just make out faint shapes, and as they reached the shallows he saw weapons of all sorts; swords, spears, even beautifully crafted bronze shields bent and broken scattered across the lakebed. He turned to Emrys, pointing to the relics. 'Why is there so much ruined weaponry down there?'

'They're votive offerings to the Gods of this place,' he said without looking back. 'When a chieftain died in the past these offerings were given to one with knowledge of this place and placed here to help ease the journey of the deceased in the afterlife.'

Arthur nodded in understanding and lapsed into silence.

Shingle ground underneath the hull as both men clambered out onto the shore. The light from their flickering torch reflected brightly from the cavern's walls as they made their way up a gentle slope until they reached a large rectangular stone, of at least four tons, in the centre. It was heavily carved all over with unfamiliar patterns that seemed to flicker and move in the strange light.

'This,' said Emrys solemnly, 'is the tomb of the founder and first great king of Cambria. His name was Camber and he was the second son of a great hero and a Goddess who came from far to the east, long before Rome was even a dream.' His eyes clouded briefly with memory. 'He brought knowledge and culture to the wild men of this land and instilled in them a love of music and poetry, and encouraged an oral history of the people to be handed down from generation to generation. It was a golden age of great deeds and even greater heroes. But. Time flows like a river and people forget and become savages once more, consumed by base desires like greed and power. Although if you look closely, you can still find vestiges of that age lingering in places such as these.' He indicated the cavern.

'Incredible. I never realised that Cambria was anything but some muddy backwater at the edge of the Empire,' said Arthur in wonder. 'But it still doesn't answer the questions – who are you, and why am I here?'

The old man sighed and sat with his back against the stone block. 'My name is indeed Emrys, or rather that was the name I was given by my parents when I was born. I've been known by many since then, much like you, Artos, or is it Arthur now? Although, neither are your real name are they, Ambrosius?'

Arthur started and jumped to his feet. 'How could you know that?' he demanded.

'I've known all about you for years, Ambrosius Aurelianus. For you are special. You have the blood of King Camber flowing in your veins, and as such, you are tied to this place, unknowingly on your part. But to those of us who keep watch, the knowledge of your lineage is as easy to follow as a footpath clearly marked.'

Arthur stood in stunned silence, trying to digest what he had just been told. 'Who are you?' he asked again in a whisper.

'I am who I am. But not who I seem,' he said cryptically. 'In these lands and especially in places like this I'm simply known as The Merlin.'

'The Merlin?' said Arthur.

'Yes. It's a title that only one may possess, and it is never passed on until the previous Merlin relinquishes their claim to it.'

'But what does it mean!'

'It means,' Emrys said, sitting forward, 'that I am the keeper of the knowledge and lore of this land, and all its secrets and magic, going back all the way back to King Camber and beyond.' His voice strengthened and rose in volume. 'And as such I have the right to go wherever I wish unhindered and under the protection of my title. Great men may seek my counsel and I give it freely and with impartiality. I have done so for countless years, serving only the land. But you – you are a horse of a different colour, Arthur. You have come here now, at this time of internal conflict, led by the will of God to free these lands, save the people, and restore Cambria to its golden past.' He deflated like a ruptured bladder and slumped against the block. 'Or that's the plan,' he said. His face creased into a tired smile that clearly showed his great age.

'And just exactly how am I supposed to do that?' asked Arthur after a few silent minutes had passed.

'It starts with this.' Emrys slapped his palm against the stone slab before standing and tracing his fingers over the surface.

Arthur joined him. 'What are we looking for?' he enquired.

'Ahh,' said Emrys, bending forward and blowing a cloud of dust from the stone's surface. 'This.' A narrow slot was clearly visible in the centre of the block. 'Now,' he said, 'place your sword in there.'

Arthur drew his weapon and carefully placed the tip into the gap; it slid in easily to about halfway, then stopped.

'Right,' said Emrys, 'when I say, pull with all your strength.'

'But that will bend the blade,' he protested.

'Just do it. You'll see,' the old man said. 'Now. PULL!'

Arthur heaved with all his considerable strength and wasn't surprised when the blade suddenly buckled and bent almost in half. He let go with a curse and, turning to the old man, pointed at the now-ruined blade. 'Now look at what you've done!' he shouted. 'You've ruined a perfectly good blade, and for what?' He threw his hands in the air angrily and walked off a few feet.

'I didn't do anything,' said Emrys. 'You bent your own sword, not me!'

'Because you told me to!' Arthur fumed.

'Semantics,' said Emrys. 'Anyway, what's done is done. The earthly power of your sword is broken. Now pull it from the slot and throw it into the lake. I'm sure Nimuë would gladly accept your offering.'

'Who?'

'Nimuë, she's the spirit of the lake and she guards this island from all but The Merlin and the rightful King of Cambria.'

'I don't worship the old ways,' said Arthur sceptically. 'I follow the path of the Christ, as do my men. This is nonsense.'

'Humour an old man, just this once, would you?' said Emrys.

Arthur shrugged and pulling the now ruined weapon from the notch, threw it far out into the black waters. They both watched the damaged blade spin away, but just as it touched the surface there was a bright flare of white light, and just for a second Arthur could have sworn he saw a slim hand reach above and grasp the hilt of the sword before returning to the depths without a ripple.

Impossible, Arthur thought, staring out across the water, blaming the low light for tricking his eyes. He looked over at the old man who was also gazing out across the lake, but his eyes were unfocused and his lips moved silently in prayer.

'That didn't just happen, did it?' said Arthur.

Emrys shrugged. 'You saw what you saw; deny it if you choose.' He turned back to the stone slab. 'Here, help me with this.' He grasped one end as Arthur took the other. 'Now, let's see if your offering has been accepted. Heave!' They both strained against the huge block. Nothing happened at first, and then with a groan of inevitability, the top of the stone came free in a blast of dust and grit and slid off to one side. Coughing and waving away the cloying dust cloud of ages past, they both looked inside.

Staring back at them from the depths of the tomb was the mummified body of King Camber, still in his armour, clutching in his hand a magnificent sword the likes of which Arthur had never seen. Even after hundreds of years the metal shone brightly, a twisting pattern running up its length, and the golden hilt clasped in the bony grip of death had a large, deep red garnet fixed into the pommel.

'The sword of a King,' Arthur said in hushed, reverent tones.

'This sword is called Caliburn, though sometimes it is referred to as Caledfwlch or Caladbolg, but that's the Hibernian name. It means hard lightning, which is a good name as this sword was forged from star metal, a rare element. So it is harder than iron, stays clear of rust, and never loses its edge in battle. A truly kingly weapon that any chief who wishes to claim this land covets above all else, even gold. Go on, take it.' Emrys indicated that Arthur should pick it up.

Arthur reached in and gently touched the withered hands that still clasped the sword in death. As his fingers touched the dry, brittle skin the hands opened, as though offering the blade to him. He gently took it and raised it, and as he did there was a sighing sound from within the grave and the body in the tomb crumbled to dust, leaving not a trace of what had once been there. Emrys bowed his head in respect to the long-dead King of Cambria, then turned and bowed once more to Arthur, saying, 'Hail, Arthur. The once and future King.'

The words echoed round the cavern, growing in intensity until the walls shook and waves appeared on the placid lake. Rocks started to fall from the ceiling, crashing to the floor and splashing into the waters.

'Our time here is done. We must go!' yelled Emrys over the noise, and grabbing Arthur's arm they ran to the canoe, jumping in and paddling towards an opening that had just been formed by collapsing rocks.

'This is our way out!' he cried.

'How do you know?' Yelling above the noise Arthur paddled with his hands, his desire to not be buried alive conquering his fear of drowning.

'Because that used to be the entrance before it was sealed, now paddle.'

Digging in to the churning black water, the canoe sped across the lake before grinding up onto the far shore where the two men leapt onto the beach and ran into the gaping tunnel as clouds of dust and crashing boulders threatened to overwhelm them. Holding Arthur's arm Emrys blundered through the darkened tunnel until the sounds of destruction faded behind them.

Stopping to catch his breath, he bent over with his hands on his knees, coughing and gasping. Arthur was in no better shape. They stood in the darkness for a few minutes and then Arthur said, 'What now? We're trapped in a tunnel with no light and possibly no way out.'

'Have faith, Arthur,' said Emrys. 'You still have the sword, don't you?'

'Yes, though I nearly lost it over the side of that blasted boat as we diced with death yet again,' he grumbled.

'Then all will be well. Didn't I tell you that there's a plan for you? You are the rightful ruler of these lands, and God won't fail you for there is too much yet to be done. Now let's get out of here.'

Arthur heard the old man poking around in the darkness, and then with a cry of triumph there was a digging sound and a shaft of welcome sunlight bathed the passage.

Stepping from the earth into the early-morning sunshine both Arthur and Emrys were momentarily disoriented after the darkness behind them. Looking back at the narrow hole they'd just crawled from, Arthur asked if they should seal it again, but after poking his head back in the old man reassured him that the crystal cavern was probably sealed off permanently. 'It should be safe for now,' he assured. 'We'd best get back to your men. I'm sure they're worried by your disappearance.' And with that, they set off.

Arthur's men couldn't believe their eyes when he and Emrys approached the cave from the outside, crunching their way through the fresh snowfall and surprising Lionides, who was on guard while Kai slept alongside him.

'How on earth?' stammered Lionides.

'Don't ask,' replied Arthur, brushing off his cloak and tunic as dirt and dust fell about him.

Chapter 10
Clan and Kin

Conor MacDuid had been unconscious for several days after making it back to his chief's camp near the west coast. Luckily his man Fionn and a few stragglers had discovered him unconscious several miles from the site of their battle with Arthur. Rigging a makeshift stretcher from pine boughs and cloaks, they'd taken it in turns to carry him on their long journey home.

His fever had burned fiercely, stealing the flesh from his bones, and the Druid who cared for him said he'd live only if the fever broke before the next full moon.

Fortunately for Conor his great strength and will sustained him, and two days before the full moon the fever broke, leaving him weak but still able to bawl out his men for their apparent abandonment of him. Fionn told him repeatedly that they'd searched for him after the fight was over, but on finding no sign they'd assumed he was dead and started the return journey to the clan's main camp, to regroup and see to their own wounds. He told Conor, of the forty men they'd set out with fifteen had died in the fight, with a further seven succumbing to their wounds days later, including Darragh, whose foot had turned green and stinking and eventually caused his death. Some had just not been found. Maybe they were lost or decided to desert.

Conor raged at the very thought of the man who'd taken his hand. A hand he could still feel when the pain ebbed enough. He could still feel his fingers, and having once tried to pick up a cup of water and sent it crashing to the floor he screamed his frustration, tears of anger and loss streaming down his face.

By all the Gods, he swore to find this Arthur and kill him slowly. Taking him piece by piece just like his hand. Then when there was nothing left, he might just choose to let him live. This brought a smile to Conor's haggard face. Yes. That's what he'd do.

He'd leave behind a stump of a man, left to beg for scraps. For the first time in days, he laughed in genuine pleasure.

'So, you're feeling better now, are you?' Conor stood before his chieftain, his father. Feargal. A dark, brooding man with iron-grey hair braided either side of his bearded face. Gold and silver torcs wrapped around his heavily muscled arms that swirled with tattoos of mythical beasts and patterns of power. His large, scarred hands rested lightly on a sword that lay across his knees as he leant forward in his seat to talk to his son, in the large hall that was the centre of his power in Western Cambria.

The smoke-laden air filtered out through a gap above the fire pit as motes of ash sparkled in a shaft of light.

'So you're telling me that forty of my men led by my own son were defeated by twenty men and a village full of farmers?' Feargal's grip on the sword became tighter as his anger built. 'And my own son, who I trained from birth, loses a hand – his sword hand, no less – to some damn Roman horseman.' He stood, his own sword hanging loosely by his side. 'And to top it off, you're telling me your own men deserted you.'

'Yes, Father.' Conor knelt before his chief, head bowed. Not knowing what more to say, he kept his silence. His father's anger was an explosive and dangerous thing that couldn't be controlled once released, and from his kneeling position he could feel that rage building as he stalked around the hall.

'FIONN!' Feargal bellowed the name of Conor's second-in-command. Fionn came rushing into the hall at his lord's call.

'My chieftain.' He dropped to a knee in supplication.

'Fionn. Fionn. What am I to do?' He tilted his head, examining the man knelt before him, sword resting on his shoulder.

'My lord?' Fionn looked up quizzically.

'Stand. Stand, my lad.' Feargal offered a hand and raised him up. Throwing an arm around his shoulders, he walked up the hall. 'I have a problem, Fionn.'

'A problem, my lord?'

'Aye. Ya see, I can't punish my own son.' He twirled his hand about as if trying to grasp a thought. 'He's my blood, you understand.'

'Yes, my lord.' Fionn started to shake with fear as the chieftain's grip on his shoulder tightened.

'And after all, he's lost his bloody hand. Careless. Careless, indeed. So. Someone else must take the blame. Any ideas, lad?'

Fionn tried to stammer a reply but his tongue suddenly felt too large for his mouth.

'No ideas then?' Feargal let go of Fionn and walked up towards his chair. 'Disappointing you are indeed, lad. You can leave now. Go on. Go.' He made a shooing motion.

With a sigh of relief Fionn bowed and turned to leave.

As his back turned, Feargal sheathed his sword and picked up a spear that was leaning against a pillar. He hefted it and threw it with all his strength at Fionn. The point ripped through his back and burst from his chest in a spray of blood and gore, splashing over Conor's face as he still knelt before his father's rage.

Fionn lay on his side gasping for breath. A thin trickle of blood ran from his mouth and onto the dirt floor. As he lay there, his life draining away, he heard Feargal step alongside him.

'You failed my son, and that means you failed me.'

Fionn looked up into his chief's blazing eyes and spat, 'Fuck you!' Feargal's blade sliced down and lopped off his head in one cut. Reaching down, he picked up the severed head and turned back to his son.

'Stand. You useless little shit.' He threw Fionn's blood-dripping head at his son, who caught it by instinct with his one good hand. 'These are the consequences of your failures.' He stormed forward and grabbing his son's injured arm, gave it a hard squeeze. Conor let out a pitiful whine and dropped the head, which tumbled along the floor to rest by its own body. 'He,' Feargal pointed at Fionn's corpse, 'he was a better warrior. A better man than you could ever hope to be. And he died because of you! Do you understand?' He slapped Conor hard and sent him reeling to the floor holding his cheek. 'Count yourself lucky that you still have a purpose here, otherwise you'd be joining him.'

'Am I to hunt this Arthur down then, Lord?' Conor asked eagerly.

'Ha. You couldn't hunt down a dead fucking sheep. Leave that to the real warriors.'

Conor's face darkened in anger and hatred for his father.

'No. I have another, more pleasant task for you. One that even you shouldn't mess up. A wedding!'

'Wedding?'

'Yes. You're getting married.' Feargal laughed, then turned deadly serious. 'While you've been out getting my men killed, I've been in talks and have recently received an emissary from Uther Pendragon in the north. He's offering a truce between our peoples in return for us no longer invading his kingdom. He won't attack us in the rear as we head eastwards. And to seal this truce, you, my son, are going to marry his beautiful niece, Gwenyfar.'

'You must be mad,' said Conor. 'I'm not marrying some Cambrian whore!'

Feargal grabbed his face in a vicelike grip and squeezed. 'You'll damn well marry who I tell you to, boy,' he spat. 'This truce will cement our future success in this realm, and you are not going to fuck this up. And anyway, once we've defeated the other tribes, there'll be nothing to stop us from taking Uther's throne, and then you can do what you like with your new wife.'

'Really. So that's your plan?' Conor felt the familiar tingle of pleasure he always had when he was allowed free rein to inflict pain and torment. He smiled a cold smile.

'Of course. But keep your desires in check until the right time.' Feargal loathed that dark part of his son's soul, but was prepared to indulge it for now. Conor wouldn't be allowed to know his whole plan. That would come later. Feargal smiled his own cold smile.

Two days later Conor, with a company of ten men set off north to the lands of the Pendragon, accompanied by Uther's emissary. The cold air of the mountains brought a chill wind and flurries of snow that caused the men to wrap themselves in their warmest cloaks, with hoods pulled up to cover wind-chapped faces. Their mounts, the sturdy ponies that lived in these hills, plodded on heedless of the cold and icy conditions. Their heads dipped as they wound their way up mountain tracks through pine forests and barren hills covered with a dusting of snow and frost.

Conor watched as an eagle hunted high up in the sky for small game like hare and ermine. He traced its flight as it circled, riding the wind like a God of the sky. He envied its freedom. The eagle answered to no one; it lived, it killed, and that was all. Its instincts were for survival and the breeding of its progeny.

He sat back in his saddle and thought about his pending marriage. It wasn't something he desired; he was always happier in the company of men. That was something he understood. But women? He could never understand them, they seemed a breed apart. An unfathomable mystery. His mother had died in childbirth with his younger brother so he had been raised by a father who at best was indifferent to him, until he became old enough to wield a weapon.

Gods, he hated his father. As he rocked in his saddle he fantasised about killing him and taking the title of chief for himself. But some small part was always filled with doubt and fear. He dug his heels into his pony and it squealed as it broke into a gallop. He grinned at its pain and delighted in the cold air rushing against his skin. 'Let's pick up the pace!' he shouted. He'd marry that Cambrian bitch and then kill her father and take the crown for himself. He laughed wildly as the party chased along behind.

Chapter 11
Wolves of the North

'I still don't understand how you ended up out there.' Barcus stood in the mouth of the cave staring in disbelief at Arthur and Emrys outside in the fresh snow.

'Magic,' winked Emrys with a mystical wave of his hands. He'd made Arthur promise not to reveal too much about his destiny, and Arthur had agreed as long as he helped to rescue the lost patrol.

'And where did you get that bloody sword from?' Arthur looked down at the King's sword clutched in his hand.

'Would you believe I found it in a stone?' he asked.

'Bollocks. Look. What's going on, Arthur? I woke to find you and that vagabond,' he indicated Emrys, 'gone with not a trace. We searched the entire cave. Twice. And found no sign. You didn't leave by the cave mouth as it was guarded at all times. So what happened?'

Emrys coughed and stepped forward. 'Your worry for your commander is admirable, Barcus. But all men have their secrets to keep, and this is his and mine alone!'

'Again,' said Barcus, 'with respect, sir, bollocks. How can we protect each other if some of us,' at this he gave Arthur the eye, 'clear off and don't tell anyone? In case you hadn't noticed there's Uther's men and bands of marauding Hibernians, not to mention packs of wolves in these hills. How are we expected to protect you? Each other?'

Holding up his hands in surrender, Arthur said with a smile, 'Of course, you're right, Barcus. We shouldn't have gone off without telling you, but it couldn't wait and anyway we're back now, so no harm done, eh?'

With a grudging acceptance Barcus returned to the cave to ready the men to leave.

'Why can't we tell the men yet?' Arthur questioned.

'Because all the pieces aren't in place. Look. If you were to stand in front of these men of yours and declare yourself a King from a lost lineage they might accept you and follow you. But they'd only see you as another self-proclaimed warlord in this troubled land. What we need is for a recognised tribal leader to come forward and legitimise you as the heir to the throne of Cambria.'

'And how do we do that? Who would declare themselves loyal to someone they'd never met? Even if I have this.' He waved the sword for emphasis. Caliburn glinted in the morning sun, the light picking out engravings running down both sides of its blade. Arthur stopped to examine it. 'I hadn't noticed these. What do they say?' He passed the sword to Emrys, who turned it over and examined the runes.

'This is an ancient script,' he said, then read on with some difficulty. 'This is an ancient dialect, older than Rome by many centuries. It says…' He squinted closely at the blade. 'It says, "Take me up."' He then flipped the sword over. 'And here it says, "Cast me away."'

'Well that makes no sense,' said Arthur.

'Of course it does,' Emrys replied. 'It means there is a time to take up arms and fight for what is right, but you must also realise there is a time to cast away your weapons, when peace has been won. It's a warning to remember your duty to the people, and not to give in to petty greed and desires. Wise words indeed.' He handed Caliburn back and then bustled into the cave to retrieve his pack, leaving Arthur alone.

Kai and Gavain were sent ahead to scout for signs of Uther's patrol of the previous day but found no tracks that would indicate they were being followed. Later that afternoon as they skirted the edge of the great forests of Cambria, the now familiar howl of a wolf pack set the hairs on their necks prickling. They'd found the spoor of a pack not too far from their cave, but the creatures had left them alone in search of easier prey. The rocky track wound its way steadily north sometimes crossing over fast-flowing streams of icy mountain water, whose frozen crust would crunch under hoof, and sometimes through narrow boulder-strewn gorges where some of the rocks towered above their heads. The going was slow and the monotony was only broken infrequently by a startled animal that would suddenly bolt cover, causing the men to string bows and bring down the occasional game bird for the cook pot. Or Alcaeus singing some bawdy tavern song he'd heard or made up eliciting laughter from his friends. They were, Arthur had to admit, a happy company even this far into hostile territory.

His reverie was broken by the sound of small rocks tumbling down the upslope of the path they were following. Turning in his saddle, he looked up and caught a glimpse of grey fur amongst the rocks above.

'Look to yourselves,' he called, pulling his spear from its holder. 'We've got company. Those wolves are above us.' The men looked about, expecting an imminent attack, weapons drawn and held at the ready.

'They're behind us too!' came a call from the rear.

'Close up, men!' Arthur shouted, and they bunched up as they moved slowly along. Suddenly there was a howl from in front of them, causing them to stop, and that was soon joined from all sides. The horses, spooked by the sound snorted, tossed their heads, and spun around looking for a way to escape. The men sawed at the reins struggling to control their mounts, spears tangling with straps, causing chaos in the ranks.

The howling continued all around them and Arthur, fearing the men losing control of the horses and being thrown, shouted for them to follow and giving his horse its head, shot forward round a bend in the track.

As he rounded the corner grey-furred figures rose up around them. But they weren't wolves; they were men wrapped in wolf skins brandishing crude spears. As he bore down on them, they jabbed at him and his men, trying to drive them into a narrowing gully.

'Don't let them trap us!' Arthur bellowed. He looked about for Emrys, fearing the old man would be left behind and easy prey, but of the old man there was no sign.

He threw his spear, catching a wolf man in the chest, lifting him off his feet and slamming him into the bank with the force of his throw. His men followed suit and were soon busily engaged with more of these strange warriors. Without his spear and unable to reach his javelins he drew Caliburn from his belt and charged forward with a cry. As he swung down on his target the man's face seemed to blanch as he fell back from Arthur's attack. The wolf man let out a snarling shout and the rest of his pack disengaged and vanished back into the hills and trees like smoke, leaving behind several of their brethren dead or dying, and a very confused company of horsemen.

'What the hell just happened?' said Barcus.

'Maybe they lost too many men?' said Alcaeus.

'Unlikely,' added Lionides. 'They must have outnumbered us, and had the advantage of surprise. I don't understand why they fled. They looked scared!'

'It happened when I drew my sword,' said Arthur. 'They were all over us until one of them saw this.' He held up the glinting blade, turning it this way, then that.

'Sir!' One of his men pointed down the track where a lone wolf man had stood quietly, his spear grounded by his side, just staring at Arthur.

'I think he wants to talk,' said Emrys, who re-appeared from nowhere.

'Where the bloody hell were you when this kicked off?' Arthur angrily faced the old man, who looked up at him with a grin.

'You didn't need my help, and it seemed prudent to stay out of the way while it sorted itself out. Now go and talk to him. But make sure he sees the sword.' He slapped the rump of Arthur's horse and it trotted down the track towards the waiting figure.

'Who are you to carry the Sword of Kings?' the wolf man demanded flatly. 'Are you some Roman thief? Did you desecrate our holiest place?'

'I am Arthur, and we are not bandits! And this sword,' he held it aloft, 'was given to me from the hands of King Camber himself in the crystal cavern.'

Emrys, who had followed him, stepped forward. 'And I am Emrys, known as The Merlin, and what this man says is spoken true. For he is of the line of Anaeas, father of Camber and true heir to the throne of Cambria.'

The man looked startled and coming forward, he looked from Emrys to Arthur and said, 'Merlin. You are known in these lands and your word is trusted, as are you. If you say this man is the heir, then it is so.' With that, he called forth his men and they dropped to their knees in front of Arthur to pledge their fealty to him.

Back down the track Kai leant forward in his saddle and whispered to Barcus, 'What just happened?'

'Fucked if I know,' he replied with a shrug.

The Clan of the Wolf, as the tribal leader Idris introduced his people, were not a part of Uther's realm, but a distant member of what had been the Ordovices. They had little to do with them as a whole, preferring to live in the ways of the ancestors. 'Ach,' he spat into the fire later that evening. 'Gutless shits, they are. Preferring to trade with the Roman legions. Or latterly ally themselves to that asshole Pendragon, who's claimed himself King. Ha. He won't come here though. Too bloody scared, he is. Do you know, he sent a hundred men up here to clear us out after we refused to join him? Well, we sent the goat fuckers back, didn't we, boys?' he yelled to his men who roared back, waving cups of ale as they feasted around the fire pit. 'They marched into our lands, bold as you like, waving their dragon banner and blowing their horns, and do you know what we did?' Idris raised a quizzical bushy eyebrow. Arthur shook his head. 'We skinned the bastards and sent them back home tied to their ponies. With their own skin tied to poles flying like flags.' He slapped his thigh and hooted with laughter at this.

Around the fire Arthur's men looked about with distrustful eyes at the host surrounding them.

'Oh don't you worry, lads!' chuckled Idris. 'We're brothers now under our new King.' He raised a cup to Arthur and drank. 'We're going to spread the word and raise the mountain men, and come down on Uther like a fucking landslide to wipe that sheep turd off these green hills.'

Arthur looked over at Emrys, who sat in the gloom on the far side of the hall, his eyes shining like polished stones.

'I have men of mine held prisoner at Uther's hill fort,' said Arthur. 'I was hoping to negotiate their release somehow.'

Idris, who was a short, dark-skinned, stocky man like most of his tribe, looked over his cup at Arthur and sipped thoughtfully at his ale. 'Your men are dead, my King, and if not they're not far from it. He'll have them working that Gods-cursed mine of his in search of gold.'

'How do you know this?' Barcus leaned into the conversation.

Idris looked over at Arthur's second-in-command and gave a sad smile. 'Because that's where he took my men when he captured them in a raid. We followed them all the way into Pendragon's lands and watched them be shackled and led underground. We waited for days for a chance to rescue them. But the only thing that came out of that hole into hell was gold and corpses. Our men are no more, of that I'm sure. And your men will be the same, Arthur.' He turned to look him straight in the eye. 'But we can avenge them!'

Arthur bowed from the waist. 'Thank you for your generous offer of aid, but I'd like to try my way first, see if I can use the influence that Rome may still have to get my men back.'

'Then you're a bloody fool!' Idris snapped and draining his cup, he got up and left the feast. In the gloom no one saw Emrys rise and follow the chief from the longhouse.

The morning dawned and the company slowly roused after a night of feasting and ale. Three grey-coated hunting dogs moved through the hall in search of scraps and Arthur fussed one as it sniffed round his sleeping pallet. The hound responded with a wagging tale and a quick lick of his face that left him laughing as he lay in the smoke-shrouded hall. 'Good boy.' He gently patted the dog's back as it trotted off in its hunt for food.

'That's a bitch,' came a gruff voice from the doorway.

Arthur rolled over and stretched, hearing his joints pop and crack. Idris strode into the longhouse and stopped in front of him. 'I must apologise for my churlish behaviour last night.' He bowed low. 'I was too deep in my cups and was too outspoken for my own good. I respect your choice to go negotiate with Uther, even if I disagree with it. If you'll have me, some of my men and I would like to accompany you and help in any way we can.'

This time it was Arthur who bowed low.

'I'd welcome the company of you and your men. That way, at least we'll be able to find our way off these rocky slopes!' He winked.

Idris looked at him for a second and then broke into a broad grin. 'I like you, Arthur. You'll make a good King.' He slapped him on the back. 'Now. Let's break our fast and we can be on our way.' He whistled low and the dog Arthur had fussed trotted over. 'Her name is Cavall, and I'd like you to have her. She's from a good bloodline, just like you, eh? She's as swift as an eagle and as faithful as they come.'

Cavall trotted back to Arthur and he stroked her silky fur. 'Good girl,' he said, and her tail wagged fiercely.

Chapter 12
Uther

The hill fort stood on a flat plateau at the base of a grey mountain, overlooking a fair valley of farmland surrounded by lush woodlands that teemed with game. A broad river flowed from its base and through the centre of the vale. Its wooden palisade sat atop a stone wall some six feet high. Stone towers had replaced the old wooden ones as the need for greater protection increased in these uncertain times. At night fires burned in braziers along the wall's length, and armed men patrolled constantly.

Inside the walls a sizeable settlement filled almost every available space, except for a great square in front of a stone-built keep, the seat of Uther Pendragon's power.

Uther paced the length of his great hall followed by a swirl of noblemen, his meaty hands clasped behind his back. At fifty-seven he was no longer a young man but age hadn't diminished his strength or his intellect. Powerfully built and of above average height, he cut an intimidating figure as he strode back and forth.

'Where the hell is that God-be-damned Hibernian party? They should be here by now.' He thumped a pillar as he passed it. Rubbing his bruised hand, he continued pacing. He knew this alliance with the MacDuid clan would strengthen his claim to the kingdom. With their men behind him no one could stand in his way. But he wasn't naïve enough to believe he could trust these invaders any more than they probably trusted him, and once he'd achieved his aim he knew he'd have to fight them. But he'd do it on his own terms at a time and place of his choosing, Gods willing. But for now, he was happy to wed his dead brother's daughter to this clan chief's son, even if half of what he'd heard about him was true. Sacrifices needed to be made for the greater good, and his ambitions were mighty.

'They're here.' A cry went up from a watcher on the wall. The party of Hibernians had just entered the valley and were making their way up to the fortress. Uther, dressed in his finest, rode out to meet them, flanked by an honour guard of fifty hand-picked men. They were chosen especially for their size and fierce appearance. A little bit of intimidation would go a long way to getting Uther what he wanted. He smiled as he looked at his men. Clad in polished leather and mail, their iron helms shining in the wan sunlight, they looked every part a King's retinue. Every other man carried a pennant tied to a spear, showing a rampant red dragon raking its white claws on a green field. Bronze horns sounded from the battlements, echoing across the surrounding mountains.

'Welcome, Conor, son of Feargal,' Uther bellowed as they pulled up to each other, clasping forearms in salute.

'Greetings, Uther Pendragon. My father sends his apologies for not attending in person, but he has many pressing engagements to attend to.' Conor gave a thin smile.

Uther nodded graciously. 'I understand. The burden of leadership is a heavy one. Now, shall we return to the comfort of my home, where you and your men can rest and later, we shall have a feast in your honour to welcome you properly? You'll get to meet your bride at last.' He winked. Conor followed Uther as he turned and walked his horse back towards the hill fort. As he looked about, the wealth of the land became apparent. Coupled with the ample defences this was a trophy indeed.

Worthy of any would-be warlord or King.

Uther gazed at Conor's right hand as they made their way along the track. 'Can I ask what happened to your hand?' he inquired. Conor looked at his mangled arm and covered it with the edge of his cloak unconsciously.

'I'm sorry,' Uther consoled. 'I meant no offence.'

'It's fine,' Conor replied in an almost petulant tone that didn't go unnoticed by the warlord. 'I lost it in combat further east not too long ago. A village we raided was protected by a Roman cavalry party. Renegades,' he spat. 'Their leader took my hand.'

'Was it a fair fight? I mean you're obviously a great warrior, I can tell, so you must have been ambushed or outnumbered to suffer such a loss.'

Conor shot a heated glance that Uther, who looking ahead pretended not to notice. He'd hit a nerve. So he pressed on.

'So, what happened?'

'It was as you say,' Conor muttered, angered at the memory. 'We were ambushed and outnumbered and their leader, who I later learned is called Arthur, tricked me and then cut off my hand before leaving me to die.'

'Indeed. Most tragic.' Uther stroked his chin to hide the smile he felt coming to his lips. This little shit stain was obviously a coward or at best a weak warrior. Not a suitable match for his niece, but he needed this alliance for his plans to work. 'Well, let us put away such troublesome thoughts for now. We're here.' The gates of the fort opened. 'Welcome to my home. Welcome, to Camelot.'

As night fell servants came to fetch Conor to the great hall for the feast. His men were billeted in a separate barrack block with stables attached for the horses.

Wearing his finest tunic and britches, woven from the best wool and dyed a dark, dark green and surmounted by a short lighter green cloak, held in place by a silver brooch, he looked every inch a prince. The outfit was held together by a belt of silver links that supported a fine antler-hilted hunting dagger and soft leather shoes covered his feet.

As he made his way to the keep the fading sun cast pools of shadow in the square and several times, he felt his feet step into some unseen muck. Anger building, he finally reached the stone steps to the heavy oaken doors with rush lights burning in sconces either side. Cursing under his breath and wiping his feet on the top step, he followed the servant deeper into the building until they entered the great hall.

As the doors swung open the warm light of dozens of beeswax candles spilled out, illuminating his now filthy shoes. The servant bade him enter, a smirk playing at his lips. The whole charade had obviously been intended to humiliate him in front of Uther. Staring straight into the servant's face, he memorised it, so that later he could exact his revenge in a most painful manner. He grinned back, the thought now giving him that familiar tingle of anticipation. The now worried-looking man started forward but Conor strode past into the hall, leaving the servant to catch up and show him to the place of honour at Uther's right hand.

'Ah. Well met, Conor. I hope you and your men are rested. Tonight, we feast and then I thought tomorrow we could go hunting. My forests are full of deer or boar, which do you prefer?'

Conor pretended to think then said, 'Well the chase of the stag is great sport, Lord. But the danger of the boar hunt puts fire in the blood, don't you think?'

'Capital!' Uther thumped the table. 'Boar it is!' He leant over and whispered in a not-so-hushed voice, 'The hand will be no trouble, I hope?' pointing his knife at the leather-bound stump.

'Indeed not, my lord.' Conor ground his teeth at the slight. 'I hunt equally well with the left.' Inside, his blood seethed. He'd burn this hall to the ground with Uther and his lackeys in it. He forced a cheerful smile and picking up a mug of ale, drained it, before thumping it down on the table and stabbing his knife into a hunk of meat. 'To the hunt!' he shouted, and all the voices in the hall echoed his cry.

Before the feast got fully underway Uther leant back in his seat and beckoned over his chamberlain. 'Where is the lady Gwenyfar?'

'I know not, my lord,' he said, his old grey head bobbing up and down like a blackbird digging for worms.

'Well damn it, man. Go fetch her.' Uther pushed him off to go search for his niece.

Gwenyfar sat in the window of her chamber. Her long, lustrous black hair hung braided to her waist, and a gown of fine blue wool covered her slender figure. She watched the sun finally dip behind the hills. With a sigh, she got up and reached for a polished bronze mirror, a gift from her late father. She looked at her reflection in the candlelight. She knew she was beautiful, with her pale skin and high cheekbones.

Her full red lips pouted slightly and her large liquid brown eyes, like amber pools that seemed to glow in the warm light. Many suitors had come to her father's court at Camelot hoping to make a match. But he had always told her she would find her own husband in time, so those men were sent away. Then, he had been killed in a hunting accident with her uncle and from that day, everything changed.

She tossed the mirror to her bed in frustration. Now she was to be wed to some loathsome barbarian who even now sat drinking in what had been her father's hall. She'd spied him from her chamber as he'd entered the gates, and the sight of him sent a shiver of fear down her spine. There was something not quite right about him, even forgetting his missing right hand. He gave off a strange aura of disquiet that frightened her.

Unbidden tears welled in her eyes as she thought back to her long-dead parents, how she wished they were here now and not that cold-hearted bastard of an uncle. A knock on her door broke her melancholy.

'Gwenyfar, are you in there?' It was that old fool Aeron, Uther's personal manservant.

'No, I'm not,' she called back. There was a couple of seconds' silence, and Gwenyfar sighed inwardly. 'Of course I'm here. Tell my uncle I'll be along shortly,' she said.

'He wants you now,' said Aeron, opening the door.

'How dare you?' Gwenyfar strode across the room and kicked the door shut. 'I might have been naked for all you know!'

On the other side of the now-shut door Aeron smiled, licking his old lips at the thought of the fair Gwenyfar naked. He wasn't that old after all!

'Pig!' she shouted as she threw open the door, and brushing past the old chamberlain, who hurried to catch up, she swept down the stairs to the great hall and her future husband.

'Ah. Here she is!' cried out Uther with mock delight. He found Gwenyfar to be a strong-willed, outspoken woman, and no amount of cajoling or punishment seemed to cure her of this. He blamed his foolish brother. Always indulging her and treating her as if she had free will to do as she pleased.

Hiding his irritation at her lateness, he put down his mug of ale and stood, beckoning her to him. 'Come, Niece, and meet your soon-to-be husband, Conor MacDuid, son of Feargal MacDuid, chief of his clan.'

Conor, feigning politeness, stood and gave a courtly bow. As he straightened he was taken aback at the beauty of the woman standing before him, and even though she looked at him with cold, hard eyes he couldn't help feeling his desire rising within.

Gwenyfar felt her skin shiver and crawl as the eyes of her suitor roamed across her. He was even more repellent close up, and even though he was dressed in fine attire it was as if some jester had placed a crown on a pig and called it a prince. A brief smile of amusement touched her lips, which she hurriedly covered.

'Look, she likes you!' Uther gestured to Conor. 'I saw that smile, Gwenyfar; you couldn't hide it from your old uncle.' Uther waved a chastising finger at her. 'See how she blushes!' he mocked.

Gwenyfar, face scarlet with anger, turned to storm out, and then against her better judgement spun round to face her uncle and all gathered and said in a cold voice, 'I see nothing to like in this half man.' She gestured at his covered stump. 'And, Uncle,' she seethed, 'if you think I'm going to marry some ugly sheep-rutting barbarian whose filthy clan have invaded this land and are even now murdering and raping its folk, then you're very sorely mistaken. I'd rather die alone in a cell or jump off a cliff.' And with that, she stormed out of the now-silent hall.

Uther hurled his mug at her retreating form, yelling at her, 'GET BACK HERE, YOU UNGRATEFUL LITTLE BITCH!'

She ignored his shouts, and once she was out of earshot she ran to her room. Locking the door and hurling herself to her bed, she burst into huge sobbing tears as the terror of what her life could be washed over her.

Back in the great hall Uther tried to hide his humiliation with a show of good humour, which Conor found delectable. Watching this so-called great man squirming with embarrassment gave him nearly as much pleasure as slitting his throat would have.

'My lord, think nothing of it,' said Conor magnanimously with a wave of his hand, the slice of meat in it flapping about in emphasis. 'I'm sure it's just nerves. After all, we've never met, and she's bound to be confused. It'll all work itself out in the morning, I'm sure.' He took a bite from the meat in his fist, and chewing slowly he thought of how much he was going to enjoy breaking that spirit of hers. Maybe a few bones, too, before he was finished with her. A slow, cruel smile spread across his face, and throwing the meat to a dog, he raised his ale mug and saluted Uther's generosity and friendship. Their alliance would be strong and enduring, he assured, draining the dregs of his cup and calling for more. The servant who had brought him to the hall leant over to fill his mug. Recognising him, Conor reached out and grabbed the man between the legs from behind, hard, squeezing his manhood. The servant groaned in pain as the ale jug shook in his hand, splashing the liquid over the table.

'Here, steady, you fool,' Uther snapped. 'You're spilling good ale.' He cuffed the man hard, sending him sprawling across the floor.

Conor laughed as he watched the man get up, bowing

apologetically while trying to massage his damaged groin. 'Good servants are hard to find, my lord,' he sneered loudly, staring pointedly at the fraught man who was trying to hobble away. 'Maybe you should send him to this famous gold mine I've heard tell of?'

'Maybe I should.' Uther rubbed his nose and looked over at the now terrified servant, who seeing his doom approaching was now attempting a limping run from the hall and the gaze of his lord, Conor's laughter ringing hard in his ears.

The following morning under a grey-blanketed sky heavy with the promise of snow, the gathered nobles assembled for the promised day's hunting. Servants handed out boar spears, long-hafted with a leaf-shaped blade and two wings protruding from the socket to prevent it from penetrating too deeply into the beast. Packs of dogs howled in anticipation of the coming hunt and beaters waited patiently, not relishing the possibility of being gored by an enraged boar.

Uther stepped out of his hall and seeing Conor already mounted, walked over, and taking a cup of warmed ale from a servant, served him personally. 'Again, I must apologise for last night's, shall we say, entertainment. Gwenyfar is a strong-willed girl, but I'm sure once you're wed and a baby's on the way she'll settle down to it.' He smiled and tossing his now empty mug to waiting hands, mounted his horse.

Throwing his heavy winter cloak back over his shoulder, he spun his mount and cried for the huntmaster to sound his horn, and without another word the party set off towards the surrounding forest.

Gwenyfar sat in her room nursing the reddened slapped cheek her uncle had given her. He'd warned her again to be nice to her suitor, and again she'd refused.

'Why do you make me do these things?' he'd asked as she lay on the floor holding her injured face. 'Don't you see you bring this on yourself?'

'I do these things,' she shrilled back harshly, 'because unlike you I've nothing to gain but misery and servitude from this supposed union. I will NOT marry that inhuman pig!' she'd screamed.

Uther had reached down and grabbing a fistful of her hair, brought her face close to his. 'Your father is dead. DEAD, do you hear me?' he shouted. 'He may have indulged your fancies, but I'm lord of Camelot now. You. Will. Do. As. You. Are. Told,' he spat back angrily, throwing her back to the floor and storming out of her chamber.

Tears spilled hotly down her cheeks as she drew her knees up to her chest and bowed her head. She needed a way out of Camelot and soon, before she was forced to marry that fool. Then in a moment of clarity she jumped to her feet and started bustling around her room, grabbing what she could and bundling it into a small sack. She was going to leave right now! It was perfect. Those preening fools would be out all day at the hunt, which would give her plenty of time to steal a horse and flee. But where? She shook away that thought; it didn't matter where just as long as it was far away from her uncle and that pig of a barbarian. The thought of leaving her father's home saddened her, but it was no longer the sanctuary of childhood peace it had once been. It was time to become a woman and take control of her own life. She knew her uncle despised her and only kept her alive to further his ambitions. She even suspected he'd had a hand in her father's death but couldn't prove it. But for now, she would go, swearing that one day she would return with an army and take back what was hers by birth right.

Last of all, Gwenyfar picked up the small bronze mirror her father had given her, and after hugging it briefly she placed it on the top of her bundle. After pulling on thick winter boots and her warmest cloak she left the hall and made her way to the stables where her horse, Spirit, was kept. The stables were quiet since the nobles had quit the fort so she had no problem saddling her mare and leading her outside. The only issue would be the guard at the gate but she was confident she could pass through without concern.

Alwyn leant upon his spear as he gazed out from the gate, looking to the forest and dreaming of joining the hunt. Many of the garrison had gone to act as beaters for Lord Uther and his guests, but he'd been left behind because he'd upset the master at arms, yet again. He hadn't meant to surprise him asleep with one of the maids, but the master had been furious at being caught, as his wife who worked in the buttery was a fierce woman who'd probably bust his nose if she found out about it. So, Alwyn was on round-the-clock duties to keep him out of the way. The sound of approaching hooves woke him from his reverie and he turned to see the lady Gwenyfar riding towards him.

'Alwyn, isn't it?' Gwenyfar said, smiling brightly. The man in front of the gate, pleased that someone as fine as the lady of Camelot should know his name, grinned broadly and executed a clumsy bow.

'Yes, my lady,' he said. 'Are you going somewhere?' He indicated the horse, although he couldn't see the pack Gwenyfar had hidden beneath her cloak.

'Yes. I'm joining the hunting party. I felt unwell this morning and said I'd follow on later.'

'Are you sure that's wise, my lady?' he continued. 'It's awful dangerous out there on your own, and what if you come across brigands and the like? Or a wounded boar? No, miss, you'd do better waiting here where it's safe.'

He reached up to grab the horse's bridle and Gwenyfar felt her hope fading, but steeling herself, she snapped, 'How dare you touch my horse?' and pulled the beast's head away from his grasp.

'But, my lady...' Alwyn stammered, but by then Gwenyfar had put her heels to Spirit and the mare, eager to run, shot forward, tumbling the guard onto his backside as she pushed past.

Gwenyfar was elated as the icy wind blew around her as she galloped down the track in the opposite direction the hunt had taken that morning. Birds pecking for morsels flapped out of her way, squawking their protests as she left the farmland behind and headed up out and away from the only home she had ever known.

Her plan was to head east towards Roman-occupied Britannia. She had plenty of gold and jewellery in her pack, maybe enough to start again somewhere more civilised, away from the reach of Uther the usurper and that vile barbarian. She laughed at the thought of the look on their faces when they found her gone. But then she thought, what if Uther sent men looking for her? He surely would. She needed to get as far away as possible today. So, giving Spirit her head she let the mare gallop on, hoping against hope that no one would ever find her.

Chapter 13
Caught

The hunt had not gone well. There had been no sight of boar or stag that whole day. The huntmaster and his men had done their best to follow trails through the woods but had come up empty-handed as no spoor could be found. 'It's as if the ground has just swallowed them up!' one remarked.

Uther's anger and disappointment in finding no game for his guest had pushed them to range further afield than planned, and upon Conor's suggestion they had split into two groups to cover more ground, a suggestion that grated Uther's fragile temper as he had not thought of it first as host. After Conor agreed to meet back at Camelot at dusk, he and his men moved off to try their luck alone. Once they were gone Uther berated his huntmaster and rode off in the opposite direction, whipping his horse to move faster.

Conor and his men were laughing in their saddles, joking about Uther and his laughable hope of peace between them.

'He'll not last long once your father has conquered the rest of Cambria,' said Feargal's kinsman, Aodh. He was an older warrior and cousin to the chief, with flame-red hair pulled into a top not, and his beard showing the grey of long years.

'You're not wrong there!' chuckled Conor. 'The fool has no idea what's going to happen to him and his niece once Da has his victory. He'll be working in the very mine he owns!'

The men burst out laughing, roaring with mirth.

'You shouldn't underestimate a wounded boar until it's dressed for roasting, you know,' came a soft voice from the side of the track. All of Conor's men turned in an instant to see an old woman standing where they were sure no one had been a second ago.

'Who are you, old woman, to speak so freely in front of my company?' said Conor, angry that he'd been ambushed. Even if it was by this grey-hair.

'I am Morgana, Conor. Son of Feargal MacDuid, would-be King of Cambria.'

'How do you know my name? Tell me before I have you flogged to death.'

'I know a great many things, princeling,' she cackled. 'I know of your alliance with Uther. I know you plan to betray him, and I know he plans to betray you.' She cackled again.

'How do you know these things?' Conor drew his sword and levelled it at the old woman's neck.

She looked up at him and the blood in his veins turned to water. He couldn't put his finger on it, but this Morgana truly terrified him.

'Put away your weapon, boy,' she hissed, and Conor found himself slipping his blade back into its sheath with a shudder. 'That's better.' She smiled. 'Now,' she continued, 'if you're in search of game today, I'd head east if I were you. There's a pretty young doe with long black hair heading that way right now.'

'Gwenyfar!' Conor turned to his men. 'By the Gods, she's run away from her uncle. Ha. I'll catch that pretty and then we'll see who's going to be rutted.' Without another thought of the old woman Conor dug in his heels and followed by his men, headed east in search of vengeance.

Morgana smiled a cruel smile. A pity the girl had to die, but The Merlin's plans must not come to fruition. She thought she'd killed him long ago, but it seemed he was back once more, and she wouldn't allow him to wreck everything like before. This time her will would be stronger, and Uther would be King.

Arthur had followed Idris through the mountains for several days, stopping at villages along the way where he and his men were welcomed as brothers.

'How close are we to Uther's fortress?' Arthur inquired one day as they sat in a smoky hall sipping a bitter ale.

'No more than two days,' came Idris' reply. 'You were well and truly lost when we found you, you know,' he chuckled.

Arthur turned to Emrys with a sceptical eye. 'I thought you said you knew these lands?' he asked.

In answer Emrys spread his hands and said, 'Well, it's been a long time and things change.'

'Mountains don't change!' was Arthur's response.

'They do if you wait long enough.' Emrys winked and sipped his ale, grimacing at the taste. 'I hope Uther brews a better beer,' he joked. His face turned serious. 'Arthur, you need allies for the coming battle. You and your twenty-five warriors are no match for Uther's army. Why, they'd laugh at you if you rode up to his walls and demanded entry.'

'But I'm not here to fight. As I've said before, I only want the men who were taken.'

'And what then? Do you think he'll just hand them back and shake hands with you like old friends and say cheerio? Don't be naïve. He'll slap you in chains and you'll be working alongside them in that mine of his.'

'That's what Idris said,' Arthur sighed. 'I just don't know how I got drawn into this. A few weeks ago, I was a Roman decurion in some shitty little fort that the Empire had abandoned, and now I'm the would-be King of a nation I've been fighting, for years.'

'Well, nobody's perfect,' said Idris with a wide grin.

Gwenyfar had made good time, even though she hadn't left Uther's lands yet. So, she decided to stop for a short while by a trickling stream to eat and rest her tired mare. As she sat nibbling on a piece of bread and some cheese, she let her mind wander to the possibilities that now lay before her. She would need to be careful, as not all men were honourable. Even some women couldn't be trusted. And for that reason, she had taken a long-bladed hunting knife from her uncle's chamber, which was tied to a sturdy leather belt cinched at her waist. She wasn't trained for war, but still she knew that the sharp end thrust into a man's soft parts would deter most attacks. She smiled at the thought and took another bite of her lunch.

'Would you have any to spare, my lady?' came a soft voice from the other side of the stream. An old woman dressed in rags stepped out from behind a screen of bushes. 'I'm so hungry and bandits stole the last of mine days ago.' Tears filled her age-dimmed eyes and she started to sob, collapsing to the ground and looking for all the world like a pile of old cloth.

'Oh, you poor thing.' Gwenyfar jumped to her feet and splashed across the stream to where the woman lay crying. 'Here,' she raised the old lady up and pressed a small loaf and some cheese into her gnarled fingers, 'please, eat. I can't believe bandits would rob someone with so little to lose!'

'They wouldn't.' She smiled, and with that, a half-dozen rough-looking men and women burst from the surrounding bushes and grabbing Gwenyfar, bound her with ropes and started to rifle through her pack, throwing everything thing into a pile on the ground.

'You evil old witch,' Gwenyfar spat, seeing now that the frail old lady was in fact the leader of this gang.

'Don't ya be calling me mother a witch now,' said one of the women, slapping her roughly. 'We're not all lords and ladies, ya know. Ya spoilt bitch!'

'Wahoo. Will ya just take a look at this, Ma!' One of the old crone's sons held up a handful of gold jewellery. 'We're bloody rich!'

'Give it 'ere,' said the mother, grabbing the gold from her son and inspecting it. 'Ow'd ya get all this, then?' she asked, shaking the jewels in front of Gwenyfar's face.

'It's mine,' she cried. 'You can't take it, it's all I have.' She watched as one of the daughters fished her bronze mirror from the pile.

'Can I have this, Ma?' she asked.

Her mother turned to look at what she'd found. 'No, that's bronze. It'll fetch a good price when it's sold.'

Gwenyfar stared in horror as the old woman took her mirror and put it back in the sack with the gold.

'Please, that was a gift from my father. Don't take it.'

The old lady looked over at her. 'Sorry, girl, but this'll get us all through the winter.'

Gwenyfar sank to her knees, overcome with sorrow. One of the bandits grabbed her roughly by the shoulder. 'What shall we do with her?' A lascivious smile on his face.

'You'll bloody well leave her alone, ya hear!' she snapped at the bandit. 'We're not in the business of rape in this family. You let her go or I'll gut you myself.' She brandished Gwenyfar's dagger threateningly. The bandit loosened his grip on her shoulder and Gwenyfar pushed herself to her feet, rubbing tears from her eyes.

'Thank you for that, at least,' she said.

The old woman, hurrying her band together in preparation to leave, turned an eye to her. 'We don't do this by choice, you know!' she said, cutting her bonds. 'We had a farm before raiders burned it and took our livestock. Now…' She opened her arms wide. 'Now we're just common thieves trying to survive. It's nothing personal, dear.' And with a wink she turned away and melted into the woods, leaving behind the girl and her horse, which was too large to take with them.

Gwenyfar smoothed Spirit's snout, whispering to her softly, when she noticed something shining in the long snow-covered winter grass. Walking back across the stream, she bent down and from under a clump of brown weeds she pulled out her mirror. She hugged it to her chest, smiling, and looking over to where the old lady had been mouthed, 'Thank you,' with fresh tears in her eyes.

'We're in Uther's lands now,' said Idris, pointing to a dragon carved in stone. They'd dropped from the high hills into a rich land of forests and rolling farmland, all within the bowl of a vast valley that stretched for miles. 'Keep your eyes open, for danger now lurks at every turn. My men and I will hold back as you commanded, while you go talk to that arseling.' Idris smiled and after clasping Arthur's arm in salute, the Clan of the Wolf melted away as if they'd never been.

'Barcus, send out two men to scout ahead, and tell them to be careful,' Arthur said.

Barcus nodded and called out, 'Lionides, Alcaeus.' Both men turned to him. 'Scout ahead and stay clear of any trouble. And report back if you see anything.' They saluted and rode off.

Arthur called out, 'The rest of us will make our way forward behind our scouts. We're not here for trouble so stay calm unless attacked. With a bit of luck, we can complete our mission and leave by dusk.'

Lionides walked his horse carefully through the trees, followed by his friend Alcaeus, who was drinking from a water skin. 'Would you like some?' He offered it to his friend who accepted but drank sparingly.

'I don't know why we're out here on our own with our arses hanging out,' said Alcaeus. 'I mean, you could hide a flaming army in here and we could ride straight past without even seeing them. A waste of time, if you ask me.'

'Well I didn't ask, did I!' said Lionides. 'And if there was an army nearby, they'd have bloody well heard you whining by now, and we would both be dead or worse!'

Alcaeus chuckled, and then both men fell silent as they heard a sound that didn't fit. Silence. They stopped moving and strained to hear anything, but there was only silence, and then it hit them. That was the problem; the woods had gone silent, and that's when they heard the scream.

Gwenyfar had still been heading east even after her brush with the bandits had robbed her of any hope of a fresh start elsewhere, now that she no longer had any money. But she was determined to never go back to her uncle ever again. She had come to realise her suspicions that he'd had something to do with her father's death were more than likely true, and that frightened her. On top of that, she was promised to a man she despised and this convinced her that she was doing the right thing. As she rode along, she thought of how her father would have been proud of her standing up to the machinations of her hated uncle. It was then that Conor and his band crashed through the woods either side of her and grabbing Spirit's bridle, brought her to a stop.

'Well, well,' said Conor. 'Look who it is, boys, the little miss who called me a… Now, what was it?' He rubbed his chin as if in thought. 'Ah, yes. A sheep-rutting barbarian!' He slid from his horse's back and walked up to where Gwenyfar sat trembling. Reaching up, he pulled her roughly from her saddle and she hit the ground with a thump, knocking the wind out of her. Kneeling beside her, he brushed her long black hair from her face and leaning forward, said with a cruel leer, 'Now let's see who's going to be rutted.' And with that he ripped her dress, exposing her soft white breasts. 'Look at these, lads,' he hooted, grasping them firmly in a bruising grip. 'Now then,' he said, with excited drool leaking from his lips. 'When I'm finished with you, all my lads are going to take their turns until they're satisfied, and then maybe if you've been good we'll take you back to your uncle, but only,' and he gripped her mouth firmly, 'only if you keep your gob shut. Otherwise, well let's just say I enjoy other pleasures too. Though you might not find them at all pleasing.' He shoved her hard onto the chilled ground.

Standing, Conor started to unbuckle his breeches as his men egged him on with howls and cheers, eager for their turn on such a beauty. Dropping to his knees he opened her legs wide, pulling up her dress. Desperately Gwenyfar lashed out, but Conor caught her fist in his good left hand and held her down. 'Will you boys hold her down for me?' he asked as he struggled with his ties. Two of his men grabbed her arms and pinned her to the floor. Panicked and powerless against these brutes, she did the only thing she could. Gwenyfar screamed!

Lionides and Alcaeus saw the group of men surrounding the figure on horseback. As he watched, Lionides saw that it was a woman. But not just any woman, the most captivating beauty he had ever seen. He felt the thumping of his heart as the leader pulled her off her mount and threw her to the ground. He turned to his lifelong friend. 'It's eleven against two. I don't fancy their odds, brother,' and he winked.

'Have you cracked your bloody head, man? Arthur said to not get into any trouble.'

'Can't you see what they're going to do to her?' Lionides unslung his bow and knocked an arrow. 'Are you with me?' He raised an eyebrow while sighting down the shaft.

'Aye. You crazy fucker. I'm with you.' His brother in arms raised his own bow.

'We'll loose one shaft each and then charge into the confusion screaming like all the lost souls of hell, right!'

Alcaeus nodded. 'Right then. LOOSE!' Their arrows flew true and struck two of the mounted attackers, pitching them from their mounts. Dropping their bows and drawing their swords, the two knights surged forward, taking two more by surprise all the while screaming at the top of their lungs. The surprise attack had the desired effect and the other horsemen panicked and rode off in confusion. That left the three on the ground. Two sprang up while a third fumbled with his drawers. The two pulled swords and tried to engage. Alcaeus lopped the head from one and the other thought better of it as the knights thundered toward him, and turning he ran for the safety of the wood. That left one, who was still struggling. Lionides trotted up and placing his sword under the chin of the man, tilted his head back.

'What have we here, brother?' He leant forward. 'A rapist, I'm guessing. Bet your little man has shrivelled back into your balls, eh?' He sliced his sword up, cutting the man's cheek open. Alcaeus had gotten off his horse and stood beside Conor, who was shaking and snivelling in fear.

'This little cock doesn't look so big now, does he?' He punched Conor hard in the kidneys, dropping him to his knees where he gasped for air as the pain suffused his body. A kick sent him sprawling to the ground where Alcaeus bound him tightly.

Lionides, meanwhile, had gone over to the dark-haired girl who lay balled up on the ground, crying.

'There now, miss.' He saw her nakedness, and pulling off his cloak, placed it over her and sat her up. 'We'd best not linger here too long, my lady, as this fella's friends,' he nodded back towards the bound, still form of Conor lying on the ground, 'might rediscover their courage and come back for a look.'

Gwenyfar looked up into the blue eyes of her saviour.

'Thank you,' she managed between sobs. 'They would have...' She broke down again, great wracking sobs of relief shaking her as she trembled in Lionides' arms. And at that moment, Lionides knew love.

'What are we gonna do with him?' Alcaeus cocked a thumb at the prone form of Conor.

'We can't take him with us,' said Lionides. 'We could just leave him like this and put his fate in God's hands.'

'Or,' said his friend, 'we could slit his throat and let him bleed out for what he's done to the young lady here.'

Gwenyfar looked over at Conor, lying helpless on the icy forest floor. She felt a cold rage ignite and gathering Lionides' cloak about her, she stood and walked over to where he was bound. Kneeling down, she drew the fine hunting knife from his belt and pressed it into his groin. Conor stared up at her as she said coldly, 'I won't let you hurt anyone ever again.' She pressed harder, but Conor felt her resolve slipping and smirked.

'You don't have what it takes to see the job through. You're nothing but a spoilt little whore.' And he laughed in her face, spittle spraying from his mouth. She then pushed the blade up under his chin. Lionides and Alcaeus watched silently as she knelt forward, pressing her lips to his ear.

'You're right,' she whispered. 'I'm not like you. I couldn't hurt someone like that. But I can do this.' And with a hard thrust she drove Conor MacDuid's own dagger up through his chin and into his brain. His body spasmed briefly and then was still.

Gwenyfar stood, leaving the knife buried in his skull, and walked to her horse. 'Shall we be going?' she said dully as she mounted Spirit.

'She's got balls, I'll give her that,' said Alcaeus, playfully nudging his friend in the ribs. He didn't notice the dreamy look on Lionides' face as he mounted and pulled up alongside the mysterious girl they'd just saved.

'My name is Lionides, my lady.'

'And mine's Alcaeus,' his friend said over his shoulder as he turned his mount.

'I... I am the Lady Gwenyfar of Camelot. My uncle is Uther Pendragon, and I would beg you not to return me there.' She looked pleadingly at Lionides and his heart melted again.

'Whatever you desire, Lady Gwenyfar. But first we must return to Arthur, our commander, and make a report, if you'd like to come with us? We are honourable men, if that eases your worries.' She smiled at him warmly and reaching over, she touched his arm with thanks, feeling a spark fly between them both.

'I've heard the name Arthur,' she said as they made their way back to the rest of the company. 'It seems he knew my husband-to-be.' She'd already explained who Conor was and what was planned for her by her uncle. 'Apparently a few weeks ago your leader took his right hand in battle!'

'I thought the little shit looked familiar.' Alcaeus slapped his thigh, causing his horse to jump forward. 'He was the leader of that bunch of raiders who attacked Dyffren village, remember, Lio?'

'Of course.' Lionides snapped his fingers in recognition. 'He's the one who broke Arthur's sword. Well, he got what was due in the end.' He shook his head, a clouded expression covering his face.

'Why so sad for a man who would have happily butchered you?' Gwenyfar asked.

Lionides looked deep into her eyes. 'It's just. Well. Isn't it all really pointless, I mean to just go around killing? Why can't we live in peace and brotherhood? That's what Arthur preaches, and I must say I agree with him.'

Gwenyfar looked startled. 'That's a very refreshing outlook,' she said. 'I can't wait to meet this Arthur of yours. He sounds a very interesting man.'

'That's not the half of it,' Alcaeus chipped in. 'He's the King of these here lands by some weird birthright or something. He's got a magic sword too!'

Gwenyfar looked strangely at both men. 'You're joking? Aren't you?' she said. They shook their heads and the small company rode on in silence, at least two of them lost in deep thoughts of desire.

From the cover of the bushes Aodh had watched the death of Conor unfold, not that he held any sympathy for the man, for Conor was damaged inside somehow. His cruel streak had been hidden by his father time and again, but everyone knew what he was like. There were a few men who were twisted like him and they flocked to his side in hopes of doing as they wished under the protection of the chieftain's son. But Aodh despised Conor and had only gone with the party at Feargal's insistence.

Before stepping from the bushes, he checked to make sure those two men had left with the girl. He was glad she'd been rescued before Conor and the rest… He left the thought unfinished. But now he'd have to explain what had happened to the boy's father, his chieftain. He shook his head sadly at the thought that he was probably signing his own death warrant. Feargal's rage could cost him his head. But he had a couple of cards to play. One, it was Uther's niece who slew Conor, and two, he'd overheard the two men mention the name Arthur, and that it was he who'd taken the chief's son's hand weeks back.

Working quickly, he gathered two of the horses that had run off during the ambush. After tying Conor's body over the saddle of one, he mounted the other and turned its head south-west, heading back to face whatever came, but knowing a war was just starting.

Chapter 14
Razor's Edge

Emrys had left with Idris and his clan when they'd separated from Arthur. When Arthur asked why, he simply said he needed to help convince other tribes to join them in their fight. But there was another reason, one he couldn't explain to his friend right now.

He stood alone high on a rocky crag, the snow swirling around his cloaked form, seemingly unaffected by the bitter cold.

In his meditative state Emrys became aware of someone nearby, so he drew himself back into his consciousness and turned.

Morgana had known Emrys would be here. It was a strange bond they shared, being siblings, even half-siblings as they were. But it was more. The pair of them had always been special even at a young age. Gods-touched, they were called, and were sent away to the sacred island to learn the ways of The Merlin. But after dedicating herself for years it was Emrys who had been called forward and named, and from that day a wedge of bitterness had been driven between them, one that still drove Morgana to this day. She knew she should have been chosen but the old Merlin said she couldn't balance the light and the dark that dwelt inside of her, and that in time the darkness would consume her. So, she left the sacred isle and had gone in search of her own way, eventually finding the grace of Arawn, the lord of the underworld whose power over life and death dwarfed even the might of The Merlin.

She had felt Emrys' essence and was drawn to it. She'd seen him alone high upon this ridge and the desire to destroy him had driven her forward as she crept up, hidden by the snowstorm. But she wasn't surprised when he turned to her with a sad smile and said, 'Well met, sister.'

She hated him for that simple act of brotherly recognition.

'Emrys, it's been a long time.' She looked at her famous half-brother standing before her. Age had robbed him of his youthful vigour and his skin was a wrinkled nut brown after spending years wandering the world. But his eyes, even buried in that creased face, were as bright and hard as diamonds.

He bowed and said, 'Not long enough if you'd had your way, I recall. You trapped me in the crystal cavern when I stopped you from stealing Caliburn, hoping that I would die of starvation I suppose?'

She nodded in acquiescence and sorrow filled his heart once more.

His sister was still a lovely woman, though silver threaded its way through her once black hair, and her skin, although free from the signs of age had something of a grave pallor about it. He indicated her ageless face. 'I see you still use Arawn's power to cast a glamour of youth onto yourself. You were ever a vain creature, Morgana.'

'And you were always a sanctimonious bore. Brother.' She said the last as if it dripped with poison. 'So why am I here?' she asked.

'I would ask of you not to meddle in the affairs of men any longer. The world we knew is balanced on a razor's edge and your interference could tip it into a darkness that would last a thousand years.'

'And what care I for the affairs of men? They are bugs to be crushed. Do you think I haven't longed for this moment? The time of The Merlin will end and darkness will consume the world.' She cackled maniacally, and Emrys saw that she was truly mad. The bitterness of long years had twisted her mind until it had snapped, and her delusions could end the world. He shook his head sadly at what must be done, but he steeled himself against the grief that threatened to consume him.

'If my death will bring you peace, my dear sister, then do what you must.' He stepped to the edge of the crag and turning to face her, threw his arms wide.

'You do not fool me, brother,' Morgana said, stepping forward. 'Do you truly think that I could be tricked so easily? No. I will bide my time and continue down the path I've chosen, and you, dear brother, will watch as I burn down all your plans. Even now your Arthur marches to his death. A death he won't even see coming!' She screamed a maddened laugh into the roiling storm and disappeared back the way she'd come, her laughter muffled by the snow.

Emrys wrapped his cloak about him tightly, his effort to keep the cold at bay failing. He was saddened to see his sister still so twisted after all this time, but she had let slip important information that he needed to decipher. He stroked his thin beard in thought as he made his way down the mountain and back to camp, but in the morning he'd be returning to Arthur with, hopefully, some clearer idea of what Morgana planned.

'GONE? What do you mean, gone?' Uther slammed his hands down hard on the table in his great hall, rattling mugs and platters, as the young guard Alwyn trembled before him. He'd just told his lord about Lady Gwenyfar leaving the fort alone. The hunt had returned from a fruitless day searching for prey, which hadn't improved Uther's temper, and on top of that the Hibernians were still not back and the sun was sinking low. No doubt lost in the woods, he grumbled to himself.

But more pressing, that wilful niece of his had run away and this dolt of a guard had let her!

'Give me one good reason why I shouldn't have you flogged for failing your duties,' Uther said.

Alwyn felt his knees shaking as he answered in a tremulous voice, 'I... I can't, my lord. She said she was going to join you at the hunt!'

Sighing as if overcome with a great weariness, Uther said, 'Just get out of my sight, you useless prick.' He waved the terrified guard away and sat down heavily, head in his hands. 'Berwyn, are you there?' Uther asked without looking up. He could feel a headache starting.

'Yes, my lord?' Berwyn was the head of Uther's household, as he had been for his brother also. He was nearing his sixtieth year but still retained a strong mind. His bald head, skirted by a few wisps of white hair around the ears, bobbed as he spoke – like a pigeon, Uther often thought.

'Get the men out searching for Lady Gwenyfar,' he ordered. 'Apparently, she's run off. Oh, and send a few to look for that barbarian and his party. It seems they've managed to get themselves lost as well. I'm off for a lie down. Only disturb me if you find Gwenyfar.'

'Yes, Lord, right away. And if they find the barbarians?'

'Honestly? Right now, I couldn't give two fucks if they're all dead in a ditch.' He massaged his temples with a groan of discomfort.

'As you wish, Lord,' Berwyn said, bowing.

Arthur sat regarding the lady before him. Lionides and Alcaeus had returned an hour ago bringing with them the tale of her rescue from a band of Hibernians. Led by no less than the man whose hand he'd taken weeks back. Although, as both men said, that particular barbarian leader was now dead, and by this beautiful woman's hand, no less!

She smiled shyly as she recounted all that had befallen her. From her betrothal by her uncle to the eventual death of her suitor.

Arthur sat back. 'Well. That's quite a tale you've told.' He offered her some water, which she drank thirstily.

'And it's all true,' she answered, handing him back the waterskin. 'But please. I can't go back to Camelot. You don't know my uncle!'

'But I am bound there, my lady. I have business with him.'

'Yes. Your missing men. Lio,' she blushed at his name, 'and his friend told me about them on the way here. I didn't know that Uther was so cruel as to abduct people to work in his mine. I don't have much to do with all that,' she said. 'Although when it was my father's, I know he paid the local men to dig there.'

Arthur sat in thought for a minute and Gwenyfar watched him through hooded eyes. He was certainly a handsome man, if a little older than her, and there was a certain animal grace about him that she found attractive. Yes. Here was a man with a great future, she was sure. Thoughts started to weave in her mind and raised a smile to her red lips.

Across the fire Lionides watched Gwenyfar with a longing that ate at his very being. He could think of nothing else. It was almost as if he'd been bewitched by her beauty the moment he saw her. But the way she looked at Arthur, he shuddered. That was something else. If she loved Arthur and not him, he didn't know what he would do. Draining his mug of ale, he stood, his mood dark.

'Where are you off to?' Alcaeus tugged his arm. 'Sit and have another. Although it's bitter, you sort of get used to the taste.' He grinned up at his friend.

'Is that all you can think of? Drink!' Lionides hissed at his lifelong friend. He looked longingly at Gwenyfar. Alcaeus' eyes followed his friend's gaze. 'Brother,' he said softly. 'She's a lady and beyond the reach of us mortal men. She's not meant for the likes of you and me. Forget about her!'

Lionides hung his head down, a wretched look on his face. 'I can't,' he whispered, as he walked off to find solace. Alcaeus sighed and picking up an ale skin, poured himself another mug.

Emrys returned sometime in the night. He could feel the wrongness in camp as he sat by the glowing embers of the fire. Something had happened to change the equilibrium of the party. But what could it be?

He got up and wandered over to talk to one of the men on watch, an affable fellow named Bedwyr. He stood watching the dark as Emrys approached.

'A cold night, Bedwyr,' said Emrys, standing beside him where he also stared into the darkness.

'Damn cold, old man.' He smiled then returned to looking outwards.

'Anything happen while I was gone?' he inquired.

Bedwyr scratched his chin as he thought, before saying, 'Lionides and Alcaeus rescued the lady Gwenyfar from a party of barbarians. She's sleeping over there near Arthur.' He inclined his head towards his leader, and Emrys saw the small shape bundled under a blanket nearby. He sucked in air between his teeth in a hiss of sudden understanding. He studied the sleeping forms of Arthur's party, noting that they all slept soundly. No. One wasn't. He studied the camp and just out of the firelight he saw a pair of eyes watching the girl sleep. Eyes filled with a deep sadness.

Inwardly cursing his own foolishness, he bade Bedwyr goodnight and went back to the fire. This problem would need delicate handling, and he knew sleep would elude him tonight. Damn Morgana and her tricks.

Uther lay in his bedchamber, one arm thrown over his eyes as his headache continued to pound in his head. If they couldn't find his niece and bring her back, all his careful plans would fall apart. He groaned in discomfort and not a little self-pity. He didn't hear the door to his chamber open and he started as cool fingers brushed his face.

'Another headache, my love?'

Uther smiled as he heard the voice of his lover whisper in his ear. He rolled over and gathered her in his arms. 'Morcant, my beloved. Where have you been? I've missed you.' He kissed her fiercely.

'I've missed you too, my handsome lord,' she replied, pulling away gently before resting her head on his broad chest. 'But you know I have many duties that take me away from you.'

'But why? I've offered to wed you many times, and yet you still refuse. Is there someone else?' Jealousy embittered his tongue and

Morcant sat up, looking him straight in the eye, and just for a second Uther saw them flash with something more than anger.

'You doubt my love for you, Uther. I who have given my all to you?'

He raised placating hands, and even though his head still pounded he begged her to forgive him his transgression. 'I'm sorry, my heart. It's just that so much has happened since you last were here.'

She placed slender fingers to his lips to silence his apology. 'Please, Uther. Let me help you with your pain first. I have a tincture that should soothe the headache, and then you can tell me what's been going on. Okay?'

He nodded and sank back to his pillow like a grateful child as she went to fetch the promised cure.

Morcant left the bed chamber and made her way to a dark end of the great hall, and after looking around to ensure she wasn't seen she depressed a hidden switch and a low door swung inwards, revealing a dark opening beyond. She entered and struck a light as the cleverly concealed door swung back into place with a faint click. As the rush light caught, she made her way along a narrow space inside the wall until she reached the point where it touched the base of a great boulder that, too large to move, was built over with great skill by the masons who constructed Camelot years before. But even they didn't know that beneath this great boulder was a vast network of underground passages dug aeons ago by hands unknown.

Morcant applied pressure to a point in the rock and another small opening was revealed. She ducked and entered, closing the door behind her to ensure that even if the door in the hall was discovered, no one would ever be able to find her greatest secret.

A series of rough-cut but well-worn steps plunged into the darkness before her. The rush light guttered as a musty wind blew up from this hidden world like the breath of some sleeping monster of legend. The deeper she descended the damper the surrounding walls became until there was a small rivulet running either side of the steps. As she reached the end of the stairs the water disappeared into narrow fissures in the rock and could be heard dripping into a vast cavern far below that had never seen the sun or felt the presence of human feet.

The dirt-packed floor levelled out and grew in size until it became a chamber of enormous size. Here was Morcant's secret home, her sanctuary. Along the walls nooks and shelves had been carved, not by her, but some unknown ancestor. Candles filled many of these and she lit several as she made her way to her store of medicines and potions.

She brushed her slender fingers across small, stoppered stoneware pots until they landed on a stubby, dark brown bottle sealed with wax. This she pocketed and then carried on until she found an even smaller bottle of fine green Roman glass, with a cork stopper and a swirling amber liquid inside. This she opened and drank, swallowing the sour-tasting contents, which caused her to gag but she continued until it was empty. Doubled over in pain and with shaky hands, she placed the bottle back where she'd found it, noting with bitterness that only a half-dozen similar ones were left.

The acquisition of human essence was a difficult and dangerous task, but she needed it to keep her failing abilities in check. The use of magic was taxing and the older she became, the harder it was to keep those abilities. So, after years of searching, she had found a scroll that told its reader how to extract essence from a living host, preferably of the same sex, and Gwenyfar had been perfect. She was so young and vibrant that she hadn't even missed her stolen vitality. But now she had fled her uncle and these six bottles were all that remained of years of careful work. She prayed they'd be enough to see her through to the end.

'Here. Drink, my love.' Morcant held a cup to Uther's lips and he drank her medicine gratefully, knowing that in a short while the pain behind his eyes would be gone.

'You are too good to me,' he said as he lay there, the honey-sweetened taste of the liquid on his tongue.

'I only do what is necessary to help you,' she replied from beside him.

He looked into her beautiful green eyes. 'You are more lovely now than ever before,' he said, reaching to stroke a stray hair that had become loose, back behind her ear.

'Flatterer.' She laughed. A merry tinkling sound, like clear silver bells, he thought. Still laughing, she leant forward and kissed him full on the lips. 'And as you know,' she said huskily, 'flattery will get you everywhere,' and lifting her skirts, she straddled him.

Thoughts of his aching head fled and Uther placed his hands on her slender waist as she started to move rhythmically against him.

'You really are too good to me,' he moaned.

The overnight snow had stopped and a bright blue sky dotted with soft clouds greeted Arthur as he awoke the following morning. The cawing of nearby rooks was brought to him on a gentle westerly breeze that, while still chill, didn't have the teeth that real winter possessed.

Sitting up, he rubbed his eyes to remove the last vestiges of sleep and was surprised to see the girl Gwenyfar curled up next to him. A gentle cough from the direction of the campfire caused him to look up, and there sat Emrys poking the fire with a long stick.

'Sleep well?' he asked. Arthur got up from his blankets and wandered to where Emrys sat and joined him.

'Well enough,' he replied. 'What's for breakfast?'

'Hopefully not regret,' was Emrys' terse reply. Arthur raised an eyebrow, and the old man indicated the sleeping girl.

'What? No. Nothing happened,' he spluttered. 'I wouldn't do that sort of thing!' Indignation filled his reply.

'Well, that's one good thing!' was Emrys' answer. 'You know that's Uther's ward, don't you?'

'Yes. Of course. She told me yesterday. I'm not stupid. We're taking her with us today.'

'What? Back to Uther's hall? Then you are stupid. He'll see her with you and think either you've kidnapped her as leverage, or she's plotting to overthrow him. No good will come of her being here, mark my words. She has to leave. Today!'

'We can't abandon her out here alone. She's already been attacked twice!'

'Then she should have stayed at her uncle's hall.'

'NO!' Neither man had heard Lionides come up behind them as they'd been conversing. 'She can't go back; he'll have her killed. You haven't heard what he's like. I can't let that happen!' As he spoke his hand gripped the hilt of his sword so tightly that his knuckles were white.

'Lionides.' Arthur stood before his man. 'You forget yourself. This isn't a conversation for you to be listening in on!'

'It is if it concerns the lady Gwenyfar,' he cried. 'I saved her and that puts her under my protection!' A note of desperation had entered his voice, and Emrys couldn't help but feel the unease in the camp growing like water coming to a boil in a sealed container.

He raised his hands to both men. 'Please, we're not saying she should be abandoned here to her fate. It's just that—'

'And what's it got to do with you, old man, eh?' Lionides turned on Emrys. 'Everything was fine until you joined us. I wish we'd never set eyes on you, then maybe all this,' he waved his hands around to encompass the camp, 'could have been avoided. Why don't you just leave us alone?'

Arthur thrust Lionides back as he took a step towards Emrys.

'Steady, lad.' Arthur's large hand was pressed against his man's chest, holding him back. 'I suggest you put that away!' Lionides looked questioningly at Arthur, who simply inclined his head. Looking down, he saw his sword clutched in his trembling hand. He dropped it to the forest floor and stammered an apology, and clutching his head ran from the camp.

The rest of the men who'd been watching agog clambered forward, demanding to know what had just transpired. All except Alcaeus, Lionides' oldest friend. He ran into the trees after his companion.

Gwenyfar watched all this unfold while pretending to sleep. She hadn't heard the whole conversation, just enough to know it was about her. She felt guilty, but at the same time thrilled that these noble warriors found her so appealing. She stretched languidly in her blankets and acted as if she'd just woken up.

'Good morning, Arthur,' she greeted him from across the fire pit as she brushed her tousled hair with her fingers. He felt his stomach lurch with desire for this woman. *In God's name how does she do this?* he wondered.

She smiled at him, aware of his discomfort and secretly revelling in it. She'd quietly moved next to him in the night so she'd be the first thing he saw when he awoke. She felt a twinge of sadness for Lionides, as she knew he had fallen for her at their first meeting, and maybe if things were different they could be together. He was, after all, handsome and brave. But the one thing she'd learned in her young life was that if she wanted to be truly free, she would have to make her own way in this man's world, and if that meant pursuing this Arthur for her own ends, then so be it!

Lionides sat on a rock, aimlessly throwing stones into a small pool. He watched the ripples as they grew, eventually dissipating when they reached the edge. He heard his friend come up behind him and a faint smile touched his lips. They'd seen and been through so much in their lives that a bond closer than blood bound them tightly together.

Alcaeus plonked himself down beside his friend and picking up a stone, he threw it out across the pool, missing the water completely, and watched as it hit the opposite bank with a muddy splat. Chuckling to himself, he said to his friend, 'Remember that slinger, you know the one that came from near Jerusalem?'

'I know what you're trying to do and it won't work!' Lionides said.

'Maybe so. But what was his name?'

Lionides sighed. 'Joshua. His name was Joshua.'

'That's right. Joshua. God's breath. He could sling a stone, couldn't he? Eh?' He nudged his friend. 'Remember that time I bet him a month's wage I could outshoot him?'

'I remember. I also remember that you were drunk too when you made the bet.'

'Yeah,' Alcaeus laughed, 'we all were, back in those days. Only way to drown out the misery!'

'You lost, if I recall.' Lionides looked over at his friend who was laughing at the memory.

'Not really,' he said, wiping tears from his eyes. 'I mean, we didn't get paid for over six months, did we? And by that time Joshua had been sent to Africa. Never saw him again. I wonder if he's still pissed at me for not paying up.' He chuckled.

'I wonder if he's still alive!' said his friend.

'Fair point,' said Alcaeus. 'But what I mean is, we've been through a lot together, you and me.'

'Mostly booze on your part!' said Lionides with a grin. His mood began to lift.

'Yeah. And mostly women on yours,' retorted his friend. 'But we've always stuck together, and you know that whatever you do, I'm right beside you, all the way. But this doesn't feel right. Arthur has never steered us wrong in all these years.'

'It's not about Arthur.' His friend turned to face him. 'It's about me. Why can't I be happy? She's the most…' He ran out of words, his mouth opening and closing like a landed fish.

'How many women have you had? Seriously, Lio?' his friend asked him. 'It must run into the hundreds by now. What makes this one any different? Okay, you saved her, and I'm sure she's grateful and that, but maybe you want her because you can't have her. Have you thought of that?'

'I can't explain.' Lionides shrugged. 'I feel... Well, I don't know what I'm feeling. But I'm sure I've never felt this way about any woman before her. I'm going crazy, brother. She's all I see when I close my eyes, and the way she looks at Arthur... Why won't she look at me that way?' He scrubbed his hands across his face. 'I'm sorry, Alcaeus. But if she chooses Arthur, I don't think I can stay with the company anymore.'

This admission rocked Alcaeus to his core. The thought of leaving his brothers and Arthur filled him with dread. He stood and after patting his friend's shoulder in silence headed back to camp to talk to the one person who could help.

Gwenyfar sat by the fire eating some stale bread that had been soaked in ale. Arthur and the old man had left camp shortly after the confrontation and the rest of the men seemed to be avoiding her, and to be honest she felt better being left alone. A polite cough made her jump and she turned to see Lio's friend, the squat fellow called Alcaeus, standing awkwardly behind her, wringing his hands in nervousness. 'Please excuse the interruption, my lady,' he said.

She laughed lightly and patted the ground beside her. 'Please, sit. Alcaeus, isn't it? I'm sorry I didn't get to thank you properly yesterday for saving my life from those brutes.'

Alcaeus blushed self-consciously. She looked at the obviously uncomfortable soldier and it thrilled her to think that she could so easily unsettle a man who'd seen combat and killed men without a second thought. This revelation unlocked something that had been hidden deep in her being. A desire for control and, yes, power. After all, why not?

She looked at the blushing soldier and fluttered her eyelashes just for fun. Seeing him squirm, she smiled and said, 'How may I help you?'

'Sorry?'

'You said, "Excuse me," so you must want something, or is it you just want to sit by the fire?' She laughed again.

'I am sorry, my lady,' he began, 'but it's my friend, Lio. You remember him, don't you? Yesterday. He – I mean we, saved you from that one-handed bastard. Begging your pardon, miss.' He shuffled his feet in the dirt, kicking a small twig into the flames where it caught and burned brightly for a few seconds, before collapsing into the ash pile. 'That one-handed son of a bitch.'

'Yes, I remember you both very well. Is your friend alright? I saw him leave camp earlier and he didn't look happy.'

'Well in all honesty, he's not, miss. You see, it's like this. He... Well, I mean... Well, what I mean to say is...' He rubbed his hair, disturbing dust and dirt from his scalp so that it showered down around his shoulders. 'He's in love with you. There, I've said it.' Alcaeus smiled as if he'd just discharged an onerous duty.

'Oh.' Gwenyfar put her hands to her mouth. 'But he can't be. We only met yesterday.'

'Well. Facts is facts, and the fact is, the silly sod's smitten with you. Begging your pardon.'

Gwenyfar sat and studied the rough-looking man before her. He was a solid presence and his friend was lucky to have such a companion, who'd go and fight for his cause in his stead.

'Do you want me to go and talk to him?' she asked.

'Oh, yes please, if you would. That'd be great.' Alcaeus sighed in relief.

'It's really no problem.' She smiled and stood. 'I'll go see him now. Where is he?'

'Oh. He's down by that little pool just east of camp.'

'Yes. I know exactly where that is,' she said, smiling once again.

'Let him down gently, won't you, my lady?' Alcaeus said, his deep affection for his friend plain to see.

Gwenyfar bent down and gave him a peck on his dusty cheek. 'You're a good friend to him, you know,' she whispered. Alcaeus' head turned a bright shade of red as he flushed in embarrassment.

She found Lionides exactly where his friend said he'd be. Sat there like a lovesick child, throwing stones into the water. She sighed inwardly as she studied the handsome man with his back to her. Should she burn this particular bridge or should she nurture his feelings for her? She tapped a finger on her lip in indecision. He was a fine man with broad shoulders that led her on to his muscular arms and strong hands. His skin had an olive sheen that she found appealing, and she felt herself getting warm inside as she looked at him.

Making up her mind, she stepped out from concealment and made sure to make enough noise that she didn't surprise him, as she knew men didn't like to be caught off guard. Silly, really, she thought.

Lionides looked up from his brooding at a sound and turned to see Gwenyfar standing there with that inviting smile on her lips. Leaping to his feet, he tossed the rest of the stones into the pool where they fell with a loud splash that made her giggle as the water doused his boots. Smiling self-consciously, he executed a passable bow and said, 'It's so good to see you again, Gwenyfar.' His handsome smile brought flutters to her chest.

'And you too, Lio. I can call you Lio, can't I? We're friends now, aren't we?'

'Oh yes, of course you can. All my friends call me Lio.' He cursed himself inwardly at that. Calling the woman he most desired in the world, friend.

'Good,' she said. 'Can we sit?'

Lio pulled off his cloak and laid it on the ground for her to sit on.

'You're just like a knight from legend,' she said, sitting down on the thick cloak. Lionides blushed and sat beside her.

'Do you find me beautiful, Lio?' she asked him shyly.

Lio stammered and then gathering himself, grasped both her delicate hands and brought them to his lips where he kissed them softly. 'You are the most beautiful woman I've ever met,' he breathlessly answered.

'So, you've been with many beautiful women then?' she teased, arching an eyebrow.

Lio flushed with embarrassment. 'Oh. I didn't mean it like that,' he started, and she burst out laughing.

'I'm only teasing you.' She grinned. Then leaning forward, she whispered, 'Thank you for saving me yesterday,' and kissed him full on the lips. Feeling her passion returned as he pulled her into his embrace, she placed a hand firmly against his chest and pushed him back. He looked at her in confusion.

'I'm sorry,' she looked away, sadness in her eyes, 'but we can't. Not here. I'm the Lady of Camelot. Uther's niece. It wouldn't be right. We need to be careful. If we're caught my reputation will be ruined.' She brushed tears away from her luminous amber eyes and looked into his of piercing blue that trembled with tears of their own.

'Tell me you understand?' she pleaded.

Gathering himself, Lionides said, 'Of course I understand.' He held both her hands in his. 'I'll do whatever you wish. Just say it.'

'Then be patient,' she said. 'A time may come soon when we can be together properly, but it is not yet, and you may see things that will make you doubt how much I care for you. But I do.' And with that promise lingering in the air she kissed him once more and left him sitting there in stupefied wonder. As she reached the edge of the clearing she turned back to him. 'Promise me you won't tell anyone about us, won't you?'

Lionides, his heart full as if it would burst, replied, 'Of course I promise. I swear on my life that I'll tell no one.' And he crossed his heart. Gwenyfar blew him a kiss and left the clearing, a smile of satisfaction on her face.

Chapter 15
Camelot

'My Lord Uther.' Berwyn knocked hard on the door of the bedchamber. 'Riders approach!'

Uther lay in bed alone. Sometime in the dark hours Morcant had slipped away again, with the promise to return soon falling from her lips. He didn't know how she came and went, and when he thought about it he felt a knot of worry twisting in his gut that there was a secret entrance to Camelot he knew nothing of. As he lay in the soft drowsiness of waking, Uther thought the first thing he'd do when she returned was ask her to show him the secret to that door.

The insistent banging finally roused him, and as he sat up, rubbing the sleep from his weary eyes, he realised with relief that his headache had gone. Sending a prayer of gratitude to Morcant he stood and splashed water from a nearby bowl on his face.

Throwing on his clothes he finally opened the door to reveal Berwyn standing there with his fist raised ready to knock.

'Good morning, Berwyn. I hope you slept well,' he said with a smile.

'Yes, my lord, and you?' The old man still had his hand raised.

'No, Berwyn, I did not sleep well. I was awakened by an insistent banging on my door!' Uther gave him a stern look.

The old man's face registered fear as his lord stood there with his arms crossed, and a face like thunder that soon broke into a broad grin. 'I'm joking, man. Have a sense of humour!' He clapped Berwyn on the shoulder. 'And for God's sake, put your hand down!'

The old man stared at his still-raised hand with a look of confusion, and then smiling at his master's jest dropped it to his side and repeated, 'My lord, riders approach Camelot.'

'At last,' said Uther, clapping his hands with delight. His men had found no trace of the Hibernians or Gwenyfar. On returning to the fort empty-handed and finding their master confined in his chambers, they had opted to seek the comfort of their barracks and head out before dawn to continue searching.

'Those damn fool barbarians have found their way back. I don't know how they managed to invade Cambria without getting lost at sea.'

The lord of Camelot laughed and strode out to the walls to watch them arrive. 'Well, let's go welcome these fools back like conquering heroes. Much still depends on the union of our peoples,' he called back to the old man who hurried after him.

Arthur and his men had left their camp two hours after dawn and reached the great plains of Camelot's valley where, in their freshly polished mail coats and oiled leather armour, they trotted in unison towards the hill fort with pennants flying and helms glinting in the bright morning sun. As they approached the walls, they could see a few armed guards standing along its length pointing and shouting back into the fort, and although they couldn't hear what was said, no doubt they were being treated as a threat.

'Sound the buccina,' Arthur commanded. Kai raised the bronze horn to his lips and sent a flurry of clear notes across the valley. 'Barcus. The flag!' he commanded, and his second rode forward with a white square of cloth tied to a lance.

'Are you sure this is wise, Arthur?' he said, worry clear in his face.

Arthur took the flag from his friend and said, 'All will be well, my brother. Don't worry. Even a warlord respects a flag of truce, and if he doesn't, well, we'll have a head start on any pursuit, won't we?' He winked. 'And let's not forget,' he followed up, 'we're not alone in this.

Idris is not far away, and he's straining at the leash to kill this bastard!' He dug his heels into his horse's flanks and leaving the line of men, approached the walls with flag in hand and an arm raised in peace.

Uther stared out across the plain at the unknown body of horsemen that had entered his lands. He'd realised immediately that it wasn't Conor and his men. These were too well disciplined and dressed like soldiers of Rome. He turned to his guard captain, a grizzled warrior with a broken nose and few teeth. 'Cadoc, haven't the legions left these lands?'

The hulking captain shrugged in reply.

Uther turned back once more as a horn sounded and a lone rider rode forward carrying a flag of truce. 'The legions have gone. So, who could these men be?' he said to no one in particular. 'Deserters? Or maybe opportunists?'

Berwyn supplied in way of reply, as he stood beside his lord, 'And it appears they have a woman with them.' He pointed to a slight figure sat behind one of the stationary horsemen.

Uther gripped the wooden palisade with both hands and leant forward in the hope of seeing better. 'You're right, Berwyn, well spotted. I bet it's that bitch Gwenyfar. These men have obviously found her wandering lost and brought her back for a reward. Capital.' He slapped the woodwork. 'That's one half of my problem solved. OPEN THE GATE!' he bellowed as he ran towards the steps to the courtyard. 'And get my horse saddled!'

Cadoc turned to Berwyn. 'We've only half a garrison here. The rest are out looking for her and that barbarian. If we're attacked it'll be a close-run thing. As you know, the bulk of Uther's army have returned to their villages to over winter.'

'Yes,' Berwyn sighed, 'that was Uther's idea to save grain and foodstocks in case the winter was harsh. But it might prove his undoing. Cadoc,' he said thoughtfully, 'could you send some runners out in secret to gather the host just in case this is a trap?' Cadoc nodded at the old man's wisdom, and turning, summoned a couple of his fastest horsemen, and after whispering hurried instructions sent them on their way.

The gates of Camelot swung open and Uther trotted his horse down the twisting path to the plain and the waiting horseman. From the wall Cadoc watched his lord make his way to the still figure at the bottom of the hill, the white flag snapping in a strong breeze that blew from the east like some herald of destruction, bringing change to a land in turmoil. Invaders from the west. Warriors from the east. Peace and prosperity seemed a long way off, he thought as he stood there with an ill feeling roiling in his guts.

The harsh cry from a raven broke his musings and he turned to watch the bird hopping along the roof of the great hall, and while he watched, the dragon banner of Uther's house, which flew there, suddenly broke free from its pole in the strengthening wind and floated down to the muddy ground below. Cadoc felt the blood drain from his face at this ill portent.

'Someone pick up that bloody banner and get it back up!' he bellowed to the servants in the mud below. He prayed Uther hadn't seen the flag fall, and with it the certain sign of the fall of his house. Pulling a small Christian cross from his tunic he kissed it and sent a prayer to the Christ that all would be well, before tucking it furtively back inside.

Arthur waited patiently as a lone figure wound his way towards him. The strengthening breeze chilled him as he sat motionless in his saddle, the only sound the crack of the white flag snapping in the wind. His horse stamped a hoof and tossed its head in protest of being still too long, and he whispered words of comfort. As he waited, he took time to study the man coming towards him. Older than him by a score of years at least, the rider, most likely Uther himself, still cut a powerful figure. Emrys had warned him privately that he couldn't be trusted and to watch for treachery. He'd also insisted on returning to the camp of Idris after his meeting with Gwenyfar the day before, as he had told Arthur that he knew Uther of old and his presence might jeopardise any talks. 'I'm meant to be impartial,' were his parting words.

Uther stopped just short of the waiting horseman and looked him up and down. His size was impressive but he'd killed bigger men before, so felt no fear facing this mail-clad warrior.

'Who are you,' he demanded, 'to ride into my kingdom with armed men?'

'My name is Ambrosius Aurielanus, Decurion of the Ala Primae Thracum. Or what's left of it. But I go by the name Arthur in these lands.'

Uther mused for a few seconds, tapping his lip as if in thought. It was a useful technique to see if the other party would continue to talk to try and fill the empty silence and give away important information by mistake. But Arthur just sat there, his head slightly cocked to one side, waiting.

'It seems to me,' Uther posed, 'that the name Arthur has reached Camelot already.' He smiled. 'Are you that Arthur?' he asked.

The man before him shrugged. 'Perhaps?' he said. 'What have you been told?'

Uther ground his teeth. This Arthur was giving nothing away. 'Oh, not too much. Just that you and your knights are honourable men and that you stand with Cambria against the Hibernian invaders. I heard tell you slaughtered a band of them some weeks back and maimed their leader. Is that true?'

'We stopped a village being ransacked and destroyed, that much is true. But the reason we're here is that you took some of our men prisoner while they patrolled your eastern border.'

'Hmm.' Uther thought back to the ragged group of Romans some of his men had brought back some weeks back. 'Yes. Yes, I seem to recall they were captured well inside the borders of my lands. Looking for my gold. One of them told me when asked.' He smiled a cruel smile, and Arthur knew they'd been tortured.

'And do any of them still live?'

'Hard to say,' replied Uther. 'Why? Do you want them back?' He smiled again.

'I would indeed.'

'And what would I get in return for this…' he rolled his wrist as if trying to find the right word, 'boon?'

'My men and I will leave your kingdom and not return. You have my word.'

'I know nothing of your word,' he snapped. He stared Arthur in the eye. 'You ride into my domain and demand the return of men who I captured in my lands, and offer me nothing in return but your promise to leave. What kind of fool do you take me for?'

Arthur bridled inwardly at Uther's temper, but showed calm.

'I understand your feelings,' he said, 'for I have nothing to offer you in return but my gratitude.'

Uther smiled a snake's smile. 'And just how grateful are you willing to be?'

This caught Arthur off guard. 'What do you mean?'

'I have lost something precious to me that I'd like back.' Uther smiled. 'My beloved niece, Gwenyfar. I have men out looking for her. But if you help track her down, I'll consider returning your men. How does that sound?' Uther knew he had him. He'd have to return his bloody niece or lose his men to the mine. A cold smile curled his lip. 'Well? Do we have a deal?' He held out his hand.

Arthur cursed. He'd been tricked. Emrys had warned him that Uther was devious. He must have seen Gwenyfar riding with Lionides. *Damn, I should have left her at camp with a couple of men. Or better yet sent her off with Idris*, he swore to himself. He needed to buy some time to think.

'I need to talk to my men, if that's alright?' he asked.

'Talk to your men? Who commands? In my household I say and

my people do, that's it!' Uther said.

'Nonetheless I will talk to my men about helping in the search.' And before Uther could reply he spun his horse and cantered back to his companions, leaving Uther alone on the plain with a broad smile of victory painted over his face.

'We can't give her back,' Lionides pleaded after Arthur explained what had transpired.

'My uncle's a snake,' Gwenyfar broke in. 'He won't return your men, and he'll probably have you all murdered.'

Not for the first time, Arthur wished Emrys was here to give counsel. Then a thought occurred to him. When had he become so important to decision making?

'I understand your concerns,' Arthur said, 'but we came here to find our men, and we're not leaving without them.' Lionides started to protest, and Arthur raised a hand to stop him. 'We must return Gwenyfar to her guardian, and that's final!'

'You can't!' Lionides looked distraught at the prospect of losing his love.

'I'll just run away again,' Gwenyfar cried, tears welling in her eyes.

'That will be your choice,' said Arthur, a stone settling in his chest at the thought of not seeing her again. Or worse, the idea that Uther might kill her. His resolve wavered. 'But for the sake of my men's return, you must go back.'

Gwenyfar looked from Arthur to Lionides and could see the desire for her in both of them. She looked at them and said, 'Promise me that you will save me from him once your men are returned. Promise, please,' she begged.

Lionides looked to Arthur for help but the head of his leader hung forward, his shaggy hair hiding all expression on his face.

'Say something, Arthur!' Lionides pleaded. 'For the love of God, man, she needs our help as much as those men!' Arthur remained quiet. 'Well, if you won't, I will.' Drawing his sword, he waited, breathing heavily.

Arthur, with sadness in his eyes looked at his man. 'Can't you see we have no choice?' he said. 'He has a fortress full of soldiers. I won't risk any of you against that many; it would be suicide!'

Lionides looked over at the wall at the men staring back at them and heaved a sad sigh. 'You're right, of course,' he said, sheathing his sword. 'I'm sorry. My passions got the better of me.'

'Don't be,' Arthur spoke. 'You're a brave man and I love you for it. Your desire to do the right thing marks you above men like Uther. Never forget that.' He grasped Lionides' arm in salute.

Uther had returned to his hall to await Arthur's reply, knowing what the answer would be before he'd posed the question. His mood had brightened considerably even though there was still no sign of the Hibernian and his party.

He had summoned Berwyn and ordered him to bring the Roman slaves immediately from the mines. The old man had bustled off and returned a while later with three skeletal men hung heavy with chains, their dirty, wasted bodies covered in loosely hanging tattered rags that used to be uniforms.

Uther stood from where he sat behind a long table and walked over to the ragged men, ordering one of his guards to unchain the prisoners. As the guard released the manacles, he stood with a slice of roasted beef in his hand. The aroma of the fresh-cooked meat set the slaves' stomachs rumbling.

'Oh, do forgive me,' he said with mock solemnity, 'would you like some food?'

The men looked nervously at each other before one spoke up. 'I'd rather die than eat with you, you goat-fucking bastard!' And he spat on the floor. The other two men shuffled nervously away from their companion, frightened of the repercussions.

'Well, well,' Uther said. 'Your time in my mine still hasn't crushed your spirit. That's good. You'll need that to get home safely!'

The three men looked at each other, not comprehending.

'Yes, home. You're being rescued, or returned. However you choose to see it.' Uther took a bite from the meat in his hand, chewing noisily. He read their confused looks and smiled. 'Your friend Arthur has travelled all this way on your behalf. So, please, we're all friends now. Come. Eat.' He beckoned them to his table.

'Arthur. Who's Arthur?' asked the man who had spoken up.

Uther smiled. 'Ahh. You probably know him as Ambrosius. The decurion of your Ala Primae Thracum.'

Recognition dawned on their faces. 'Oh. You mean Artos? He's here? Come to save us?' The three men were greatly cheered at this news. The thought that Rome hadn't abandoned them lifted their spirits, and they fell on the food Uther had provided for them. Between mouthfuls they grinned at one another as the grease ran down their chins, joking about good old Artos here to save them. Uther watched all this slyly from his seat, sipping from a mug of warmed ale, and when the men had eaten their fill, he beckoned them over to the fire and bade them to sit at a bench by the blazing logs to await the coming of Arthur to fulfil his part of the bargain. As they rested, all three men slowly became drowsy and their heads began to nod in sleep as the tension of past weeks was released. Uther rose and left the hall, minding the guards to keep an eye on the dozing slaves. When he pushed through the hall's entrance he could see the construction he'd commissioned being completed by bemused-looking carpenters. 'Nearly ready, are they?' he called across the yard.

'Almost, my lord,' called back one of the worker men. 'What are they?' he asked.

Uther tapped the side of his nose. 'All in good time, my man. All in good time.' And he winked conspiratorially.

'Well, at the very least I want my own horse back,' demanded Gwenyfar. 'I'll not enter Camelot sat behind some sweaty warrior!'

'Of course,' Arthur acquiesced. The attempt to hide her behind the bulk of Lionides had obviously failed so there was no longer a need to try and keep up the ruse. He turned to Gavain and asked him to bring up Spirit, Gwenyfar's mare.

The party approached the winding track at the base of the hill fort, and staring up, they all realised how difficult it would be to storm the walls without the aid of Roman artillery.

'Halt!' came a cry from the ramparts. 'Only Arthur and the lady Gwenyfar may enter.'

The men grumbled at this. There was no chance Arthur was entering that snake pit on his own. Barcus spoke up for the men. 'That's insanity, Arthur. You can't go alone. Ask if you can at least have an honour guard?'

'Well thought of, brother.' Arthur clapped him on the shoulder then bellowed up to the walls.

Cadoc turned back to Uther, who was standing in the courtyard below. 'He wants an honour guard, my lord.'

Damn, thought Uther, who was hoping to bring him in alone. Arthur obviously wasn't a man who trusted easily. But he couldn't let him know that the garrison was woefully undermanned at this time, leaving Camelot vulnerable to attack.

'My lord,' a familiar soft voice called from close to the wall.

Uther turned, a smile brightening his grizzled face as Morcant stepped from the shadows. 'My love. You're back. Thank the Gods!' he cried as he stepped forward to embrace her slim form.

From the wall above Cadoc coughed loudly to attract his attention to the waiting horsemen below.

Uther released Morcant from his embrace and stepped towards his captain to answer.

'What's going on, Uther?' Morcant asked, before he had time to talk. He turned to her.

'Gwenyfar has been found and returned to us by a party of Romans led by a man named Arthur,' he said.

Morcant hissed at the mention of his name.

'Is everything alright, my dove?' Uther took her hand, a look of worry writ large upon his face.

'I must see.' She gathered her skirts and nimbly climbed up to the palisade. Staring down the slope, she saw Gwenyfar on horseback alongside a tall, powerfully built man in mail. At least twenty men were arrayed behind him, all dressed for battle. As her gaze swept the host, she noticed one who stood out. All the men were looking up at the fort, tensed, as if ready to hurl themselves at the walls. But not this one. He sat staring at the back of Gwenyfar. Morcant smiled and turned to Cadoc.

'What are their demands?' she asked.

Cadoc looked at Morcant, and then down at Uther, who nodded that he should answer her. 'Lord Uther wanted the big man to come alone with the lady Gwenyfar. But they refused.'

'I don't blame them,' she answered. 'Only a fool would enter a wolves' den alone and unarmed. So now what are they asking for?'

'An honour guard, my lady,' replied Cadoc.

Morcant mused this over for a few moments before turning to Uther and saying, 'Give him his honour guard. But one man only. If he baulks at this, then tell him trust goes both ways.' She smiled, then looked over at Uther's handiwork standing in the courtyard. 'I take it these are for Arthur?' She indicated the wooden structures.

'In a manner of speaking, my love. The reason he came here was to rescue some of his men who were captured in my domain and put to work in the mine. I thought to use them to show I don't give in to demonstrations of strength or threats!'

Morcant smiled, a wicked-looking thing that both scared and thrilled Uther equally. 'A capital idea,' she chuckled. 'Then, in the confusion, you overpower him, kill his honour guard and seize Gwenyfar while leaving his men stuck outside! Powerless. Soon the

JASON ROBERTS

rest of your men will return, and you can sally out to join up with them and defeat this Arthur's men. That is a great plan, my dear,' she said silkily.

Uther beamed at the praise, unaware that it wasn't his plan at all.

'Cadoc,' he shouted up to his guard captain, 'tell him he can have his guard. But one man only!'

'Yes, my lord.' Cadoc saluted and shouted over the wall to the waiting men below.

'One man? You can't accept these terms. It's madness!' Barcus bridled with indignation after hearing the reply from above. 'Somethings not right here. I say we leave and gather Idris and his warriors and take this place by force.'

'And the lives of our men?' Uther had paraded the three remaining captives along the ramparts as proof of life.

'I'm sure they'd rather die than see you captured and killed because of them.'

Arthur shook his head. 'No, my friend, this is how it must be. God has a plan for all of us, and this is mine.'

'Then I'll come with you as honour guard,' Barcus offered, sitting proudly on his mount.

'No, you must stay here with the men and if things go wrong, get them away and go to Idris. Tell him what's happened, he'll know where Emrys is, and then leave this place and find a new way of life. Promise me.'

Barcus stared at his commander and friend of nearly twenty years with a lump in his throat. But he nodded in acceptance, as was his duty. 'I'll take Lionides with me. He and the lady Gwenyfar are friendly with one another and that may help to keep her calm to face what's ahead.'

Barcus turned and shouted for Lionides to form up on them.

Lionides' head jerked up as he was yanked back from wherever his mind had drifted to. 'Sir?'

Barcus frowned. 'You're going with Arthur as his honour guard. So keep your bloody wits about you. If you let anything happen, I'll gut you myself. Is that clear?'

'Crystal, sir.' He snapped off a salute. But his soul sang at the thought of being with Gwenyfar a while longer, and maybe a chance would arise to pull her from this particular fire and then they could leave together!

He pulled up alongside Gwenyfar's horse and gave her a sidelong glance, which she returned with a sweet smile. Sitting up straight in his saddle, he felt as if he could storm Uther's castle alone, so full was his heart.

'Right. Let's do this.' Arthur looked at Lionides with a warm smile on his face, and then kicked his heels and started up the track.

The gates to Camelot swung open as Arthur and his small party approached. Uther stood to one side, smiling and waving them in. Lionides scoured the walls for any sign of betrayal but could see hardly any men on duty. Frowning, he turned to Arthur. 'Sir,' he said, 'where are Uther's men?'

'I thought the same thing. Stay alert,' he said as they crossed the threshold and entered the courtyard.

'Welcome to Camelot,' Uther cried. 'I have something that will please you, I'm sure.' He laughed, and indicated the far side of his courtyard where three wooden crosses stood, on which the men Arthur had come so far to rescue had been crucified. 'Just like your Christ God. No?' He chuckled at his perceived wit.

'What treachery is this?' Arthur spurred his mount across the yard to where his men hung mewling in pain as blood ran from wounded limbs.

'Arthur, it's a trap, we must leave.' Lionides grabbed Gwenyfar's bridle and pulled her to him as they turned to head back through the gate. But it was swinging shut as they moved towards it and men armed with spears and bows now lined the wall above.

Arthur, roaring like a wounded animal, spun his mount, hooves slipping in the mud, and drawing his sword he levelled it at Uther. 'Betrayer!' he shouted. 'Father of lies!' He dug in his heels and surged towards Uther, who shrank in fear as the enraged knight charged upon him.

'Loose!' a woman's voice screamed, and a volley of arrows rained down around Arthur and his horse, which screamed in agony as it was skewered by half a dozen shafts. As his mount crashed to the ground, Arthur, who had narrowly avoided being hit by sheer luck, pulled his feet from the stirrups and rolled free of the thrashing beast's legs. Coming up, he caught a spear tip with his blade, knocking it up before driving his point into the man's breast. Arrows still rained down but he dodged and few got near him as he slid under the guard of a warrior with a large-bladed axe and sliced his throat with an uppercut that sent a spray of blood high into the air.

Lionides, seeing his commander in trouble, reluctantly let go of Gwenyfar's reins and drawing his own weapon joined in the fray, attacking those who would get behind Arthur, using his mount to knock men out of the away.

'Get to the wall!' Arthur shouted above the noise of battle. 'You must warn the men, and get yourself away. Save Gwenyfar if you can.'

'I won't leave you!' Tears of frustration ran freely down his face as he cut another man through the neck, nearly taking his head. He felt his horse stumble and looked back to see a fletching deep in its rump. Pulling his feet free, he dropped beside Arthur. 'Well met.' Arthur grinned, battering a spear thrust aside and then stepping into the space before hammering the pommel into the surprised face of his attacker, who dropped like a stone.

'We need to get to the wall,' he reiterated. 'Where's Gwenyfar?' Both men looked about and saw her swiping at grasping hands as guards swarmed around her only a few feet from the gate.

'Let's move.' Grabbing the tunic front of a stunned guard, Arthur propelled him backwards using his body as a shield as arrows thumped into it. Letting the corpse sink to the ground, the two warriors battered aside the guards who surrounded Gwenyfar and using her horse as a ram, pushed towards the nearest steps up to the wall.

They were going to get away. Uther couldn't believe it. Thirty-five against two! The odds seemed impossible but this bear of a man fought with the strength of ten, and his companion showed a skill with the sword that was unmatched here in Camelot. He stared in disbelief as they reached the rampart, slaying any who came near. The archers who had stopped shooting as their quivers emptied drew swords and joined the fray.

Arthur turned back and pointed his sword at Uther, shouting something unintelligible. The blade shone in the sunlight, and from the entrance to the great hall, Morcant stood in stunned disbelief, her eyes not accepting what she was seeing. This man. This Arthur wielded the Sword of Kings, the blade of King Camber himself. In an instant her plans changed.

'Uther!' Her voice carried across the courtyard and above the clash of blades. Uther looked over to see Morcant pointing wildly at Arthur from the door of the great hall, and shouting above the din, 'The sword, Uther. The sword. Don't let him leave with it, it's important,' she cried over and over.

Arthur and Lionides, with Gwenyfar between them had reached the top of the wall and looking out, he could see his men. Signalling for them to come at once he turned back to see Uther rallying his remaining men and coming at them with more organised determination.

'We need to get over this wall and away,' he said, looking over at the twelve-foot drop on the other side.

'That's an ankle breaker if ever I saw one,' Lionides replied. The base of the wall was a rocky jumble of stones and small boulders before a ditch lined with stakes.

'Any ideas?' Arthur questioned both of them.

'If we had time, we could tie our belts together and lower ourselves down. But I don't think our host wants us to leave just yet,' Lionides said with a fierce grin as he watched Uther's men cautiously approaching.

'We could jump down before the gates,' said Gwenyfar, pointing, 'and while you two defend me I could try to open them, allowing your men in.'

Arthur considered this suggestion and finding no alternative, nodded and the three of them headed in that direction as Uther's men, seeing their intentions, moved to cut them off.

Morcant grabbed Uther's arm as he headed toward the gates. 'You need that sword, Uther,' she said earnestly.

He turned to her. 'What's so important about his damn sword?'

'That's the Sword of Kings. The weapon of King Camber, the man who gave this land of ours its name. Can't you see? It's a powerful symbol for the people. If you possess it, you will be the ruler of all these lands. With that blade in your hand, you will be unstoppable. You'd no longer need to alliance yourself with that Hibernian chieftain. The peoples of Cambria would flock to your banner. You'd have an army of thousands at your command, Uther. Can you imagine?' She let the words hang in the air a moment until she saw the light of avarice spark in his eyes. 'Get it,' she whispered.

Uther bellowed at his men, pushing them forward. 'Stop them leaving at all costs!' he shouted. 'And bring me that sword!'

Arthur heard Uther's command and knew time was running out!

'We need go, now!' he shouted as the lord of Camelot's men formed a shield wall and started a slow advance, beating weapons against iron rims over and over.

'I'm working on it.' Gwenyfar was struggling to lift the heavy beam that sealed the door, and little by little it slowly rose, until it would move no further. 'It's stuck!' she cried in dismay.

'Well unstuck it!' Lionides called back over as his shoulder as the first spear thrust snaked from above a shield like a flicking tongue. He deflected it with a twist of his sword and then with a lightning-fast thrust pierced the wielder's shoulder, forcing them to drop their shield. Arthur stepped forward and stabbed Caliburn straight through flesh and bone in a spray of bright blood before ripping it out, dropping the spearman and creating a gap that Lionides, working in tandem with his commander, took advantage of by stepping forward into it and crippling the men either side of their fallen comrade, before nimbly jumping back. The attack faltered again, and Uther had to threaten his men to push forward once more.

By now though, Arthur's companions who were locked outside had arrived and were beating against the gates with swords and spears trying to force entry. Arthur bellowed through a crack in the timber, 'Barcus, send some men to scale the palisade!'

'Already happening. Just keep those goat turds busy, and we'll catch them unawares. Hang on, Arthur!'

'Good man!' he shouted in reply. 'Lionides, did you hear that?'

'Yes, sir. Just keep 'em busy,' he said, his sword flickering back and forth. It seemed the tide was turning in Arthur's favour as suddenly there was a cry from the rear, and the sound of fighting caused Uther's men to look about in panic.

'Quick,' Arthur whispered to Lionides during the brief confusion, 'grab the bar.' Jabbing their blades into the ground they hefted the heavy wooden block from its seating and, tossing it into the faces of Uther's men swung open the gates to Camelot.

Barcus and fifteen of his best mounted men charged through the wide opening like avenging demons, their war cries and iron-tipped lances scattering Uther's guards like chaff in the wind as they clattered across the courtyard, spitting enemies without mercy. Uther's men, seeing the battle was lost threw down their arms or ran for their lives. The fight was over.

Morcant had seen Arthur's men climbing over the palisade and knew the battle was done. So she ran to Uther's side and grabbing him, forced him to follow her back to the hall, calling for Cadoc and half a dozen men to follow as they fled into the rush-lit gloom.

'This way,' she directed, and led the small group into the dark corner of the hall where she opened the same small, secret door she'd used just recently to return to Camelot. Grabbing torches, Morcant led Uther and his men through the narrow space, making sure the door was firmly shut behind them.

'Keep quiet,' she hissed as the men muttered in fear. She led them a short way down the passage. 'The walls are thin here and they'll hear us if we don't keep the noise down.'

They shuffled along in silence until she reached that same familiar rock in the wall. Pushing against it again, another opening appeared and they followed her through into a wider space. Not the one that led to her solace, but a cave only ten or so feet across.

'We'll wait here until dark, then make our escape through the mine and into the hills,' she said.

Uther looked amazed. 'I never realised this was here. I knew there must be a way in and out for you to vanish so easily. But this?' He shook his head in amazement.

'My lord,' Cadoc said. 'This morning Berwyn asked me to summon the dragon host, for we were undermanned and ill prepared to fight any kind of encounter.' He bowed low to his lord, expecting retribution, but Uther just chuckled softly.

'That old man is a better strategist than I'll ever be.' He shook his head in wonder. 'He had already anticipated this outcome and prepared for it. Incredible.' Uther stalked around the small space, stepping over his tired men. 'Tonight, we make our escape, and then tomorrow or the next day we'll meet up with the dragon host and take back what's ours!' He thumped his fist into his palm. 'And after that,' he wagged a finger at Morcant, 'we kill Arthur and take his bloody sword!'

Idris sat by the fire in Uther's great hall drinking ale plundered from the Pendragon's stores. 'So let me get this right.' He took a foaming sip, then wiped an arm across his mouth. 'It only took two of you to capture Uther's stronghold. I don't believe it!' He laughed, beating the table before him with the flat of his hand. 'Oh. This will go down in legend. Ha. The bards will be singing songs and telling stories about you for years to come!' He drummed his hands on the table again. 'So where is Lord Goat Turd then?' he asked, looking around in case Uther popped out of thin air.

'It seems,' said Arthur, a booted foot resting on a stool as he sipped his own drink, 'that, somehow during the fighting he managed to slip away. But no one knows how or where!' He drained the bitter ale and leant over to get the jug to refill his mug.

'Well met, Arthur. Idris,' said Emrys, striding into the great hall. He'd arrived with Idris earlier, but had been poking around the keep looking for Uther, Arthur supposed. 'A stunning victory. Thank God Uther had sent most of his garrison out looking for the lady Gwenyfar,' he laughed, picking up a spare mug and helping himself to some ale. 'Or you'd have been dead or stuck down a mine by now!'

Chapter 16
Vengeance

Feargal's man, Aodh, reached his chieftain's war camp the same day Uther was driven from Camelot. He had ridden day and night and the exhausted mounts were near collapse as they walked past the pickets and straight to the central barn in the sea of tents and rough shelters Feargal used as his command and living quarters.

Almost half the area was used as stabling, while the rest, curtained off for privacy, was where the chieftain made his battle plans and slept.

Nearly dropping from his saddle with weariness, Aodh handed the reins of both animals to a groom and asked him for help to lift Conor's cloak-wrapped body from where it had been tied over the other animal's back.

Feargal wasn't in his quarters, so runners were sent to find him and after an hour, in which Aodh managed to get something to eat and rest a little, the fiery-tempered chief resplendent in his battle array walked his horse to the barn before removing his helm and ducking through the door.

Aodh got to his feet from where he had been resting on a low stool, and dropped to a knee, head bowed as the chief entered.

'My chief,' he started, but Feargal cut him off.

'Where is my son?' he asked in a low voice, rough with emotion.

'We laid him in your sleeping area, my chief. We didn't think anywhere else suitable.'

'Good. Good, Aodh.' Feargal filled a mug with water and offered it to his man. 'Please, sit and drink, and tell me what happened to my son. Then, we'll see what must be done.'

Aodh told his chief the tale of what had happened, only omitting a few details he thought would send his lord into a black rage. When he was done, he sat back and waited in silence as the man he feared and respected came to terms with the death of his only son.

'So,' he said after several minutes of pacing, 'that bitch niece of Uther's murdered my son! And was then taken away by men who fight for someone called Arthur. Is that correct?'

Aodh nodded without speaking.

'The question is, is this Arthur in league with Uther? Or is he operating alone? If he's alone, then I'll find him and kill him. But if it's some trick that Uther has pulled…' Feargal stopped and looked out through the open doors and into some unseen distance, 'then I'll raze that bastard's kingdom to the ground and sell all his people for slaves! And as for this Gwenyfar!' Feargal removed his helmet and hurled it across the room. 'She's going to burn on a pyre like the witch she is!' he roared.

Aodh shrank back on his stool in fear as his chief's dreaded anger flared like the sun. Seeing his man cower so, his fury abated and he smiled, reaching over and gripping both his forearms in a warrior's salute. 'You did well, cousin,' Aodh saw the sad smile on his chief's worn features, 'bringing my boy back to me for proper burial.' Taking a large silver torc from his arm, he bade Aodh to rise and placed it around his own. 'We are brothers now.'

A large mound overlooking a bend in a river marked the burial place of Conor MacDuid, Son of Feargal, chief of his clan. A steady rain of sleet and snow driven by a cold wind flapped cloaks and battered dull iron helms with icy rain as the might of the clan, four hundred men, filed past in silence out of respect, on their way to Camelot to exact revenge for the killing of the chieftain's son.

Feargal stood alone by the grave, cold rain running through his hair and beard. He'd sent his Druid away, preferring to be alone in his mourning. He gazed down at his muscled arms noting the twisting tattoos of faded blue writhing along them. Mythical beasts and patterns of power, the map of his rise, all etched into his skin. *And for what?* he thought. He had no heir but Conor, having failed to conceive another child after trying for years with various women, and now he was gone. Was this some cruel punishment by the Gods? He looked up through the rain, barely feeling it burn his skin with its cold touch, searching for an answer that he knew wouldn't come.

With eyes closed he turned around, feeling the sleet and rain splashing his eyelids. Round and round he turned, and a hoarse laugh built in his throat until it burst forth into a madness of sound. Soldiers passing by the mound looked at their leader, worry clear on their faces. Had he gone insane, they wondered?

Feargal's crazed spinning stopped suddenly and his eyes snapped open, bright and clear. He bounded up the mound, mud squelching beneath his feet as he slipped and slid to the top where he stopped and looking skyward cursed the Gods and their capricious ways. Pointing a finger shaking with emotion at the dull grey heavens, he shouted for all to hear, 'Gods of this land, hear me. In the name of my dead son, I curse you all,' and he spat. 'And swear my vengeance.' He pulled a knife from under his sodden cloak and sliced across his chest, feeling the warm blood ooze down his skin. 'My life's mission will be to destroy this land and to burn your priests wherever they might hide. Do you hear me?' he screamed in defiance as he rubbed his own blood across his face.

He looked down at his passing army and started beating his chest and shouting, 'Vengeance. Vengeance!' over and over until the men, not knowing what else to do, started to join in, hammering spears and swords against shield rims and taking up the cry. Soon the whole army roared this new battle cry. Birds startled from their roosts took to the sky, cawing and crowing their outrage, adding to the cacophony until the hills rang to the cry of, 'VENGEANCE!'

As promised by Morcant, Uther and his men slipped away unnoticed from the walls of Camelot through passages in the gold mine above. After leaving by a hidden exit they'd made their way to the western edge of the valley and up into the treeline before turning south and following the ridge throughout the night, only dropping lower down when the weather became colder and forced them to seek shelter from the biting wind-driven sleet.

'I should be warm and dry in my hall rather than freezing my balls off out here,' Uther grumbled the next day as they continued to trudge through the damp bracken that clumped in shades of green and brown between the pine trees. A light air frost had painted the delicate fronded leaves with a crystalline beauty that fell like snowflakes as they brushed past.

'Grumbling won't help us, my lord.' Morcant wrapped an arm through Uther's and rested her head against his shoulder as they walked along a narrow trail.

'I know. But I can't help feeling that I'm out of favour with the Gods somehow.' He patted her hand gently as they continued on.

'Maybe you shouldn't have had those men crucified like the Christ God?' Cadoc said from up front as he kept watch.

Uther halted and shrugged Morcant off his arm. 'Are you questioning my decisions, Captain?' he growled.

Cadoc stopped walking and turning back to his lord, spoke simply. 'I'm just an ordinary man, my lord. I'm not privy to the dealings of great men such as yourself. But, I wonder if mocking God, any God for that matter,' he uttered quickly, 'isn't a good way to fall under their notice and bring punishment down on our heads?'

Uther mulled this over for a while before saying, 'You have a point, Captain. But never question me again. It's lucky for you that I have need of you right now or I'd have you crucified like those bloody Romans, and be damned the consequences!' He pushed past Cadoc and hurried along the path, shouting back over his shoulder, 'And when I'm reunited with the dragon host, that fucking Roman sat in my fucking hall, by my fucking fire, will join his men on those crosses, and we'll see if his Christ God will save him. Now come on!' he bawled, striding away.

Feargal and his army rode steadily north-east through the worsening weather. The men grumbling that the campaign season was well and truly over and that they should be back home to tend their homesteads were silenced with beatings and floggings, as his desire for revenge burned like a furnace. 'It won't be long, boys!' he shouted when they had stopped for a rest. 'Once we have Camelot, we can overwinter on Uther's stores and then return home for a while. What do you say?'

The men cheered, knowing they had little choice and no chance of returning home without their clan chief's ships.

Feargal sat on a small stool in a stitched leather tent taken from a sacked Roman fort some months earlier. 'What do the men really think, Aodh?'

Aodh sighed, scratching his armpit and flicking a louse into the fire where it popped on the flames. 'They miss their kin and lands, Lord,' he answered truthfully. 'They say they need to start planting seed for next year's crop or their families will starve!'

'Do they think I'm mad?'

Aodh looked into his chieftain's face. 'No, Lord. They know you're grieving. They're just not used to being abroad at this time of year, and they worry. That's all.'

Feargal sighed. 'Maybe I was rash in marching on Uther this late in the year. But it's too late to turn back now. Once we've taken his stronghold the men will stop griping, I'm sure, and that bastard's niece will keep them warm as she burns.' The light from the brazier shone in his eyes as he stared into the flames.

Arthur woke rested and refreshed in what had been Uther's bedchamber. The rest of his men along with Idris and his wolves had rounded up Uther's remaining men and servants and thrown them from the hill fort, fearing those still loyal to the former owner of Camelot could create mischief. And as Idris had said to them as they protested their loyalty, 'Well at least you're alive!'

Upon inspection Uther's gold mine was a grim place full of dead or starving slaves working in the worst conditions imaginable, tunnelling away the rock in search of the precious red gold of Cambria. These men, women, and children were freed and sent to Camelot to be looked after. The gold itself, and there was an enormous quantity of it, was stored in sacks and barrels in a locked stone undercroft beneath the great hall itself. Arthur mused; there really was a dragon sat on a mountain of gold!

Gwenyfar sat in her old room staring out of the window onto the courtyard of Camelot. The view was the same, but so much had changed, she thought, watching the bustle below. Her breath caught suddenly as two familiar men started to practise with swords and shields. Alcaeus and Lionides faced each other and began to circle, taking testing swings and slashes at one another. Neither could break down the other's guard and it soon became a waiting game to see who would make the first mistake. By now the two men, sweating despite the cold, had drawn a small crowd who were busy wagering on the outcome. Seeming to tire first, Alcaeus dropped his shoulder, letting his shield dip. Half the crowd groaned at the expected defeat of their man. Lionides, seeing the opening thrust his practice sword over the top, but it was a feint and just as the tip snaked over the shield's rim, the stocky warrior suddenly bent his knees, dropping dramatically, causing Lionides to overbalance and in a smooth, practised movement he pushed up and forwards, knocking him off balance and sending him crashing to the mud where he lay with his friend's sword tip resting against his chest. 'Do you yield?' Alcaeus asked, a grin of victory on his scarred face.

'Aye. I yield. This mud's too damn cold to lie in long,' his friend replied with a laugh, reaching up to grasp Alcaeus' offered hand. There were cheers and groans from the crowd as money changed hands and they drifted away back to whatever duties they had been doing before the bout started.

'Fancy swordwork is all very good,' said Alcaeus as he walked with his friend to wash up, 'but sometimes the best swordsman can be undone with a simple trick.' He winked.

'I'll remember that for next time!' Lionides said as his teeth started to chatter after the soaking.

Gwenyfar had watched the bout and was surprised when Lio was beaten. She had thought him invincible, but his friend tricked him easily. She pursed her lips, gently tapping a finger against them in thought. Then she rose and headed outside.

Emrys had finally found Morcant's secret door after much searching, but he was more surprised at the extent of the tunnels around and beneath the hill fort, and as he stood in her inner sanctum looking around, he couldn't help but wonder who she was. That she had a knowledge of potions there was no doubt, but there were piles of scrolls and wax tablets filled with knowledge from across the Empire. She was no simple hedge witch; she was a powerful sorceress in her own right. But he had no memory of her; she simply did not, could not exist. Unless…

Emrys headed for the exit but a grinding, grating sound filled the chamber and a great stone block came crashing down, sealing the way. Through the cloud of choking dust he could see he was trapped. She'd done it again. 'MORGANA,' he wailed futilely.

Many miles south, Morgana smiled in triumph.

'What is it, my love?' Uther tilted Morcant's delicate features and kissed her lips tenderly.

'Nothing,' she said, 'I'm just happy.' Morgana turned back to stare in the direction of Camelot. *Rot in hell, Emrys.*

Everyone in Camelot felt the ground shake as the huge stone sealed Emrys in the cavern below, but no one knew what it meant. 'I've felt these before,' said Arthur. 'In Rome they happen regularly. But I've never known one to happen in Britannia.'

'What are they?' Idris asked, fear etched upon his face.

'Honestly? I've no idea,' said Arthur. 'There's theories it's the Gods shaking the world. Or it might be natural, linked to mountains that spew fire and liquid rock into the sky!'

'Mountains that spew fire?' Idris said in amazement. 'No wonder your lot invaded here. The bloody rain would put out a fiery mountain!' Both men laughed at this inescapable truth.

Emrys waited patiently for the dust to settle before studying the rockfall. Long years had taught him to be patient, as often a solution would present itself if you just waited long enough and did not panic. Sitting cross-legged in front of the blockage, he studied the problem. The size of the boulder meant he couldn't move it by force. There were several smaller rocks wedged around it, and maybe if he were younger he might have been able to move them, but that was no longer a possibility. Thankfully, there was a tiny gap through which a slight breeze blew, causing his torch to flicker and dance.

'Well at least I won't suffocate,' he said to the silence.

Standing, he explored his surroundings and taking note of the supply of candles in various niches around the walls, he said, 'Plenty of light for now, too. But no water!' That would be a problem if he was here too long. He tapped his chin with a forefinger while looking around. The scrolls and tablets looked interesting and he searched through several while his mind worked the problem of escape.

Time passed in the dim cave and the pile of scrolls had increased considerably as he studied them, lost in their contents. There was wisdom and knowledge from all across the known world. Morgana had not been idle these long years, it seemed. The works on dark magics he put to one side, not interested in them. These he would destroy before he either left the cave or died in it.

The others that dealt with potions and healing, he wrapped and put safely in a satchel he carried.

Feeling tired, he lay down to sleep, but lit a few of the candles first in order to preserve the precious light and the feeling of safety it provided.

Time passed and he woke to find his torch extinguished and only a couple of the candles guttering faintly. How long had he been asleep? Several hours at least, he guessed. Getting up and feeling stiff joints crack, he lit more candles and lacking water to moisten his parched throat he returned to studying the wax tablets neatly stacked on a small chest containing clay pots of various powders. These he sniffed and occasionally dipped a finger in, tasting bitter and unknown elements. He spat, hoping none of these were poison, although most of those were kept separately on a shelf nearby.

Leafing through the tablets, he found some interesting tales of travel far to the east of the known world, to the land of silk. Serica. Reading on, he discovered something remarkable and put down the tablet to search the small chest again.

'Ha!' he cried in triumph and jumping to his feet he started to rummage in earnest through Morgana's collection of apothecary paraphernalia. Finding what he was looking for, he went back to the rockfall and once more sat in front of it with legs crossed as he studied carefully.

After several minutes, he rose and going to a bench, he started to prepare for his escape.

'Lio. Lio!' Gwenyfar waved after spotting the handsome warrior washing the mud from his clothes in a bucket of warmed water from the kitchens.

'Lady Gwenyfar. It's good to see you.' Lionides stood in just his breeches, his muscular chest damp as he towelled himself dry. She stared at him in open admiration and he felt himself blush with embarrassment at her brazen stare.

'Are you shocked, sir knight, to see a lady look at you so?' A half-smile played across her full lips, and Lionides felt his passions ignite.

Hiding his embarrassment by pulling on a fresh tunic, he looked at Gwenyfar and said, 'Lady, it's not seemly for one as highborn as you to act so.'

She laughed her light laugh and stepped forward, placed her hands on his chest and standing on her toes, kissed him. He pulled back in shock, looking about in case they'd been seen.

'What's the matter, Lio?' she teased, standing with one hand on her hip like she'd seen the kitchen girls do when talking to the guards. Lionides swallowed hard, feeling his desire rising.

'Please,' he said. 'You can't be seen with me. I'm just a common soldier.'

'Nonsense,' she answered. 'I'm the Lady of Camelot, and this is my home, and I'll do what I want in it!'

A cough came from in the kitchen and they both jumped. Gavain stood there, and bowing to Gwenyfar, turned to Lionides and said, 'Arthur has summoned us all to the great hall at once. It seems we're not alone in this valley!'

Gwenyfar returned his bow and asked what he meant. 'I'm not sure I should say, miss. Arthur has just sent me to gather the men.'

'Typical,' she yelled. 'This is my home, not his, and I will not be kept out of meetings just because I'm a woman!' She stamped her foot in frustration and swept past Gavain towards the hall.

'In God's name, she's a fiery one!' Gavain chortled.

'You have no idea,' replied Lionides, slapping his comrades back. 'Let's go see what all this fuss is about, shall we?' The two of them set off after her.

Arthur sat in Uther's throne – a heavy oak chair carved with twisting dragons at the far end of the hall. An enormous fire pit blazed in the centre of the room sending dancing shadows writhing across the walls. Gavain, followed by Lionides, entered and they made their way to the side benches where the rest of the men had gathered.

Gwenyfar, Lionides saw with a smile, was seated next to Arthur in a slightly smaller version of the throne.

'Men.' Arthur stood and stepped down from his seat. 'This room is too large for us to talk plainly without shouting. Please, join me around the fire pit, where at least we'll be warm.' He smiled.

The men rose and made their way to form a circle around the crackling blaze. 'That's better!' he announced, warming his hands over the flames. 'We are all together in this room because you followed me on a doomed mission to bring back our fallen brothers. A fool's errand on my part, I think.'

Barcus looked across the fire to his commander. 'No, Arthur. We followed a leader who brought us all this way unharmed.'

Gavain nudged Lionides and whispered, 'Unharmed? You nearly drowned.' He winked.

'You still owe me a silver denarii!' Lionides grinned back.

'When I next get paid,' Gavain groaned in defeat.

'It's not your fault Uther is a treacherous turd. You couldn't have known he'd do something so cruel as to crucify those men,' Barcus continued, impassioned.

'I was warned.' He indicated the chief of the Clan of the Wolf. 'Idris tried to warn me and I didn't listen. And even Emrys had his concerns.'

'No offence, sir,' Kai broke in, 'but we didn't know Idris then.' He looked to the hill man. 'No offence meant.'

'None taken, I'm sure.' Idris raised a mug in salute.

'And where is Emrys?' Kai continued. 'Isn't he supposed to be your adviser or something?'

'Indeed,' Arthur said gravely. 'But no one's seen him since yesterday when the earth heaved.'

Suddenly the whole hall shuddered as the ground shook, tossing men to the floor and sending sparks from the fire swirling up to the rafters in a spinning chaotic dance. 'What in God's name?' Arthur got to his feet, seeing many of his men doing likewise. 'Twice in two days?'

'This is just like what happened in Pompeii!' Bedwyr cried over the clamour of voices. 'This whole damn mountain might explode!'

Idris, who'd dropped his mug and lay flat on the floor, looked around white-eyed, expecting molten rock to suddenly come pouring through the doors. 'Explode!' He leapt to his feet and headed for the door. He rushed outside and looked up behind the hall to see the grey mountain quietly sitting there with a cap of snow resting on its peaks. A swirl of mist wreathed around its lower reaches and he could see birds flying unconcerned above the green of the pine forests that climbed its steep flanks. Gripping his chest in relief, he walked back inside to see a very dusty and disarrayed Emrys standing next to Arthur holding a pot of something in his gnarled hands.

'The mountain's not exploding,' he revealed, a grin broad across his weather-tanned face.

Emrys looked up at him as he entered. 'Of course the mountain's not exploding, that was me!' And taking a pinch of powder from the pot, he threw it into the fire where it erupted in a flash of light.

'Incredible,' Arthur said as the men crowded round to see what this miraculous powder was.

'What is it?' Kai asked as Emrys showed them the contents.

'I'm not sure. But it certainly is useful for getting out of tight spots!' His mirth was lost on the men who looked at him as if he had gone mad.

'I'm glad you've returned to us, Emrys. But we've a more pressing matter at hand.' Arthur looked at the men with a levelled gaze. 'Scouts have returned and they tell of not one but two armies approaching Camelot. They'll be here by this time tomorrow or maybe the day after.'

'It's got to be my uncle.' Gwenyfar spoke up. She was shaken by the earlier explosion but refused to show it even after Lionides had appeared at her side to help her off the floor. She brushed a dusty lock of hair from her beautiful face and continued. 'When you arrived here, he'd already sent his army home to their villages for the winter. You only saw a few guards that were left behind while they searched for me. Many folk frightened more by the invaders than my uncle sought protection here beneath his banner, and he was happy to give it to swell his ranks with fighting men. The rest worked the land or hunted for game.'

'How many men does he have at his command?' Lionides asked, gazing into her soft brown eyes.

'At least three hundred, maybe as many as four hundred, it was hard to keep up with the amount of refugees that showed up constantly.'

'God's teeth,' Alcaeus cursed. 'Even behind these walls we can't take on that many!'

'And that's just one army,' Arthur said. 'Scouts reported two!'

'I'm guessing,' Emrys stepped forward, 'that the second army consists of our friends from over the water.'

Gwenyfar's hands shot to her mouth. 'It's Conor's father, Feargal. He wants revenge for the death of his son. He wants me!' She looked imploringly at Lionides, and then much to Lionides' chagrin, Arthur.

'My lady,' Arthur bowed, 'you are under our protection. We won't let him or your uncle harm you while we still live.'

'But what if you're all dead?' she cried. 'There must be close to a thousand men out there heading this way. What can twenty-five knights do against that host?'

'She's right, Arthur,' said Idris who'd been listening carefully. 'You and your men, even aided by me and the few lads I brought along, can't stand against two armies. May I suggest we quit this fort, sooner rather than later, and take to the forests and mountains? I have kin not too far away and they can take us in and hide the slaves you rescued from the mine. They'll never find you up there!' he said with pride.

'Idris has a point.' Emrys pulled on his beard as was his habit when in deep thought. 'We need to get the freed workers away from here, beyond anyone's reach. Us, too. Feargal thinks Uther is still in Camelot so he's heading straight here to confront him about the death of his son and seek retribution against the lady Gwenyfar.' He looked at her and nodded in recognition of the part she'd played.

'Also, Uther knows you're here. He's raised his army to take back his home. So, let's give it back to him. We leave Camelot immediately so that Uther can reclaim it, and when Feargal arrives they can sort out their differences while we make good our escape. What do you think?'

Arthur thought about Emrys' plan. 'Well, men?' He turned to his trusted companions. 'We're all in this together as equals now, so what do you say?'

'Let the goat fuckers fight it out between them,' Alcaeus stated, and many of the men joined in with agreeing to the plan. The rest swore to follow Arthur wherever it led them. So it was agreed that they'd leave Camelot immediately.

'Right, men,' Barcus hollered across the fire. 'Get your shit together; we leave in an hour.'

Chapter 17
Escape and Alliances

Uther had met up with the dragon host late the second day after losing Camelot. The bulk of the army had greeted him led by a trusted commander called Kynan, a hard-faced warrior who'd spent his life leading men into battle. His face and chest showed the familiar swirling blue tattoos that painted the skins of the people, and large gold hoops decorated his ears.

'Well met, Kynan.' Uther gripped his forearms in salute.

'Lord Uther. I've called the host as summoned.' He returned the grip fiercely. 'The rest should be here in a day or so.'

'I've no time to wait. How many spears did you bring?'

'Around two hundred so far. But give me time and it'll be closer to four!'

'No. Two hundred should be enough. We march straight away.' Anxious to move, he drummed his fingers on his thigh.

'Where are we headed? If you don't mind me asking. I've not had time to find out what the summons is about!'

'Camelot was taken two days ago by trickery,' Uther lied, 'and I want it back.'

'Gods above. Camelot? Fallen? How did they get in? Tricked, you say, how so?'

'Under a flag of truce. I let them in and they butchered my garrison.' Uther thumped his chest as he spoke.

'Treacherous bastards. Don't worry, Lord, we'll get these fuckers, you'll see!' Kynan growled, then turned to his trumpeters. 'Sound the horns, we're moving off!' He climbed onto his horse.

Uther helped Morgana mount one of the spares Kynan had brought, then jumped onto his, kicking in his heels and turning back towards his home, followed by a sea of spears. 'Let's see how you fare now, Arthur,' he muttered under his breath, the fire of battle in his heart.

'Scouts report a large army heading just east of us, my chieftain,' Aodh reported.

'Who the fuck are they?' Feargal scratched his head. The army had made good time and were almost within striking distance of Camelot. He pulled a louse from his beard and crushed it between two of his thick fingers. 'I wonder who Uthers pissed off as well,' he pondered.

Aodh shrugged in ignorance. 'They couldn't get close enough to see the banners, but they think it's a local army, not another clan from back home.'

'Now that's interesting!' Feargal swayed gently in his saddle as the animal walked slowly along the trackway. 'If they're a rival tribe, maybe we could join together and destroy that upstart between us. I mean, the enemy of my enemy...' He left the saying unfinished as another scout rode up.

'Well!' Aodh barked at the man. 'Report!'

The man stiffened in his saddle. 'My chieftain, I managed to get close enough to the enemy force without being seen. I saw the banners.'

Feargal pinned the man with a look. 'Well? Who's banner is it?'

'Uthers, my chief. It was the dragon banner of Lord Uther!'

'And was Uther there?' Feargal trembled with excitement at the possibility. 'Yes, sir. I saw him myself, at the front.'

Feargal reached into his pouch, pulled out a piece of hack silver and tossed it to the man who caught it deftly. 'Well done, lad. Good job. Now go rejoin your mates!' The scout turned his horse and galloped back down the line of warriors.

'What can this mean, my chief?' Aodh asked, confused.

'Well, it could be one of two possibilities.' Feargal held up two fingers. 'One,' he folded one down, 'the fool could be coming out to attack us, but that's unlikely as we seem to be heading in the same direction. And two,' he folded the other, 'he's been kicked out of his stronghold and has raised an army to take it back.' He rubbed his weathered hands together with glee.

'So what do we do?' Aodh speculated. 'Do we attack him while he's on the road?'

'What? Gods, no, that'd be a mess. They'd spot us and have time to prepare long before we got anywhere near. No. Here's what we'll do. Send four of our fastest scouts ahead and see who holds Camelot. That's the lynchpin. If we can, we'll ally ourselves with them and wait for Uther to arrive and then give him a lovely warm welcome home.'

'What if they won't join with us? We'll be trapped between two forces!'

'True enough, Aodh. But fortune favours the bold, and anyway, I fancy wintering in Uther's hill fort, more appealing than hunkering down in a rat-infested barn!' he laughed.

Gwenyfar looked back sadly as Camelot disappeared from view, screened by the surrounding forest. She couldn't believe she'd lost her home for a second time after only just returning. The sorrow was overwhelming but the fact was, she would be far safer with this band of warriors than she had been in a long time. She knew they'd willingly sacrifice their lives for her, and that was a great comfort.

She looked up ahead at Arthur as he sat straight in his saddle, talking low with Idris, who rode a stocky mountain pony by his side. He was definitely a desirable mate. If he survived, she mused. Then there was Lionides. Her heart belonged to him, his beauty was a song in her soul, and he loved her, that was clear. But he would never be able to raise her up to where she would be free to live her own life. She sighed; the way ahead for her was fraught with sadness and risk.

But she needed to choose with her head and not her heart. A small tear slid down her cheek at the thought of what lay ahead.

'Why so sad, Gwenyfar?' She hadn't noticed Arthur drop back to talk with her.

Brushing away the tear with the back of her hand, she answered, 'I've lost my home once again, and I'm not sure if I'll ever return there.' This was a simple truth that she didn't feel the need to embellish with a lie.

'It's only temporary,' he replied, wiping away another tear with his thumb.

She gripped his hand and kissed it softly. 'Thank you.' She looked deep into his eyes, and he felt a surge of affection for this brave young woman.

'I don't know how you stay so strong,' he murmured huskily, his throat choked with desire.

'It's easy when I'm surrounded by such heroic warriors and their brave leader.' Her reply, equally husky, surprised her. Arthur felt a confusion inside that he didn't understand. He'd been with plenty of women in his life, and one or two had been special. But this? This was different and he needed time to work out his feelings, so begging her leave with an excuse that he needed to check the way ahead, he rode off, leaving Gwenyfar with a flush to her cheeks and a smile of satisfaction on her face.

Feargal was stunned by the news that Camelot was empty and the gates were wide open. The scouts had returned before sundown with the report and he'd urged his men to keep marching past dark, hoping to reach the walls before dawn.

'But the men are flagging,' Finn, one of his captains, argued. 'They can't go on without a break.'

'I'll give them an hour's rest to eat and drink a little, but no more. We must make the fort before Uther!'

'Understood.' Finn bowed and left to give the command to stop.

'Will we make it?' Aodh asked, staring up at the darkening sky. 'Looks like more snow is due tonight.'

'Then more reason to make Camelot. They won't grumble so hard when they've a roof over their heads and ale in their bellies. So come, let's grab a bite and a mug before we move on.'

'Sweet lord above,' Cadoc cursed, lying on his stomach overlooking Feargal's army as it rested. He crossed himself then kissed the small forbidden cross he always wore under his tunic. He'd been given it by a priest of the Christ, who came to Camelot years ago to try and convert Uther's brother. The old King had imprisoned him to stop him spreading his truth and a young Cadoc was set to guard the cell, and so the priest had talked to him, telling him about the teachings of the one God, and slowly but surely Cadoc had seen the light of truth, and in the secrecy of the dark, dank cell had been converted to the true faith. The priest had then given him this tiny cross, carved, he claimed, from the one true cross on which the lord Jesus Christ had been crucified in Calvary.

The priest had died of a fever some weeks later and Cadoc heard his confession before he died. The feeling that he'd let his mentor down bothered him to this day, so he treasured this tiny cross more than all the gold in Uther's mountain.

Creeping back into the cover of damp ferns, he slipped away to the waiting scout who held the horses quietly in a fold in the land. 'You were right, Llew. That's Feargal's battle host. He must have heard about his son's death somehow. Let's get back to Uther and give him the bad news!'

Uther paced around his tent, a tent that Kynan had relinquished to him when he arrived. 'Gods above. He's after my blood. What am I going to do?' This last was more of a rhetorical question so Cadoc and Kynan remained silent while their lord continued to rant. 'And how many men did you say he had, Cadoc?'

'At least four hundred, sir.'

'We're outnumbered, then.' Uther stopped his pacing and turned to face Cadoc, who stood to attention. 'And do you think he knows we're here?'

'Undoubtedly, my lord. If our scouts managed to locate his force, then they must have spotted us by now.'

'Then why hasn't he attacked yet?' Uther resumed his pacing, chewing the inside of his cheek as he thought the puzzle through. 'Oh, Gods!' He abruptly stopped. 'He doesn't want to face us.' His face drained of colour as realisation dawned on him. 'He's making for Camelot. He plans to overwhelm Arthur's men and take my hall for his own. Kynan. Get the men ready. We march for Camelot with all haste.'

'But it's dark, sir. Most of the men are asleep.'

'Then wake them the fuck up. We've got to beat Feargal to my fortress. If that cock sucker gets there first we'll have a devil of a time winkling him out, if at all!'

Uther's camp burst into life as the men were roused and called to marching order. Within an hour they were on the move as fat flakes of snow started to drop out of the heavy sky.

High above the valley, sheltered in a deep glen thick with pine, Arthur's much smaller party sat around several small fires trying to stave off the cold. Very little of the snow filtered through the thick canopy and the needle-strewn ground stayed mercifully dry. The ex-slaves had formed a separate group and burrowed deep into the bed of needles for warmth as they huddled, sleeping in a group, closer than family. Idris looked across at their dozing forms with sorrow clear on his grizzled face.

'No man should be treated like this, Arthur.' He pointed with his knife as he whittled a small piece of wood by the fire's glow. 'It's not right. Not in my eyes!'

Arthur turned to his friend. 'You're right, Idris. The teachings of the Christ say all men are born equal. He preached to "do unto others as you would have them do unto you."'

'Wise words indeed, friend, Arthur.' Idris then sat in silence, his hands working automatically as he carved away slivers of wood by touch.

After a few minutes of silence filled only by the crackling of fires and the soft murmuring of muted conversation, Idris put away his knife, placed the small carving into a pouch and said plainly, 'If they pursue us, whichever army it should be, then these poor folk here,' he indicated the sleeping refugees from the mine, 'won't stand a bloody chance, and neither will we if we're caught together.'

'What are you suggesting?'

'I'm suggesting that half a day's march east of here, or thereabouts, there's a village of my distant kin. I've six good lads with me, and I think we should send them off with our friends over there to safety. I'm sure they'll be looked after, as we all have cousins and the like in the village.'

'That sounds like a solid plan, my friend. At first light we'll send them off with whatever we can spare, and blaze a wide trail west for a few miles before circling back to see if we've been followed, and if they take the bait!'

'Aye. That'll do it.' Idris nodded. 'I'm for my bed now.' He patted Arthur's shoulder as he stood. 'Say a prayer to your Christ for us heathens, eh!' And with that, he wandered off to find his blankets. Arthur watched his friend leave with a smile.

The following morning brought more snow as the party moved out from the protection of the trees. In places it was knee deep and the rescued slaves shivered even in the clothes that had been handed out before they left.

'They won't make it much further in these conditions,' Gwenyfar said as she sat on her horse, Spirit, who had survived the fall of Camelot. She rode beside Arthur at the vanguard of their small force.

'They'll be looked after fine. Idris' men are going to take them to a village east of here. It's half a day's march so they should get there unscathed.'

'But look.' Gwenyfar pointed at a girl of no more than seven, who although swaddled in a large cloak, had rags tied around her feet. 'The poor thing.' Genuine sorrow for the child's plight touched her heart. As she watched, the clan chief, Idris, walked over to the girl and smiling up to her, handed her a small token wrapped in a piece of leather.

'What's he got there?' she wondered aloud.

Arthur turned to look and saw the little girl smiling and playing happily with a beautifully carved image of a bear. He smiled. 'He's a good man, true and kind.'

'And generous,' Gwenyfar added.

'Yes. Generous. I watched him carve that bear last night. I wondered what he was doing. He had noticed the girl's sadness where I missed it.'

'Don't be too hard on yourself.' She rested a hand on his arm and gave it a squeeze. 'You've a lot more on your plate than he does.'

'What do you mean by that?'

'Well, I've heard the talk in camp, about you and who you really are. The once and future King. You've a nation to bring together.'

Arthur laughed. A cynical sound. 'You listen to the gossip of a crazy old man, and a few desperate farmers. How could I forge a nation with twenty-five men? Answer me that.' He placed his hands on his hips, challenging her to answer.

'Hey, laddie, you've more than twenty-five men now, you know.' Idris, who had heard the conversation, chipped in. 'The people I represent number in the hundreds, and there's hundreds more in the valleys and plains here about. Mark me, when you need them, you'll have an army of well over a thousand. What do you say about that then?' And mimicking Arthur, he planted his hands on his hips and bellowed a laugh. Arthur laughed along but soon turned serious.

'But most are just farmers or hunters, not trained soldiers!'

'Ach. You're talking of fighting against trained legionnaires. Most of those bastards back there are no more soldier than any of the rest of us. They're just opportunists who flocked to this banner or that for the promise of plunder. Trust me, Arthur, when the time comes and you show them that sword, they'll follow you. Mark my words!' Turning his horse, he walked it away to send off his men with the refugees.

Gwenyfar put her arm through his and leant against him with a contented sigh. 'I believe in you,' she whispered. He looked down into her eyes, feeling his emotions rise within him. She gazed up, gently snaked an arm around his head and drew him down into a lingering kiss. He pulled back slightly and in a breathy voice raw with passion, said, 'I think I love you, Gwenyfar.'

She smiled into his handsome face. 'I love you too.' And she kissed him with a fierce desire as he crushed her to him.

From some distance away Lionides saw the coming together of his one true love and his friend and leader. A deep anger rose from within, and a strong desire to be alone. Without a word he dropped back in the marching line and disappeared from sight.

Feargal, at the head of his army came into sight of Camelot. Impressed by its location at the top of a flat plateau that eventually became the mountain behind, he led his men up the twisting path that led to the wide-open gates, between which on horseback sat one of his scouts with a foaming mug of ale in his hand. As the war chief rode past and into the courtyard of the deserted fort, the scout passed him the mug, which he drained, and thanking him, tossed it away as he leapt off his horse and strode into the great hall, which sat cold and silent, just a thin trail of smoke rising up from the fire pit to show that it had ever been inhabited.

'This'll do nicely,' he shouted, calling for Aodh to bring the army into the fort and find them barracks and food. 'Yes. This'll do very nicely,' he said as he dropped into Uther's seat and swung a leg over one arm. 'And bring me more ale,' he called out with a laugh.

The men of Hibernia filled the fort to capacity with horses, oxen, and a host of chickens and sheep that were kept for the pot. The sound of celebration filled the air as the men, cheered by the fact that they had shelter and a ready supply of alcohol, relaxed for the first time in months.

Feargal, flanked by Aodh examined the defences, walking along the length of the rampart looking for weak spots. Finding none, they made their way to the solitary lookout tower that faced the valley, giving an elevated view of the land below. Down in the courtyard no one knew what to make of the three wooden crosses that now stood empty, so they were pulled down and broken up for firewood.

'Oh!' barked Feargal as he stood high up in the freezing, windswept tower, pointing to a smudge in the distance. 'It looks like our host has arrived home to find the fires still burning!' Aodh laughed along with his chief at the thought of Uther being stuck out in the chill winter snow that lay thick over the landscape. Just in sight of his hearth but unable to reach it. The two men stood for a while watching as the smudge got larger, finally revealing itself as Uther's army.

'What do you think he'll do?' Aodh wondered aloud.

'My guess,' said Feargal, 'is that he'll try to parley, and should I?' He rested his arms against the railing, watching as the force before Camelot spread out. 'How many do you reckon?' He turned to Aodh.

'Maybe three hundred, possibly a few more. But they won't be able to stay there long. It's bloody freezing, and food and fodder for the animals is going to be scarce!'

'Hmm. That's why I was thinking… Well, let's just wait and see what happens, shall we? I fancy a warm mug and bright blaze to chase the chills away.' He laughed again and slid down the ladder, swiftly followed by his second.

Uther cursed his misfortune. How could those goat fuckers have beaten him to his own stronghold? Cadoc had reported that the army was at rest when he returned with the scout. Maybe they were mistaken, or perhaps they were in league with the Hibernians. *No, that's ridiculous*, he thought. Cadoc was loyal to his king. But king of what now? He cursed again as he stood there in the snow, staring up at the smoke from his own fire curling up above the walls.

'Fuck. Fuck. Fuck!' he screamed. Men nearby shrank away from their leader's anger lest it be directed at them. 'Cadoc. Kynan! Get over here!'

The two men ran to their lord, eager to soothe his temper before he did something rash.

'What are we going to do? Hmm?' Uther paced the ground in front of them both. 'Come on. Any thoughts?'

'We could parley?' Cadoc shrugged. 'They might listen!'

'Or they might fill our asses with arrows.' Kynan snorted. 'I say we wait for the full host to gather then assault the walls and take back Camelot by force!'

'Both are good suggestions, and I think we'll do a little of each. But we can't afford to wait too long. There'll be no fodder for the animals soon and if the food runs out, the men will start to slip away.' Uther tapped a finger on his cheek. 'Let's see if they'll parley while we wait for the rest of the men to arrive. If they agree, then good. If they don't, we go in hard and kill every last mother's son!'

Kynan pumped his fist at this, cheering.

'And if they agree to parley?' Cadoc asked.

'Then hopefully they'll let us in, and like that fucker Arthur we'll somehow open the gates...'

'...And kill every last mother's son!' yelled Kynan, filled with bloodlust.

Uther laughed and punched him lightly on the arm. 'You old war dog. You can't wait for the fight, can you?' They all laughed.

Feargal and Aodh were sat in Uther's hall, eating his food and drinking his beer, when a guard entered. 'Men approaching the gates, my chief!' He saluted and then waited.

Feargal put down the chicken wing he'd been gnawing and wiped his greasy hands on his breeches before standing, and with a belch, said, 'Well, that answers that, then. The shit kisser wants to talk!'

'You said he would.' Aodh was still sat eating as he spoke, spitting bits of bread over the table. 'I say let them wait. Come, my chief, finish your meal. Let them cool their heels.' He laughed at his own joke and Feargal joined him, wiping a tear of mirth from his eye.

'Oh, that's a good one. Cool their heels. Oh ho!' He grabbed his sides and fell back into his seat. Looking up at the waiting guard, he said, 'Tell our visitors that we're at supper and can't see them until later.' He grabbed another piece of chicken and began to chew noisily. 'Oh. And be sure to thank Uther for his hospitality. He sets a fine table!' He winked at Aodh and both men fell into laughter again. Amused by his leaders, the guard saluted and left to relay the message.

'That'll piss him off,' Feargal said. 'But he owes me, and I intend to collect before this is over!' He threw the piece of chicken away and watched as two dogs fought over the morsel.

'Cheeky fucker!' Uther fumed as he sat in his tent in the hastily erected camp, after hearing the reply. 'Making me wait while he eats my food! Argh!' He flung his poor meal of porridge across the small space, where it splashed up the sides and ran in thick clumps to the floor. 'I've a good mind to attack now, consequences be damned!'

'It's getting late in the afternoon, my lord. We can have no more than two or three hours of sunlight left. Maybe it would be wise to wait until the morning?' Cadoc pleaded. He had no stomach for wasting good men in a punitive attack.

'Two hours is plenty, you old woman,' Kynan mocked. 'Maybe you should go back to your embroidery!'

Cadoc bridled and stepped forward, both fists clenched. 'Enough!' yelled Uther. 'Cadoc is right. There's no point wasting men tonight; we'll achieve nothing except bleeding our army. We'll see what tomorrow brings. And where the hell is Morcant?'

Lionides wallowed in his misery as he rode aimlessly through the forest, uncaring of his destination. His mount pushed through bracken-filled gullies and snow drifts, following her master's directions until they stopped and the horse came to a standstill in a bright glade with a thin rivulet of cold mountain meltwater trickling through it.

The animal bent her neck to drink and almost toppled Lionides over, so lost in his thoughts that he hadn't noticed he'd come to a halt. Leaning forward, he patted her neck lovingly and said, 'Sorry, girl, I just don't know what I'm doing right now!' He slipped from his saddle and sat by the stream, listening to it gurgling as it wound its way towards the river in the valley far below.

'Maybe I should follow this stream to the sea and board a ship to a far land?' He looked up at his faithful mare, and the horse seemed to stare back at him in disapproval. 'No, you're right,' he said. 'I know you wouldn't enjoy a sea voyage. Sorry.' He reached into his leather scrip and pulled out an oat cake, which he offered up. The horse's ears pricked up and she walked over to slowly lip the cake from his fingers, snuffling contentedly as she munched.

A crackling in the bushes warned Lionides that someone was near. He stood, drawing his sword, scanning for threats.

'There you are!' a familiar soft voice chimed, and Gwenyfar stepped between two tall pines and into the clearing.

'What do you want?' Lionides snapped, angered by her presence.

'Don't be like that!' She stepped forward and tried to cup his face in her hands. 'How can you be so cruel?'

Lionides gripped her shoulders as if he wanted to shake an answer from those sweet lips. 'I saw you with Arthur. I heard what you said. So why are you here?' Confusion mixed with longing warred across his handsome face.

Gwenyfar stepped back and studied his face, a strange look in her eye. 'I'm here... because I love YOU!' she pleaded. 'Arthur heard what he needed to hear. I don't love him. It's you I want.'

'I'm sorry.' He fell to his knees in front of her and wrapped his arms around her waist. 'I've been such a jealous fool. Can you forgive me?'

'Of course, my love.' She dropped to her knees and held him close, brushing his soft golden hair like a comforting mother. 'Lay back.' She placed a hand on his chest and pushed him onto his back where he lay with warm tears making tracks down his cheeks. Gwenyfar climbed onto his hips and leant forward, kissing him deeply. Lionides felt himself responding as if in a dream as she undid his breeches and slid onto him. He gasped as she started to move rhythmically on top of him. 'Are you sure?' he gasped, overcome with desire.

'Yes, my love, just relax,' she said, as he groaned in pleasure.

Lionides lay back on the chill ground unaware of the coldness around him as he bathed in the warm afterglow of their lovemaking. He looked to Gwenyfar and was surprised to see her getting herself ready to leave. 'Where are you going?' he demanded. 'Stay.' He reached for her but she danced away from his grasp with a throaty chuckle.

'I must go. You've been missed and Arthur and the men are out looking for you, and no doubt they'll miss me soon as well!' She finished lacing her dress and stepped towards the gap where she'd entered the dell not so long ago. 'Go back to Arthur and act as if nothing has happened. Just tell him, I don't know, you got lost?' She smiled that smile that made his heart sing before stepping through the gap and disappearing from sight.

Once away Gwenyfar leant against the bole of a large lone oak and clutched her chest, feeling... nothing. The glamour slipped away and Morgana smiled in triumph. The seeds of Arthur's destruction were sown, and all she needed to do was wait until they blossomed. She patted her hair back into place and headed back down the mountain to where her own horse was tethered. She needed to return to Uther soon, but she had one more stop to make before she went back to him. She raised her hands high and howled in joy, quickly joined by the voices of nearby wolf packs.

With Emrys trapped or dead her plans wouldn't fail, and that young fool Lionides couldn't tell her from the real Gwenyfar, their other meetings had proved that. 'Love blinds even the mightiest warrior until he's as helpless as a babe,' she cackled.

Lionides rejoined the rest of Arthur's men and was surprised to see them all together and not out looking for him.

'Where have you been?' Alcaeus had spotted his friend and ridden over to him.

'I, err, I was unwell,' he stammered.

'That must've been some shit. You've been gone ages. But don't worry, you weren't missed. I covered for you.'

Lionides looked at his best friend, perplexed. 'What?'

'Nothing,' he replied distractedly, noticing Gwenyfar at the front with Arthur, deep in conversation. 'Umm, thanks for having my back.'

They rode on in silence.

Chapter 18
Pursuit

Feargal spent a restful night in Uther's bed but was woken in the early hours by a clamouring outside his chamber. Throwing off the covers he drew a dagger and, naked, threw open the door to see flickering torches and men rushing around with excited faces. As one passed he grabbed him by the collar. The man gasped in shock, seeing his chief step out of the dark naked and holding a knife.

'What's going on?' he demanded to know, shaking the man. 'I was sleeping!'

'My lord.' The guard struggled to bow as he was held firmly in Feargal's fist. 'Gold, my lord. One of your men has found heaps of gold!'

'Show me!' Feargal released the guard who led him to a small door that wound down to a locked undercroft, which now stood open.

'Where's the man who found this?' he demanded. A red-faced warrior, obviously drunk, was brought to him and stood swaying as he fought to keep balance.

'Well? You wine sack, what were you doing down here in my hall?' He gave him a hard stare.

But the drunk man just chuckled and said, 'You're naked!' before belching and almost falling over.

'For fuck's sake, hold him steady.' Feargal's ire was rising. Guards grabbed the drunk and held him upright. He gripped the man's neck and slapped him hard across the face. 'You'd better start talking. What were you doing down here?'

The man looked about as if just realising his situation and slurred a response. 'I... I was looking for something to drink...'

'Looks to me like you've already had enough,' one of the men holding him muttered.

The drunk looked at him before continuing. 'I came into the hall but there was no ale, so I went in search of the kitchens and found this door instead and thought it must be where Uther keeps his drink. But it wasn't. It's full of gold!' His sweating face tried to smile at his lord, but the grim face staring back froze him in a rictus of fear.

'Did you take any?' The question was loaded with menace, and the drunk man felt his bowels loosening in fear. A thin trickle of piss ran down his leg to pool between his feet.

'There was so much,' he blurted pleadingly, 'I didn't think you'd miss a little.'

'Have I not been generous to you all?' Feargal roared. The point of his knife hovered in front of the man's eye.

'Ye...Yes, my lord. I'm sorry, I'm sorry,' he cried, his hands reaching up, begging.

'I despise thieves,' he said calmly, and sliced the man's ample belly open with a slash of his blade. Purple entrails spilled out onto the floor as blood washed down the man's legs. His shocked eyes stared at his own guts as he tried to hold them in with his hands. The guards holding him stepped aside and the drunk sagged to the floor amongst his own insides, his lifeless eyes staring into infinity.

'Get this mess cleaned up!' Feargal wiped his blade on the dead man's back and stepped over the gore-covered floor and into the undercroft.

'Immediately, sir.' Both guards reached down and grabbed the corpse by an arm each and dragged it off.

'And send for Aodh!' he bellowed after them.

Alone in the gold store, he marvelled at the wealth before him. 'A fortune,' he mused. 'No, ten fortunes, fifty, a hundred!' He turned around in the large space and everywhere he looked he saw barrels and sacks full of gold.

'Gods above,' a voice from behind him spoke. Aodh stepped into the room.

'Is it not a wonder?' Feargal laughed. 'We have the wealth of a kingdom here. Our whole invasion has been paid for a thousand times over!' He threw a fist-sized gold nugget at his friend.

'Indeed.' Aodh tossed the weighty nugget from hand to hand. 'So what? Are we going to take all this and leave?' He threw the lump back to his chief, who tossed it back into a barrel.

'Yes and no. We're going to take all this, for sure. But if Uther thinks I'm going to leave when there's the possibility of a rich seam of gold somewhere in the mountains, then he's going to be mighty disappointed. I want that rat bastard to lose everything!'

'And I can help you!' Both men spun round in surprise at the feminine voice behind them.

'Who the fuck are you?' Feargal stood naked and unabashed in front of a stunningly beautiful woman with fiery red hair that seemed to him to glow with an inner light. 'And where the hell have you come from?'

'My name's Eilonwy, and until recently I was a prisoner of Uther. The Roman freed me, but when he left with Uther's niece Gwenyfar I stayed behind. And then you arrived and I hid.'

'Uther's niece? Where were they headed? Do you know? Speak, woman!' Feargal took a step forwards and Eilonwy shrank back in fear.

'Don't hurt me, Lord,' she begged, and Aodh stepped between them.

'My chieftain, best not to frighten her to death with the size of your...' He nodded down, indicating Feargal's nakedness.

The Hibernian warlord laughed out loud, all threats of violence forgotten.

'You must forgive me, my lady,' he made to bow. 'I've been away from the comforts of a good woman too long, and I forget myself. Please.' He indicated to follow him out of the storeroom. 'Aodh, secure this door and post a guard on it. I want no more drunken fools thinking they can steal what's mine. Do you hear!' Aodh nodded and trotted off to do his chief's bidding.

Feargal led Eilonwy back up to the great hall where he sat her down at Uther's table and begged her to wait while he threw on some clothes.

'That's better,' he said, his boots beating a tattoo on the flagstone floor. 'Can I offer you something to eat or drink?'

'Oh, yes please,' she answered, smiling, showing surprisingly white teeth. 'I'm starving. I haven't eaten since you arrived.'

'That can soon be rectified.' Feargal called out and men rushed to do his bidding, bringing food and drink and placing them in front of their lord while he served his beautiful guest.

'Now tell me,' he urged, watching her as she ate, chewing delicately. He felt his lust rising as he watched this gorgeous creature sat alongside him. 'Where was Arthur heading? Did you hear?'

She stopped eating and placed her food back on her plate, wiping her mouth with a piece of cloth. 'They headed north and east up into the mountains. I can show you the trail they took, as I watched them leave the other morning.'

'Good. Good.' He poured her some ale. 'Please drink, and in the morning you can show me where they went.'

Eilonwy smiled a bright smile. 'With pleasure,' she said. 'You've been so kind to me.'

She blushed in a way that made Feargal hard. *Gods above,* he thought. *I haven't felt like this about a woman in a long time.*

As she lay in the darkness of the bed chamber that Feargal had given her, Eilonwy smiled, a predatory grin. Having locked the door of what had been Gwenyfar's room, Morgana stretched languidly in her bed and went to sleep.

She awoke to a gentle knocking on the door. Taking on the appearance of 'Eilonwy' again, she opened the door to find a burly Hibernian with a sheepish grin beckoning her to attend the great hall where Feargal was waiting to speak with her.

'Good morning, my lady.' He stood and welcomed her to his table to break her fast. 'I hope you slept well?'

'The best night's sleep I've ever had!' she answered smoothly. 'And you, my lord?' She bowed while looking at him seductively, which only enflamed his desire even more. He swallowed hard.

'I sleep little these days,' he said, 'since the loss of my only son.' A sadness crept into his eyes and Morgana smiled inwardly.

'Tell me,' she insisted. So Feargal, the war chief and leader of Clan MacDuid, told this strangely alluring woman all about his son and what had happened to him at the hands of Gwenyfar.

'That's terrible.' Eilonwy covered her mouth in horror. 'I see now why you wanted to know which way they had gone. I'll happily show you now, if you'd like. I'm not really that hungry.' She rose from her seat trailed by Feargal, who hung on her every word.

Outside, the two of them followed by faithful Aodh climbed the watch tower and stood looking out over the lands that used to belong to the Pendragon. A man much reduced and forced into camping outside his own hill fort.

'That way, my lord.' She pointed out a track to the north-east that cut through the forest and up towards the high reaches of the surrounding mountains. 'I believe there's a pass not too far away that drops down into another valley and then from there it's only a few days' ride to the river that marks the edge of Uther's domain.'

'Thank you, my lady.' Feargal turned to Aodh. 'Take a party of a hundred men and track them down. I want Gwenyfar alive, you can kill the rest.' Aodh looked worried. 'What's bothering you, my friend? Don't you think you can take Arthur and his men with a hundred of ours?'

'It's not that. Aren't you risking your position here in Camelot by sending so many off in pursuit of one woman?'

'Don't you worry about us here, we've more than enough to hold back Uther's pitiful warriors, plus we're behind stout walls and they're freezing their bollocks off in the snow.' He pointed to the camp that was just stirring, with cooking fires sending columns of smoke spiralling into a crisp blue sky.

'You'd best get a move on before the camp is fully awake or they'll be chasing you into those hills for sport,' he laughed. 'Go on, be off with you.' He pushed Aodh back towards the ladders.

'One more thing, my lord.' Eilonwy grabbed Feargal's arm before he started down the ladder. 'I heard them talking about Arthur's sword, like it was something special. It had a funny name, something like Caladbolg.'

Feargal's eyes lit up at this revelation. 'Caladbolg, are you sure?'

'Yes, I'm sure.' Eilonwy looked confused.

'Gods above. Aodh, hold up, I've another task for you.' And he clattered down the ladder after his man, leaving Morgana at the top of the tower alone staring eastward. An incantation barely above a whisper slipped from her lips in clouds of white that grew and swelled, and as it reached the sky above, it turned a dark, foreboding grey and sped away from Camelot and over the mountains, to where Arthur and his knights were making their way through the high passes. Her work done, she lightly climbed down the ladder and made to rejoin Feargal in the great hall.

Uther watched the company leaving Camelot flanked by Cadoc and Kynan. As surprised as he was that men were quitting the fort, he was pleased it was so, as it meant a greatly reduced garrison and an opportunity to retake his home.

'Where are they off to?' Cadoc scratched his chest where he'd been bitten by a louse.

'If I had to guess,' Kynan said thoughtfully, 'I'd say they know where Lady Gwenyfar is heading and are going to bring her back.'

Uther looked at his two commanders. 'I want my home back. But having said that, I also want the head of Arthur and my bloody niece back with me so I can kill her myself. Cadoc, take a small hand-picked band of ten men and track those bloody barbarians. Use our best scouts and trackers. I want you to stay close, but don't engage with either party if possible. Once you've found them, I want you to wait and see how it goes, then take advantage of the situation, understand?'

'Yes, my lord. I'll play the role of scavenger and pick over the carcass of what's left.' His feral grin showed that he relished the idea. He bowed and left the two leaders.

'Kynan. I want a battle plan drawn up for the recapture of Camelot as soon as possible. The thought of another night out here freezing my arse off isn't something I find appealing. Get to it!'

Kynan nodded and went off to plan his attack, leaving Uther alone watching as the gates of Camelot swung closed with a heavy thud that carried over the still valley.

Arthur had always enjoyed the solitude the wilderness provided. Even in the company of his men, out here he had a sense of freedom that he couldn't find anywhere else. He looked across at Gwenyfar, who was staring out into the wide forest enjoying the same sensation as himself. He smiled. This was a woman he could settle down with, and, maybe, raise a family? He squashed the thought, knowing his path might surely lead to his death.

They had been walking their horses for several hours since dawn had broken with no sign of pursuit. Men who'd been sent back along the trail reported that the path behind was clear for at least two miles. Arthur reined in his tired mount.

'Right, men,' he hollered. 'I think we've led a merry dance far enough, don't you?' The company sat in silence. 'I'm hoping by now that the folk we rescued are safe at the mountain village Idris sent them to.' Idris nodded in agreement. 'So now we turn back, and if Uthers or that barbarian and his men are tracking us, well, we're going to give them a nasty surprise.'

His men pumped their fists and cheered at this; running away from a fight wasn't in their nature.

'I will not let anything happen to the innocent lives that Uther cruelly ripped from their homes and forced into his mine, and even if we die today, or tomorrow, we die knowing we did the right thing. Are you with me?' He threw the question out like a challenge and his men responded with vigour, cheering and screaming their assent. He called Kai and Bedwyr to him. 'My brothers. My friends,' he said softly. 'I have a separate task for you both. I wish you to take the lady Gwenyfar and head towards Caerleon, where she'll be safe. If all goes well, we'll meet up there soon. If not,' he pulled a heavy leather bag from his saddle bag, 'there's enough of Uther's gold here for all three of you to find a new life away from the troubles brewing in Britannia.'

His two men begged for him to reconsider. The thought of not riding with their brothers tore at their hearts. But Arthur refused their pleas, extracting a promise from each of them that they'd protect Gwenyfar from harm at all costs. Sadly, they gave in to his demands and left to say their goodbyes to men they'd ridden with for years.

'I won't go!' Gwenyfar glared at Arthur, lightning flashing in her amber eyes. 'And you can't make me!' she shouted.

'I could have you tied to your horse. My men would do that for me.' A tired smile played on his lips.

'You wouldn't dare!' she cried, outraged at his suggestion.

'I won't have to if you go peacefully.'

She suddenly deflated like a burst bladder. 'But I don't want to leave you.' Tears started to brim in her eyes.

'I know,' he held her hand, 'but I can't fight Uther's men and worry about you!'

'But you said yourself, there's no sign of pursuit. We might be free of them.'

'I only wish that were so.' A sigh escaped him. 'Long years have taught me that jealous men don't let their possessions go without a fight, and you've two jealous men who want you back, maybe for different reasons. But you can't be here when we meet, as meet we surely will!' He looked into her eyes intently, hoping to see understanding. She stared back, resignation clear in her face.

Exhaling a relieved breath, Arthur said, 'Good. I'm glad that's decided. Thank you.'

Gwenyfar leant across and kissed him lightly. 'Until we meet again, my love.' She followed Kai and Bedwyr who were waiting nearby.

Lionides, upset that Arthur hadn't chosen him to look after Gwenyfar, stared balefully at his commander as he instructed his two friends to take his lover away. But at the same time, he loved him too, for sending her away to safety.

Emrys, who'd been studying the scrolls he'd retrieved from Morgana's lair, sat quietly on a moss-covered rock looking westwards. He had a deep feeling of wrongness in his gut that he just couldn't figure out. So, he shut his eyes as the horsemen bustled about nearby, and slipped into a deep trance, his walking staff across his spindly legs. His mind flew away from his body as he sent his essence soaring above the forest, where it circled skyward like an eagle riding the wind. Then, with the swiftness of an arrow it shot west, scanning the surroundings. He saw with his mind a large party of horsemen winding their way towards Arthur. Not Uther's men, he noted. So the barbarian was after them too. That was problematic. He sped on further, stretching his abilities; another smaller party following the Hibernians came into his sight. More problems. But none of this was the sense of wrongness he'd felt earlier. Then he saw it. Boiling up from Camelot, a bank of dark grey clouds heavy with snow was heading towards Arthur and his men. But this wasn't natural. Morgana, it had to be. This was very bad. Emrys withdrew his essence back into his body, and his eyes snapped open.

Arthur had been watching the still form of Emrys for ten minutes after noticing him sat on a rock motionless. When his eyes suddenly opened Arthur jumped in surprise.

'We're in trouble,' he said, getting up. 'Gather your men. We need to find shelter fast!'

'What's the matter?' Arthur said, worried by the old man's agitation.

'There's a storm coming, a bad one. An unnatural one!'

'Unnatural?'

'Yes. There's some things I need to tell you. But first we must find shelter, then I'll explain everything. Come on, Arthur, move.' Emrys clapped his hands and Arthur, as if breaking from a trance leapt into action, calling the men together.

'Idris, you know these lands better than I. Are there any places we can go that will shelter all of us from a snowstorm?'

The heavy-set Cambrian stood thoughtfully for a few moments, trusting Arthur's judgement. 'Yes, I think there's a place nearby that should suit. It's not much, but it's the only place I can think of.'

'What of Kai, Bedwyr, and Gwenyfar?' Lionides spoke up.

'My God.' Arthur slapped his forehead. 'I sent them away a while ago now. Lionides, please, can you go find them? We'll mark the way so you can find us.'

'Of course.' He jumped on his horse with a light heart at the thought of seeing her again. 'She'll be safe with me, Arthur!' And he sped off in pursuit.

'Right, Idris. Lead the way.'

The party hurriedly mounted and following the mountain man, set off to find shelter as heavy clouds covered the sky above, sending the first fat flakes of snow swirling around the trees.

Aodh had found Arthur's trail easily enough, and his men increased their pace as they caught scent of their quarry. Hurrying up the steep valley he noticed the darkening storm overtake him and his men and head off east. He worried over its unnatural size and speed but was happy that he wouldn't need to face it any time soon. 'Come on, lads,' he encouraged his men. 'They're not that far ahead, and I've a feeling we're going to catch up to them far quicker than we thought!'

Cadoc and his lead scout Llew watched the Hibernians from a rocky outcrop above the track. They'd overheard Aodh talking, and nodding silently to Llew the pair crawled back to the rest of the men.

'We'll give it ten minutes then follow them from along this animal trail that runs parallel to the main track. Keep the noise down and stay out of sight. Got it?' The scouts and trackers nodded, grinning.

'Are you trying to teach us to suck eggs?' one of them jibed.

Cadoc laughed softly. 'I wouldn't dream of it. You fuckers are more animal than human anyway.' They all joined in laughing as they set off.

By now, high up, the wind had increased, driving a stinging blizzard of snow and ice into the eyes of Arthur's party.

'We need to find this shelter soon, Idris!' Arthur was forced to shout to be heard above the howling gale. The trees around them bent and clattered together in an alarming manner, and visibility was down to just a few metres as the thickening snow threatened to overwhelm them.

'It's close by now, I'm sure.' Idris staggered as he led his horse by its bridle. They'd been forced to dismount some time back as the branches whipped about them in a frenzy. Two of Arthur's men had been unhorsed already as the frightened mounts high stepped and tossed their heads in fear, and although only receiving a few cuts and scratches, it was deemed safer to lead the scared animals.

As yet there was no sign of Gwenyfar and the men with her, and they had no way of knowing if Lionides had caught up to them. Arthur fretted at not being able to help Gwenyfar but in this blizzard it was doubtful they'd make it back. Arthur just prayed they'd find shelter and weather out this storm, although with what Emrys had said, he had no way of knowing how long that could be.

Kai and Bedwyr pushed on through the howling blizzard, desperately seeking cover from the storm that had come upon them so suddenly. Gwenyfar followed behind, treading in their footsteps as she tried to keep up. Her horse, Spirit, pulled and tugged in an effort to escape the raging storm, ears flat against her skull.

'I can't go on much further!' she yelled above the storm. Neither man seemed to hear as they struggled to keep moving. She yelled again, and Bedwyr turned to face her.

His face was white with cold. Ice crystals clung to his eyebrows and beard.

'We have to find shelter, my lady!' he shouted back. 'A cave or a sheltered spot. We must keep moving or we'll die out here!' Fear touched his voice and Gwenyfar shivered from more than just the cold.

Lionides followed the path his friends had taken and thought he'd catch up to them quickly, but the blizzard had overtaken him and he'd been forced to stop and shelter in a rocky overhang. Walking his horse as far beneath the cliff as possible, he'd hastily gathered fuel and lit a fire, which now crackled and popped, casting a warm glow, and thankfully chasing away the worst of the cold. He sat wrapped in his cloak chewing at a fingernail, his worry for the welfare of Gwenyfar almost causing him to cast caution to the wind and trek out into the wall of white that swirled outside his haven of safety.

A jumbled collection of brush and pine boughs served as a barrier against the worst of the wind, and Lionides was thankful that he'd had the sense to drag them into the overhang before the storm really took hold. He looked over at his horse as it rested in the far reaches of the shallow cave. Every now and then it shivered and its whole body shook. Getting up, he reached into his saddlebag and pulled out a spare cloak, which he threw over the back of the animal. The beast's great head turned to him, large brown eyes showing gratitude for the small kindness as it went back to lipping the ground in search of roots or small tufts of grass.

'There!' Kai pointed. A dark opening appeared out of the white. 'Is that a cave?' He strained against the falling snow, but the image had vanished. 'This way. Follow me.' He turned and struggled through the knee-high drifts towards what he thought he'd seen. Bedwyr and Gwenyfar heard his call, and falling in behind, followed his lead. Suddenly they heard a cry, and the shadow that had been Kai disappeared.

Running forward as quickly as they could, the pair looked about for their companion, but he was gone. Bedwyr handed the reins of his horse to Gwenyfar and carefully stepped forward, patting the neck of Kai's horse as he passed. Just a few paces on, his lead foot met air and he quickly stumbled back. Looking down, he first saw Kai flat on his back at the bottom of a steep gulley, choked with snow-covered brush. Next, he saw that there was a narrow gap leading below the undergrowth, big enough for the horses to enter.

'Kai. Kai?' He shouted.

Kai looked up at his friend and waved as snow settled on his face. 'I'm okay. Just a little bruised, and look, I've found shelter.' He grinned and then winced as he tried to move.

Between the three of them they managed to get the horses down the steep sides without too much trouble, and once in the shelter of the brush the temperature rose, which was fortunate as they couldn't light a fire. So instead, they huddled together with their cloaks spread over them and sat waiting for the blizzard to pass.

The snowstorm was a thing of nightmares. A towering black wall of clouds that just kept on growing.

Aodh watched it sat on his horse as he followed the trail left by the fugitives. What he couldn't understand was how it always seemed to be just in front of them. Yes, it was snowing, but not heavily and it melted soon after it hit the ground. Almost as if it had been sent to slow his prey but not hinder him or his trackers.

They'd reached the place where the party had split, with Arthur going one way and Gwenyfar the other. The sound of the storm covered the drip of melting snow as it fell from the surrounding trees.

'I don't like this weather,' one of his men said. 'Smacks of witchcraft.' There was muttered agreement from all in earshot. Even Aodh had to agree with the conclusion.

'Whatever it is,' he looked at his men, 'it's helping us, so let's be grateful we're not in it unlike those poor bastards we're tracking.' He slid off his mount and examined the wet ground. 'Looks like they split here.' He pointed to the two sets of tracks going off in opposite directions. 'These,' he pointed to the largest set, 'look like they're circling back the way we've just come from. While these,' he pointed at the second set, 'are heading east. Three riders, one lighter than the others. I'd bet my life Arthur's sent Gwenyfar off with some of his soldiers, hoping to get her safely away before we catch up. Smart move. But the storm will have forced them to stop close by, I'm guessing.' He rubbed some dirt between his thick fingers as he thought of what to do next.

Standing, he brushed the mud from his hands and said, 'Right. This is what we'll do. We have more than enough men to split our forces and deal with Arthur and Gwenyfar. But, we're going to let him go for now.' He stared into the hard faces of his warband. 'Feargal wants Gwenyfar for killing his son. So, we go get her first, and then we come back and finish off this Arthur. Any questions?' Silence greeted his words. 'Good. Then let's go get her.' He mounted up and the band set off after Gwenyfar.

Arthur and the remainder of his men huddled together in the cave Idris had found. It was cold and damp but kept them away from the worst of the storm that raged outside. Emrys poked around at the back, looking for somewhere dry to sit.

'Funny stone, this,' he said, examining the strange blue-black rock that was split into flat layers.

Idris looked over from where he squatted, more like a boulder than a man, his cloak flipped over his head to keep the damp off. 'We call it Sglatys. Good for building with, you know!'

Emrys dropped the piece he was holding. 'It's quite brittle, isn't it!'

'Aye, that it is. But it's easily worked and strong enough, I suppose.'

Emrys shrugged and sat on a flat section.

'Any chance this will blow over soon?' Arthur called from where he stood staring out into the swirling maelstrom.

Emrys tugged his beard. 'It's no natural storm, so it will wane when the caster of the spell becomes weakened.'

'And how long could that be?'

'Shouldn't be too long now. Morgana is strong, but even she can't keep it up for more than an hour or two!'

'Yes. You mentioned that name before. You said you would tell me more. I think now is a very good time to start talking, don't you?' Arthur looked at his friend, who merely shrugged again, and then started to speak.

'Morgana is a sorceress of great power. She gets them from Arawn, the king of the underworld, and they are dark and dangerous forces.' Emrys sighed in resignation. 'She's also my half-sister.'

Arthur looked up in surprise. 'Sister!'

'Half-sister.' He raised a finger. 'We were both trained on the sacred isle, but I was chosen to be The Merlin, and she couldn't accept that and became twisted by jealousy. Ever since, she's been trying to kill me and take my place, not that it works like that. But I think her mind has been broken through these long years of hatred and envy.'

'Was it Morgana who trapped you in the cave back in Camelot?'

Emrys nodded. 'And in the crystal cavern,' he said, scratching the back of his hand. 'You remember how we entered the cave?'

'How could I forget!' Arthur shivered at the memory.

'That's how I got out. After ten days of crawling about in the darkness like a worm, I found that tiny gap, and with only my hands I dug my way through to the other side, where I wandered lost for a time until by chance, I found the cave where we stayed that night.' He sagged visibly at the conclusion, as if releasing years of pent-up fear.

Arthur put an arm around the old man. 'I don't know how you did that. I know I couldn't.'

'Aye, well I was younger then, and full of hope and a desire to live.' He smiled. 'But more importantly, Morgana wants to bring about the destruction of Britannia. She worms her way into the halls of warriors and chieftains and poisons their minds until they do her bidding, while leaving them to believe they are in control. That way, she sows the seeds of chaos and destruction while hiding in the shadows. But,' Emrys said, 'she needs the sword you carry.'

'What, this?' He slapped the scabbard at his hip.

'Yes. As I told you once before, it is the Sword of Kings, and a very powerful weapon for good, or evil. If it falls into Morgana's grip, then all will be lost and darkness will cover the land, and if she can kill you as well then all is truly lost, for I fear there is no other who could wield this blade in the name of the light.'

The men who had been listening turned away after the old man finished his tale, barely believing what they'd heard. But Emrys wasn't done.

'Arthur. I found you wandering this land in search of a lost patrol. At that time, you knew who you were and what your mission was. But that mission is over, and ever since you've been lost.'

'That's true,' Arthur said. 'But my mission now is to get my men home, and hopefully find a place for Gwenyfar to live free from her uncle.'

'Pah. That's not your mission,' the old man spat. 'You're just using your men as an excuse!'

'I have a duty to my men,' Arthur countered.

'Have you asked them what they want?'

'No. I...'

Emrys turned to the men clustered together in the small cave.

'Men of Rome,' he began. 'You've followed your leader Ambrosius to the farthest reaches of the Empire.' Twenty-two stern, battle-hardened faces nodded in agreement. 'Now, your legions have left these shores, and abandoned you to your fate!' The men muttered angrily. 'Whatever future awaits should be yours to decide. What is it you want?' He watched as anger turned to confusion.

Gavain spoke up for the men, his calm demeanour making him a natural choice as spokesman. 'What do you mean, Emrys? Our duty is to Rome.'

'But Rome has left these shores. Would you leave here to travel there?'

'No, Emrys, I wouldn't. I'm no Roman by birth,' he said, 'and neither are my brothers.'

'Then what is it you cling to?'

Gavain shrugged. 'I'll tell you. It's your brothers, the men who stand beside you in battle, and it's Arthur who keeps you all together as one. That's what you cling to, and in these stormy days of upheaval you must cling together or be ripped apart and lost in the confusion.'

Emrys sat back down on his mossy rock and waited.

Gavain looked to the men and then to Arthur. 'We go where you go, Ambrosius,' he said, using his real name, before saluting. His companions followed suit.

Arthur felt the love of his men wash over him and was moved to be amongst such faithful friends. 'So, what's it to be then?' he asked. 'Shall we leave Cambria and try to make our own way to wherever we came from? Or shall we stay and do our best to help the people fight against the forces of chaos that threaten our very existence?'

'STAY!!' they roared as one, and in that instant the spell was broken.

'The wind's dropped and it's stopped snowing!' Alcaeus said from the cave's mouth.

Chapter 19
Capture and Return

Morgana staggered as her spell suddenly shattered, sending her crashing to the floor of Uther's tent.

'Lady Morcant, are you alright?' Uther's personal man servant Aeron bent down to help the stunned woman up from the floor.

'Yes, I'm fine.' She held her head as a pain shot through her temple, and groaning, allowed herself to be helped to Uther's sleeping pallet.

'Shall I fetch help, mistress?'

'No, Aeron, I'll be fine,' she smiled weakly, 'I just need a moment to gather myself.'

'As you wish, my lady.' And he bowed, leaving the tent.

Morgana sat in the welcome gloom as her head pounded a steady drum beat inside her skull. She couldn't understand what had just happened. No one could break her spell now that Emrys was gone. Unless… She lay back on the bed and stilling her racing mind sent her essence out towards the mountains. High over the forest her thoughts swept, higher and higher, until suddenly she was rebuffed by a force she didn't recognise. She tried again. But it was as if there was a bubble protecting the spot where Arthur should be. With a sigh, she opened her eyes and sat up, recognising the futility of trying to pierce a power beyond her abilities. She needed to go and see for herself.

'Aeron!' she shouted, and the man servant ducked into the tent.

'Mistress?'

'Saddle my horse,' she ordered.

'But my lady, it's too dangerous to go out. Lord Uther is about to attack Camelot.'

'Then we won't disturb him.' Her thin smile sent Aeron scuttling out through the flap.

Uther stood with his men in full battle array. His iron helm was decorated with a solid gold dragon and his polished coat of mail gleamed in the afternoon sun. His men lined up with their round shields forming a wall, behind which a forest of tall spears bristled. Kynan stood at their head watching the walls of Camelot, counting the heads that lined it. This would be a close-run thing, but nothing short of a full-frontal assault could breach those heavily defended gates.

The plan was simple. Archers and slingers would keep the defenders' heads down while the rest of the army climbed the steep track and breached the gates. There was no use for cavalry in a battle like this, so every man carried a spear along with a long-hafted axe and heavy knife. It'd be hot, bloody work, but he'd spent a lifetime fighting, and although fear still threatened to unman him, as it should any sane man, he pushed it deep down ready to release that energy when it was needed.

'SPEARS READY!!' he roared, and started beating his sword against the rim of his shield. Almost four hundred spears followed suit until the valley rang with their clamour.

'FORWARD!' he commanded, and the dragon host started up the slope towards the gates of Camelot.

'Here they come, men!' Feargal shouted from his position just behind the gate rampart. 'Archeeeers...' He held the word for a few seconds. 'LOOSE!'

A hundred arrows filled the sky like a black rain of death.

Outside the walls, Uther's men held up their shields as the falling shafts thumped into the rawhide-covered wooden discs. Most of the arrows stuck in the wood or bounced off the iron boss but some punched through, causing flesh wounds, and others found their mark and men dropped, shot through the neck or chest. Those behind stepped over their fallen comrades and pushed on up towards the looming gates above.

'LOOSE!' The cry came from the captain of Uther's archers, and arrows and slingshot were returned with punishing force. The crack of the heavy shot hitting the palisade caused the men behind to drop out of sight, while the arrows found their targets in the courtyard beyond. Another flight crested the palisade, wreaking destruction amongst Uther's force, but in a few more strides they were out of danger as the archers inside could no longer risk shooting for fear of hitting the men on the wall.

'Archers, to the wall!' Feargal cried, and the men in the courtyard ran to the ladders as slingshot cracked off wood and iron split heads, sending bodies tumbling backwards.

The attackers reached the gate and started hacking at it with axes as there was no space for a ram to be brought to bear. Rocks pelted down on them from above and the occasional arrow found its mark as men from both sides fell, writhing in agony, their lifeblood draining onto the frozen dirt.

'Keep pushing,' Kynan exhorted as the gates swayed beneath the pressure of men trying to force their way through. 'We're nearly there!'

On the other side, Feargal's men ran forward, bracing the collapsing gate with balks of timber ripped from the great hall. 'Keep at it, boys!' he yelled. 'Finn!' He called over one of his captains. 'I want a double line of men across the courtyard, shields up and ready in case they get through. Take one in every four men off the wall and jump to it. I'll not lose this fort to that bastard today!'

Finn raced off, shouting at men up on the rampart as arrows continued to rain down on them.

Uther, shield above his head, had joined his men at the foot of the gate as they continued to hammer away at the splitting wood. 'That's it, boys. Show these goat fuckers who owns this fort. Break it in!' A splintering crash followed and suddenly the doors started to swing open.

Feargal watched Uther's men as they hacked at the gates, knowing that if they got in, it would prove costly. He hadn't had time to fully prepare for the assault before the attack started, and down a hundred men, he cursed his ill luck that his own hubris might cost him his life.

Finn ran over to his chief. 'They're breaking in. What are your orders?'

Feargal felt the indecision writhe in his gut like a serpent. He looked at the gate, then at the men Finn had lined up waiting beneath a hail of arrows, shields over their heads.

'I'll tell you what we'll do, lad.' He grinned wildly at the thought that had just crossed his mind. 'We're going to let them in!'

'We're what?' Finn couldn't believe what he was hearing. 'That's madness!'

'It is, Captain, but it's our best hope to survive the day. I underestimated Uther.' He clapped Finn on the shoulder and told him his plan.

Aodh walked through a mist-shrouded forest. The snowstorm had vanished as quickly as it arrived, leaving behind a blanket of melting snow that dripped from every branch, a sound that was muffled by the thick fog that had sprung up as the warmth of the sun hit the unnatural chill left behind after the storm. His men rode in silence behind him, all except Colm, Aodh's best tracker, who kept pace, eyes firmly following the patterns left behind by man and animal. He stopped and raised a hand; Aodh stepped next to him. 'What have you found?' he asked.

'It's faint. After the snow, but here.' He pointed to a cluster of shapeless depressions half filled in. 'They headed this way. I'm sure.'

'Good enough for me.' And turning, he signalled the men to follow as silently as possible.

Ahead in the mist-covered woods a faint sound carried. Feargal's men halted, straining to hear if it was repeated. There. The sound was heard again. 'That's a horse, sir,' Colm added.

'Aye. And not too far away, I'll warrant. Right,' he turned to regard the men, 'dismount and fan out and around to the north and south. Keep silent, and don't give our position away.'

They set off in a wide semi-circle, creeping slowly towards where they thought the sound had come from. After a couple of minutes walking Aodh signalled a halt and sent Colm ahead alone to scout the area. Five minutes later he returned.

'There's a steep brush-covered ravine up ahead. No more than fifty yards east of us. There's definitely someone in there, maybe more.'

'How many do you think?'

'It's not a large space, so no more than three or four.'

'It's Gwenyfar. I'm certain.'

Aodh would be glad to be away from these hills and the strange sense of foreboding he felt. Turning back to the men behind him, he said, 'Head back to the horses and bring a couple of lit torches, just in case they don't want to come out.' He gave a wolfish grin. His men smiled back and ran off to do as they were bid. 'No point waiting around,' he said, and drawing his sword he motioned for the men to follow.

Kai's head snapped up as he heard a sound from outside their hideaway. He nudged a dozing Bedwyr. 'Did you hear that?' he whispered.

'No, I didn't hear a thing. But I was half asleep. It looks like the storm has passed us by!' He crept up to the lip of the ravine, then slid back down, cursing. 'We've been found. I see at least sixty men out there!'

'Uthers or the barbarians?'

'Does it matter?'

'I suppose not. What are we going to do?' Kai worried, looking at the still-sleeping figure of Lady Gwenyfar. 'We can't fight our way out, and I'm not going to let them take her. Arthur entrusted us with her safety!'

'Hey! You in the hollow!' a heavily accented voice rang out, causing both men to start.

Gwenyfar, roused from her slumber was quickly told of the situation.

'Are they my uncle's men?'

'I don't think so, my lady. There's quite an accent. I believe they're Hibernians.'

Gwenyfar's lip trembled in fear. 'You can't let them take me. They want me dead.'

Bedwyr felt guilty because he knew there was very little he and Kai could do to protect her. They would probably be able to take down a few, but their deaths were inevitable.

She saw the looks on their faces and understood what was passing between them. The feeling of defeat crushed her and she sagged to the ground, shaking with fear as tears filled her eyes.

'Let them take me,' she finally said, sniffing back her grief. 'They won't kill me here. Their master wants that pleasure, I'm sure. Find a way out and tell Arthur where I'm going. I know he'll think of something.' Before either man could protest, she scrambled up the bank, disappearing over the lip.

Aodh saw Gwenyfar crawl out of the gulley and try to dart away, only to be tackled by two of his men who brought her, struggling, to him. 'Lady Gwenyfar.' He bowed, laughing as he mocked her. 'My master requests the pleasure of your company at his new fortress.'

'His fortress? How dare he? That pox-riddled worm. He'll be crow bait soon enough. Just like the rest of your inbred kind!'

Aodh stepped forward and backhanded her, sending her sprawling to the floor, dazed. 'Tie her to one of the horses,' he commanded.

'What about the ones left in the gulley?' Colm asked.

'Torches!' Aodh yelled, and the men who'd brought them up handed them over. He walked to the edge and looking down, saw Kai and Bedwyr, swords drawn waiting below. He smiled down at them then tossed in the torches, watching the two men scramble back from the fire as the flames took hold.

'Let's go.' Aodh mounted and the party galloped away from the blazing ravine.

Kai and Bedwyr, coughing, had retreated from the flames to where their terrified horses whinnied in fear as they sought escape. 'We've got to find a way out quickly, Kai.' Bedwyr covered his face with the hem of his cloak against the choking smoke. 'How far down does this gulley run do you think?'

'Not far enough,' his friend replied. 'We're trapped!'

Lionides pushed the branches he'd erected as a barrier aside and led his horse out from the overhang, stamping his feet to bring back his circulation. The storm had passed and he needed to find Gwenyfar to make sure she was safe. As he mounted his horse he caught a faint smell of smoke. *That must be their campfire*, he thought as he turned in its direction.

As he got closer, he could see smoke billowing through the trees. He dug his heels in and his steed leapt forwards. This was too much smoke for a simple campfire, and fear put wings to his heels as he drove his horse to greater effort. Leaping down, he rushed to the edge of the ravine, only to be driven back by a wave of scorching heat as the fire consumed the brush below.

'Gwenyfar!' he shouted above the noise of the flames.

'Lionides? It's us, Bedwyr and Kai. For the love of God, man, get us out of here!'

Casting about for something to use on the flames he started to throw handfuls of snow over it. But it had little effect; it hissed and spat but continued to burn. Running over to his horse, he grabbed his spear and began pulling the brush back from his friends, allowing him to see their frightened blackened faces.

'Do you have any rope?' Kai called out, coughing.

Lionides grabbed a coil of rope. 'What now?'

'Tie one end to your saddle, then throw it down here. We'll tie it off to the burning bushes, then you pull them out of the way. Okay!'

'Got it.' Lio passed the coil down to his friends as the fire threatened to engulf them.

After what seemed forever Bedwyr shouted, 'We're ready!' Lio grabbed the reins of his horse and leapt into the saddle immediately, digging his heels in hard. The willing beast shot forward, taking the strain of the rope. Then, with a great tearing sound, the flaming bushes were dragged out of the gulley and along the path out of harm's way.

Drawing his knife, Lionides cut the rope and let the bushes burn themselves out in a large snow drift.

Coughing and spluttering, Kai and Bedwyr, leading their three horses clambered out of the ravine that was nearly their tomb.

'Thank you, brother.' Kai leant forward and still coughing, spat a wad of black spit onto the ground.

'Where is Gwenyfar?' Lionides looked at the two crestfallen men.

'She surrendered herself to the barbarians to save us.' Bedwyr looked ashamed. 'There was nothing we could do. I counted at least sixty, maybe more!'

'She was amazing,' Kai agreed. 'She knew if we survived there was a chance to rescue her. We need to get back to Arthur at once!'

'Then what are we waiting for?' Lionides mounted as his companions, still wheezing and hacking, followed suit.

Cadoc had watched Gwenyfar be taken by Feargal's men. Uther wouldn't be pleased. He'd hoped there would be a pitched battle between the two forces, and during the confusion Cadoc would steal Gwenyfar away from under the noses of the combatants. But that's not how it had turned out.

'What now, sir?' Llew stood ready, as did the other men.

He sighed. 'There's not much we can do but head back to camp and tell Uther that we've failed.'

The despondent band headed back the way the Hibernians had taken, so they missed Lionides rescuing his friends from the flames.

As the three companions headed towards where they'd last seen Arthur, they found the tracks of two separate parties.

'Two.' Kai coughed, clearing his lungs of the smoke still. 'Two sets of tracks. Curious.'

'It looks like someone was shadowing the barbarians.' Bedwyr leaned from his saddle, checking the trail. 'And I guess they're not ours or they'd have stopped to help!'

'So that leaves Uther's men,' Lionides stated. 'But a small band only. If we can find Arthur quickly, we can overtake them and finish them off!' His anger at losing his love blazed brightly.

'You're right on one count. We need to get back to Arthur quickly. But to come back and slaughter these men, that's not right. It's not Arthur's way, Lio, and you know it.'

Although he was being chastised, Lionides didn't hear. The pounding of the blood in his head drowned out their words.

Arthur and the remaining knights headed back towards Uther's valley, following a different trail from the one they'd used to leave. The snowstorm had only affected a very localised area, making the return journey far easier than they could have wished for. The sky blazed a bright blue, with the sun passing towards the west as it headed for who knew where in its eternal dance. Small creatures could be heard scratching around in the undergrowth, and birds darted from tree to tree as the mounted men passed through their territory, calling alarms to any that could hear.

'It seems to me,' Idris pondered, looking over at Emrys, 'that this sister of yours was only trying to slow us down, and not kill us.'

'How so?' Emrys watched the burly chief as he walked alongside the horsemen. 'Well, this storm she sent. It dumped so much snow in such a short time that it forced us to seek shelter. If she'd wanted to kill us, she just needed to freeze us slowly as we travelled, you know, less snow but longer lasting. That way we wouldn't have stopped so suddenly.'

'So why did she want us to stop?'

'Because,' Arthur joined the conversation, 'she didn't want us to go too far and lose the chance to get her hands on this.' He drew Caliburn from its sheath and held it aloft so the dying sunlight reflected off its shimmering blade.

'She wants the blade, that's true. But she doesn't want it in your hands.' Emrys was struggling to figure out what her plan was. How did she intend to relieve Arthur of Caliburn? That was the question that would unlock the answers he sought!

Lionides, Bedwyr, and Kai returned to the spot where they'd last seen Arthur, but there was no sign of their companions. They decided to follow the track back towards Camelot and hope to catch up to the Hibernians, and see if they could somehow get to Gwenyfar before they met up with the rest of their war band.

Cadoc's band followed the barbarians from a safe distance, keeping pace with them from deep in the trees. They watched as the rearguard disappeared down the slope and around a rocky bend before they began to move on. But, unbeknownst to Cadoc, Arthur's men had seen them and were following closely.

'Do we take them, Arthur?' Alcaeus fingered the heavy spear he carried. 'We could easily catch them unawares. There's only ten of 'em!'

The rest of the men agreed, but Arthur wasn't sure.

'We might bring those Hibernians they're following charging back up to see what's going on,' he worried.

'But why are they following each other?' Emrys rubbed his chin. 'Those barbarians must have been after us is my guess, to send so many men.'

Just then, Lionides and the other two missing knights appeared out of the mist that still shrouded the mountainside. Alcaeus trotted over and grasped his best friend's arm in greeting.

'Well met, brother,' he said. 'I didn't think to see your pretty face again!'

The other men welcomed Bedwyr and Kai back, but Arthur looked to his three men. 'Where's Gwenyfar?' His voice sounded strained.

'Hibernians took her, sir,' Kai told his leader sadly. They then told all that had happened from when the storm hit, leaving nothing out.

'Damn it all!' Arthur slapped his sword hilt, gripping it with whitened knuckles. 'That's what those whoresons were after.'

'And why Uther's men were following behind,' Emrys cut in.

'That answers two questions and gives us our decision. We take down Uther's men and then try to rescue Gwenyfar before they reach their camp.'

Cadoc heard the cry of alarm from the rear of his troop as they followed the trail left by Feargal's men. The thundering of hooves caused him to turn in shock and see Arthur and his warriors almost upon them. With no time to organise a defence or to flee, Cadoc roared for his men to dismount and head for the cover of the trees.

Slipping from his saddle, he and a few of the men nearest the front avoided the initial clash as Arthur's heavily armoured knights tore through the lightly protected scouts. Screams and groans filled the air as men fell, spitted on lances or hacked with axe and sword. Soon the ground lay littered with the dead and dying remains of Cadoc's command. Only himself, Llew, and four others had survived the first contact, crouched behind the boles of large trees. He watched as the knights expertly controlled their mounts, looking around for more targets.

Suddenly a cry went up. 'Over there!' Despite the danger, the four men who'd gone with Cadoc, on some unheard word had made a break for it, running deeper into the woods. At once the horsemen went after them, crashing through briars and scrub in pursuit. As he watched from his concealed position the four men were cut down without hesitation. Looking over to where Llew was lying, almost buried in the carpet of needles, Cadoc nodded a warning as the horsemen returned. Llew's eyes suddenly grew large, showing the whites. At the same time Cadoc felt a sword point press into the back of his neck.

'Well, well. What do we have here? Up you get, laddie!' Idris poked the prone man again. 'Come on, quick as you like, and call your friend out too. I saw you trying to signal him. Where is he?'

Cadoc sighed and stood up, hands raised. Llew followed suit.

'So!' Arthur sat on a fallen tree, spinning his sword on its point, watching as the tip burrowed into the earth. 'What am I going to do with you two?' Cadoc and Llew were on their knees facing the enormous warrior and surrounded by his mounted men.

'We were only sent to watch the barbarians,' Cadoc pleaded. 'Uther was hoping we could save Gwenyfar, we—'

'Liar!' thundered Arthur. He placed the tip of Caliburn under Cadoc's chin, tilting his head back. 'Now is a time for truth, and time is running short. So, tell me. The truth.'

Cadoc crossed himself and swallowed. 'My lord,' he began.

But Arthur silenced him. 'Are you a Christian?' he asked.

'Yes, Lord.' Cadoc fumbled the tiny cross from his undershirt and held it up for Arthur to see.

Arthur smiled and pulled a similar cross from his shirt. 'So tell me,' he began, 'and swear on the cross, why you were up here.'

Cadoc was stunned to see another Christian in these lands. For most of his adult life he'd had to hide his faith for fear of retribution. Tears of joy and relief tumbled down his cheeks.

'Oh, Lord. You are a Christian too. Praise be to God,' he declaimed. 'Yes, I swear on this cross, that all we were instructed to do was to follow the barbarians and see if they captured Lady Gwenyfar, and to hopefully get her back before she's taken to Camelot. On this I swear,' he repeated.

Arthur studied the face of this unknown warrior looking for guile, but saw none.

'I believe you,' he said. 'Uther probably hoped we'd all kill each other and then you could take advantage of the situation. Am I right?'

'That's about the size of it,' Cadoc answered truthfully.

'But it hasn't answered the question of what I'm going to do with the two of you,' Arthur repeated, 'and did you say that Uther's not in Camelot, or did I mishear?'

'Yes, Lord. I mean no. Uther's not in Camelot. The Hibernians beat him there.'

'Ha!' Idris slapped his thigh in mirth. 'The goat turd lost his house for a second time in as many days!' He continued to chuckle as Arthur once again looked into Cadoc's eyes.

Cadoc swallowed, feeling as if this man was staring into his soul and weighing it against the scales of his life.

'Are you a good man? Cadoc, wasn't it?'

'I think so, sir.' His reply trembled on his tongue. 'I try to be, at least.'

'Hmm.' Arthur pursed his lips in thought.

'Ach. Be done with them both,' Idris muttered, and some of the men nodded in agreement. 'We don't have time for this if we're to save Gwenyfar!' he added.

'No. I don't think so,' was his reply. 'I think God has led us all to this point, and you, Cadoc, are part of his plan.' He looked over at Llew, who had remained silent throughout. 'And what of your friend here?'

'He's a good man, my lord,' Cadoc swore. 'Though not a Christian,' he added. 'But a fine and honest man, nonetheless.'

'I have a mind to spare you both,' Arthur started. Idris and some of the men protested, but he raised a hand and silenced them. 'If you swear on the blood of our saviour that you'll follow and be loyal only to me. So help you God!'

Cadoc, a look of relief filling his face, removed the small cross that had saved his life and swore fealty to Arthur before God and his servants.

Llew looked around nervously and swallowing, said, 'I don't worship the Christ God but Uther is not a kind man, so I don't feel as if I'm breaking oath with my lord, as I had little choice in the matter. So now I swear on all that I hold dear that I will serve only you unto death. I hope that will suffice?' he added.

Arthur stood and, offering a hand, helped both men to their feet. 'Welcome to my company. Now, we've wasted enough time. We need to find Gwenyfar.'

'They'll nearly be at Camelot now,' Cadoc said.

'What will they do to her?' Lionides' worried voice called out.

Emrys turned to look at the blond-haired warrior. 'They'll want to punish her for what she did to the chief's son. My guess is they'll burn her alive!'

Lionides cried out in anguish as he felt his heart breaking. 'Arthur. We must go now. It's imperative we save her.'

'But how?' Arthur climbed onto his saddle. 'How can we save her? We don't have enough men to take on an entire army!'

Idris walked his pony to Arthur's side. 'Is it an army you need, Arthur?' He winked, and cupping his hands to his mouth let out a long, haunting howl that filled the air, silencing the birds and small creatures that fear such beasts. As the sound faded, the company sat listening to the silence.

'So what now?' Barcus asked, impatient to be off.

'Just wait, friend, Barcus,' said Idris.

Then from a distance an answering howl rose on the wind, followed seconds later by more, seeming to come from every direction.

'What's going on, Idris?' Arthur enquired.

'Well,' began the burly Cambrian, 'it might be, that when I sent my men away with those refugees, I might have asked them to spread the word of the coming of the once and future King, and maybe you might just have an army. Look.' He pointed out into the trees where shadowy figures were starting to appear.

'Idris!' Arthur slapped his friend across the back. 'Did anyone ever tell you, you're a bloody marvel!'

Idris blushed, embarrassed by the praise. 'I just thought you may need some help. Seeing as you can't stay away from trouble!' He grinned under his bushy beard.

Cadoc added, 'There's a secret entrance into Camelot, my lord.'

Arthur turned to the newest member of his company. 'Go on, Cadoc, tell me.'

'Well,' he began, 'when you beat Uther at the gates, his mistress, Morcant—'

Emrys stepped in. 'Morcant you say?' He looked at Arthur. 'I'll bet all the gold in that mountain that Morcant is Morgana!'

Morgana had heard all that passed between Arthur and Uther's captured man, Cadoc. She hissed in anger as Emrys, who still lived, had figured out she was manipulating Uther in the guise of Morcant. She wouldn't now be able to return to him, as once her true nature was known and named, that particular glamour would no longer work. She cursed again as she heard the approach of the mountain man's clansmen. She couldn't allow herself to be taken out in the open as Emrys would surely see her dead this time. But what to do? There wasn't enough time to build a new identity. It took more effort and life force than could be imagined to fashion a successful glamour. Eilonwy was still a useful character, she mused, but Uther would take too long to seduce, and anyway, there was no time as the battle raging below was coming to a crucial point. Everything was starting to move too fast and she could feel her control slipping away. Spitting in fury and cursing her ill fortune, Morgana skulked back into the trees from her hiding place and made her way back down to the valley to try and salvage what she could of the day.

Chapter 20
Defeat

Uther roared at his men, urging them on to greater effort as the great gates of Camelot started to open.

'We've done it, boys!' he shouted above the clamour of battle. 'Just one more push!' His men heaved with all their might, feeling the wood giving way under their hands. With cries of triumph and victory they threw open the gates of Camelot and rushed into the courtyard beyond.

''Now, you whoresons. Loose!' Feargal screamed from next to his men, who were lined up just beyond the gates. As they swung wide, more than a hundred spears thrown at close range decimated the front ranks of Uther's men. 'Shields up!' he shouted, and his men obeyed, overlapping with the man to their right, forming a solid wall of hide-strengthened wood. 'Now. Forward and push those fuckers back!'

Feargal's men shuffled into the startled and confused ranks of what had been a victorious army, stepping over dead and dying men pierced through with heavy spears. The men in the rear of the advance stamped down or stabbed those on the ground, leaving a bloody smear on the hard-packed earth.

Uther's stunned warriors brought their shields to bear and attempted to push back the advancing line, but Feargal's men had the advantage of surprise and a downward slope, and slowly the attackers were driven back down the path that they'd shed so much blood to climb.

Uther had fallen back to the rear of his soldiers and was screaming at them to push harder, but the fear was taking them and he could feel a tremor running through the line as the possibility of a rout flooded his mind. Looking left and right, he spotted Kynan on the far flank. 'Bring those slingers over and get them to attack from the sides, for fuck's sake!' he bellowed at his general, whose eyes had the same startled look in them as the men's. 'Snap out of it, man. Or the day is lost!'

Kynan suddenly regained focus, the fear draining away as he once more had a purpose, and running from the flanks he screamed to the remaining archers and slingers to shift their aim to the gates.

The captain's commanding heard their general and shouting for the men to follow, scrambled to a better position to lend aid to the struggling force at the gate.

Finn sensed the sweet taste of victory as step by painful step, the army of Uther was pushed inexorably back down the hill away from the wall. He stood in the front rank facing the fear-lined faces of his enemy, his sword red with gore as it snaked out over the rim of his shield to take another attacker in the throat. Ripping it free in a spray of blood that spattered his face, he shoved his shield forwards in time with the men. The sound almost a song to his ears as the rhythmic thump and clatter filled the air. Another step. Push, stab, withdraw, repeat. Trancelike, the men of the great war chief Feargal MacDuid gained ground. Until there was a strange discord in the rhythm, and men started to scream from the flanks as black shafts once more filled the air with the hum of death, and slingshot howled out of the sky like lead hail, crushing skull caps and bones and driving fear through the invincible ranks of the Hibernian army.

Impossible, Finn thought as a white-feathered shaft appeared as if by some mummer's trick to grow from his shoulder. Suddenly feeling the strength leave his arm, he staggered back in the line and was replaced by another who took a crushing blow to the side of his face from a lead shot, which smashed his cheek and left his eye dangling down as he screamed like a child, dropping his shield to try and push his ruined eye back in its socket only to be felled by a spear thrust to the belly. This can't be! Finn thought as he tottered through the gates clutching the wooden shaft that grated against bone with every painful step.

Feargal, sensing the momentum lost, pushed his way to the front of the line to lead his men by example, a huge double-headed axe clutched in both hands. A spear licked out from behind Uther's shield wall and Feargal pushed it aside and swung a blow that split man and wood in two in a fountain of blood and bone. Then swinging his great axe in a figure of eight, he carved deep into the ranks followed by his men, who, seeing their chief fighting alongside them rallied and started to hammer back, their shouts and war cries echoing.

From across the valley Aodh and his hundred horsemen cleared the trees and saw the battle moving back and forth at the gates of Camelot, like some great writhing beast drawn from the bowels of the earth.

Sliding his sword from its sheath, he turned to his men and said, 'The battle hangs by a thread. Our lord needs our aid in this darkest of moments. Who's with me?' In answer his men beat their swords on their breasts and the cry of, 'MacDuid!' rang from their throats as they started forward. Looking over at the man who had Gwenyfar bound to his horse, he shouted, 'Keep to the rear, but stay close. She's got to pay for what she did!' The large warrior nodded mutely and followed on behind.

'To Camelot!' Aodh bellowed. His horse's ears pricked and it picked up speed, heading toward the battle. As they reached the base of the hill fort, he shouted the command and his hundred men dug in their heels, sending their mounts into a thundering charge. Clods of winter earth were tossed from iron-shod hooves as the beasts laboured up the hill, smashing into the rear of Uther's men and scattering them as swords crashed into helms and shattered shields.

Feargal, unaware of what was happening felt a ripple go through Uther's men as the fear was translated to the front of the line. Taking advantage of the momentary lapse, he bellowed and swung his blood-drenched axe into the faces that appeared before him. They all looked the same to him as they fell like wheat beneath the scythe of his wrath, dirt covered and grimacing. Yellowing teeth bared in fear or anger, it didn't matter. Death was all.

Aodh felt the momentum of his charge start to falter as he reached the thickest part of the battle. Men choked every space and soon it became hard to push his mount through. Slashing right and left at the nameless faces that came at him, he pummelled onwards. A bright polished iron helm came into his view, surmounted by a golden device that he didn't recognise. The head turned and raised its weapon and Aodh struck down with all his anger, splitting the helm and cutting into the skull beneath. The figure fell from view as he screamed his battle song, cleaving a path to safety.

Then suddenly he was through and clattering into the courtyard, followed by those of his men who'd survived the desperate charge. The man holding Gwenyfar was one of them, though he was covered in blood, and as soon as he reached the safety of Camelot's walls he slumped dead in his saddle, pierced through by an arrow.

A great cry went up and the pressure at the gates lessened as Uther's men fled the field.

'Uther's dead!' The cry continued on. 'Uther's dead. The day is won!' And a ragged cheer was ripped from the throats of those of Feargal's men who had survived.

Feargal himself staggered into the courtyard, his mail coat rent in places, and his helm lost somewhere in the melee.

'Is it true, my chief?' Aodh walked stiffly, every bone in his body aching.

Feargal took an offered mug of water and slaked his thirst. Wiping his mouth with the back of his hand, he looked over at his kinsman. 'Do you not know?' Disbelief filled his face, and he threw back his head and laughed. 'By all the Gods, man. It was you. You slew Uther!'

'Me?' Then an image of a polished helm came to his exhausted mind; the face, familiar. The gold device. A dragon. Aodh put a hand to his head in shock. *I killed the Pendragon*, he thought.

'You're a fucking hero, Aodh!' The men around him cheered and chanted his name, as the shattered helm containing the mangled head of Uther Pendragon was passed up to the gatehouse wall and placed on a spike.

'Don't look so shocked, man.' Feargal grasped his forearm. 'The battle's won. This land is ours. Uther was the most powerful warlord in Cambria. Now he's dead, and that's thanks to you.' He slapped Aodh's shoulder. 'Let's celebrate our victory. Let's get drunk together!'

'I have brought you Gwenyfar,' Aodh said with an exhausted sigh.

'Ha. I'd forgotten about that little bitch.' He walked to where Gwenyfar was tied behind the body of his fallen man. Grabbing a fistful of her hair, he tilted her head back. 'Enjoy your last night, my lady. For tomorrow you burn for what you did to my son!' He let her head drop and walked away to the sounds of her tears.

'I didn't kill Arthur or retrieve the sword, my chief. I'm sorry.'

'Don't worry about that now, Aodh. I'm too damn tired to concern myself with magic swords. I just want to wash this blood off and have a drink.' Feargal strode into the hall, unbuckling his sword belt and tossing it to a servant. 'And pick up my mail and sort it out as well!' he shouted over his shoulder as he opened the door to what had been Uther's chambers.

Arthur had watched the death of Uther from the edge of the valley and saw the horse carrying Gwenyfar enter the hill fort. Behind him and throughout the woods, more of Idris' clansmen were arriving minute by minute. There must have been over two hundred men already with more on the way, and word had spread, as runners from as far away as Dyffren village had arrived to tell him that the lowland folk were rallying to his banner.

'I don't even have a banner,' he'd joked with some of his men, and was then surprised when Idris' wife, who'd arrived with the men, presented him with a flag showing a rampant white bear on a green field, holding a sword with a crown above its head. 'That's exquisite,' he'd told Bronwyn, genuinely touched by the craftsmanship. She'd blushed and brushed it off as nothing, but he saw her shining with pride.

Emrys walked over to where he stood, leaning heavily on his staff. Age seemed to be catching up with the old man.

'Please, Emrys, sit.' Arthur stood up from the tree stump he was sat on and offered it to him.

'Thank you, my King.' He eased himself onto the log. 'It's funny. I feel old, Arthur. I think time has finally caught up with me.'

'How old are you exactly?' he asked.

'Hard to say.' Emrys smoothed his tunic where it had creased over his legs. 'I have the memories of every Merlin who's ever lived trapped in here.' He tapped his head. 'I can remember when the first of your people came to these shores, and by that, I mean the first time. Led by that pompous fool Julius Caesar.'

'That's impossible!' Arthur stared at the old man who gazed coolly back. 'That was hundreds of years ago. Don't take me for a fool, Emrys!'

'Haven't you learned anything, Arthur? Nothing's impossible; the legacy of The Merlin is knowledge, all the combined lives my predecessors lived. I'm a witness to history.' He looked at Arthur with a level gaze. 'I was there when Caesar landed, and I was there many years before when the Celts arrived. I am the land, and the land is me. I am The Merlin. Possibly the last,' he muttered. 'But all that is irrelevant in this moment. We need to be looking forward, not back. So, tell me, what's your plan?'

Arthur looked at his grime-stained hands, turning them over and studying the whorls of his fingers. 'Cadoc says there's a secret entrance into Camelot. He used it when Uther fled from us.' That felt like a lifetime ago now, he thought. 'I'm going to enter that way with some of my men while Idris leads the rest of the army against the walls as a distraction. Hopefully we can sneak in and rescue

Gwenyfar before she's murdered.'

'And after you rescue her and save the day, what then? Do you plan to stay?'

'Yes,' he replied, simply. He'd come to realise that he'd been sent here for a reason, and he was going to see it through to the end, whatever that was.

Morgana slipped into Feargal's chambers. Now that Uther was dead, she needed to strengthen her tie to this barbarian chieftain, and she'd always found sex to be a very useful tool. Men were weakest when being led by their desires. She smiled as she saw him lying on his bed, his broad chest slowly rising and falling in sleep. The glamour of Eilonwy slipped over her and she climbed onto the bed beside him, only to find a thin blade at her throat, and a meaty fist gripping her arm.

'It's me, my lord. Eilonwy,' she gasped, smiling inwardly as she felt his grip lessen.

'You shouldn't creep up on a sleeping man, woman!' he growled. 'What do you want, to wake me so? And where's my fucking guard!' he shouted the last but heard nothing.

'They're sleeping too, my King,' she whispered, running her fingers across his chest, circling his nipple.

He looked at her then threw her off the bed as he stormed to the door and saw his men asleep on the floor. He gave them a hefty kick, but they didn't wake. Spinning around, he stormed back over to her and grabbed her by the throat, picking her up until only her toes touched the ground.

'What have you done, witch?' he bellowed, shaking her.

Morgana hung choking in his fierce grip, her legs scrabbling to find purchase. This wasn't going as well as she'd hoped. 'Please!' she croaked as he squeezed tighter. Her hands gripped his thick wrists as she tried to prise them from round her neck. 'Please!' A fat tear leaked out of her eye as she realised he was going to throttle her. No.

This couldn't happen. Not when she was so close. Her hands scrabbled desperately, trying to find something to help her.

Feargal looked into the eyes of the choking woman but felt nothing but contempt for her pathetic attempt to manipulate him. A woman could never know his secret heart. He squeezed harder, and then gasped as his breath was robbed from his throat.

Letting her fall to the floor where she lay like a landed fish, he reached down and felt a thin blade driven deep into his lung. Pulling it out, he looked at its blood-slicked blade and dropped to his knees, then turned to the woman who'd undone him. She just lay there, rubbing her throat and smiling.

Feargal held his side as blood and fluid leaked around his fingers. His breath was nearly impossible to draw in, and he gasped as he slowly drowned in his own blood. Morgana sat up and drew her knees up under her chin. She watched, fascinated, as the warrior before her slowly died, his weakening fingers scratching against the floor as he tried in vain to get help.

'Not so powerful now, are you?' she whispered, tilting her head to one side like a bird studying a worm.

'All that strength. Where is it now?' She laughed as he stared at her, weak gurgling noises the only sound he could make. Standing up, she crossed to where he lay clutching his wound. A puddle of blood pooled around his torso. Kneeling, she dipped a finger and brought it to her lips. Feargal watched in horror through his dying haze as this witch woman licked his blood from her fingers.

Moving his hand aside, she slowly pushed her fingers into the gaping wound, watching his face as it contorted in agony. She explored the cavity with wicked glee as he twitched and groaned, feeling his warm blood pumping across her hand. All too soon for Morgana's liking the flow stopped and she realised that he was dead. 'How disappointing,' she said, wiping her hand on his tunic and standing. Now she faced the problem of hiding the body long enough to do what she needed to. But first, she needed to prepare a new glamour. It would take time and cost her much, but the risk was worth it to finish her journey. So, she left Feargal's body and made her way to her secret lair, and, although damaged in Emrys' escape, her potions and paraphernalia were still there, though covered in dust. But as she reached the shelves where her spells were, she found them empty. Screaming in frustration, she flung a clay pot at the wall, smashing it and spilling its precious contents on the floor.

'Emrys!' she screamed, pulling at her hair in frustration. She no longer had what she needed to form a glamour. All was lost! She tore around the cavern like a tornado, smashing pots and destroying items that had cost her years to attain. Why was this happening? And why now after all her careful planning? It had all been for nothing. Morgana slumped against the wall, sliding to the floor where she wept at her failure.

This was the end. Or was it? She looked up, drying her eyes on her sleeve as an idea germinated in her mind. Crossing her legs where she sat, Morgana breathed deeply, trying to centre her being. She felt the rapid pounding of her heart and slowed it until a wash of calm drifted over her. There was a way out, but it needed to be thought through carefully. She closed her eyes, a smile curling her lips as she meditated on the problem.

'Murder. MURDER!' Eilonwy ran through the great hall screaming at the top of her lungs. Her shift torn and bloody and a livid gash across her breast. The forms of Feargal's warriors sleeping around the fire in the hall woke with a start from their ale-addled dreams, and grabbing for knives and axes, the men got to their feet in a rush of confusion as Eilonwy dropped beside Aodh, the dead chieftain's second.

'He's dead!' she cried, tears streaming down her beautiful face, a face now twisted by anguish.

'Who's dead? What's going on, woman?' Aodh gripped her by the shoulders and gave her a shake. 'Who's dead?'

'Feargal. Feargal's dead,' she sobbed, tearing at her clothes.

'How?' Aodh shook Eilonwy again. 'How did he die!'

'Assassins. I was sleeping in our lord's chambers when they came in. They'd killed his guards and then came for him. I awoke and saw them just as they reached the bed. They murdered him in his own bed. He didn't even have time to defend himself!' She sobbed again, snot running from her nose, which she wiped on her torn clothing.

'Who did this?' Aodh stood tall, radiating hatred. 'WHO DID THIS?' he roared at the cowering woman.

In a small voice, she said, 'I heard them say, "For Arthur!" as they stabbed him.'

Aodh leapt into action, shouting for the men to rouse the fort and search it from top to bottom in case the killers were still inside.

'Find them!' he bellowed as he ran to his master's chamber.

Feargal lay half in his bed, ragged holes all over his torso from the many stab wounds that had been inflicted. His lifeblood was pooled across the floor. Aodh sat by his chieftain and friend, twisting the heavy silver torc he'd been given not so long ago.

Tears ran freely down his face as he mumbled over and over, 'I failed you, my chief. I failed you.'

Eilonwy had followed Aodh into the dead chief's room and now stood behind, massaging his shoulders and whispering into his ear. As her poison words enchanted his mind Aodh felt his desire for revenge ignite like a blacksmith's forge, burning to a white-hot heat.

Throwing her off, he stormed back into the great hall where the men waited, having found no trace of the intruders.

One of the war captains, Niall, a thickset man with white hair and a milky eye, stepped forward and said, 'There's no sign of the murderers. They must have fled after their cowardly attack, my chief!' He knelt on the floor followed by all present in the hall.

'What foolishness is this?' Aodh demanded. 'I'm not your chief. He lays in there!' And he pointed back angrily as his grief threatened to overwhelm him.

'I'm sorry,' the captain explained, 'but you're his cousin, and with no other kin present this invasion is finished unless you take over command now. If not, we'll be at each other's throats by moonrise tomorrow trying to claim a piece of that fortune that lies beneath our feet.'

'And will the men all follow me?' he asked.

'Yes. The other captains and I have discussed it, and we're with you. We're deep in a foreign land. Trapped. We need to leave here as soon as possible and take a ship back to our homeland before it's too late. If you'll do this, then we will follow you.'

Aodh stood in front of these warriors, his emotions warring within him. 'Yes,' he said humbly, 'I'll lead us home. But I ask one thing only.'

'Name it, my chief,' War Captain Niall answered.

'I want Arthur dead!'

Chapter 21
Victory

Arthur's army numbered over three hundred men, many of whom were mounted on the stocky mountain ponies that fitted so well into this rugged landscape. Dawn wasn't far off and they were all aware that time would run out for Gwenyfar if they didn't act soon.

They had gone over Arthur's plan to sneak into the fortress, and they'd argued about him leading men into certain danger. 'We need you outside in the attack with us!' Idris had protested loudly. 'If the men can't see you, they bloody well can't follow you, now can they!'

'He has a point, Arthur.' Emrys stood beside the stocky chieftain. 'I say send one of your best warriors to lead, say, half a dozen of Idris' men into the passage, while you make a show of a frontal assault. It makes sense if you stop and think about it!'

The argument went on until eventually Arthur conceded and agreed to let Lionides and Cadoc lead the secret assault into the hill fort, accompanied by his friend Alcaeus and five of Idris' men.

'Hopefully,' he said, 'we'll be able to break our way into the fort, as the gates are too damaged to be much use as a barricade, and meet up with you.' He gripped both of Lionides' shoulders and gave them a squeeze. 'Be safe, Lio, and rescue Gwenyfar.'

Lionides saluted his commander. 'I'll save her. Or die trying,' he swore.

'I'm going with them as well,' Emrys said, stepping alongside Lionides. He held up his hands as Arthur started to protest. 'No,

Arthur. I must go. Morgana is still alive and I feel she's in that fort. She'll try to kill Gwenyfar just to spite you. I know it. And God knows what else she's been up to.'

'Fine,' Arthur conceded. 'But be careful. All of you.' He gripped the arm of each man in the small party before they set off under the cover of darkness.

'Now comes the hard part,' he said, turning to the rest of his men.

The morning finally dawned and Aodh sat on the throne that had once been Uther's, and briefly Feargal's.

Niall marched into the hall in his armour, his helmet under one arm. 'My chieftain.' He saluted. 'A large body of warriors has just come into the valley from the east. We think it's Arthur.'

Aodh looked up at his war captain. 'And the pyre?'

'Did you hear what I said, my lord? Arthur's coming!'

'Yes, I heard you,' he snapped, 'but I asked if our chieftain's pyre is ready!'

'It is. As you instructed.'

'Good. Good.' Aodh stood and headed for the courtyard. 'Come, we've a farewell to make.'

Out in the courtyard a huge log pyre had been constructed, atop which sat a funeral bier containing Chieftain Feargal MacDuid's body, in his armour and with his unsheathed sword clasped in his cold hands. His sunken, waxen features showed little of the man he had been in life. At the foot of the pyre a large stake had been driven into the dirt and stacked with faggots of wood.

'Fetch the girl,' Aodh commanded, and men rushed off, returning with Gwenyfar who struggled and screamed in their arms.

'You can't do this!' she pleaded. 'It's not my fault. Conor tried to rape me!' Her cries fell on deaf ears as she was lashed to the upright.

Aodh approached her as she twisted against the rough rope, the harsh fibres tearing into her skin. He leant forward. 'It's nothing personal,' he said. 'It's just that this was my chief's wish. He wanted you to pay for the death of his son.'

'No. No!' She kicked and fought against her bonds, but to no avail.

A horn sounded from beyond the walls, and all eyes turned towards it.

'Men approaching!' someone shouted from the rampart. Aodh looked to the gates where they hung loosely closed.

'This fort is no longer defendable!' he shouted. 'We'll meet these whoresons on the plain and show them how real warriors fight!' He pumped his fist in the air and shouted, 'MacDuid! MacDuid!' over and over. The familiar battle cry lifted the spirits of the Hibernian warriors who joined in shouting and chanting their battle cries. As the gates opened and the men filed out past the funeral pyre, Aodh took a lit torch from a waiting hand and thrust it deep into the brush at the base, watching as smoke and then flame took hold before turning his back and following his men.

Cadoc led the small party through the secret tunnel to the back of the great hall. After dousing the rush lights they'd brought he pushed against a hinged block, and a section of the wall swung open into the heart of Camelot. Whispering so as not to be heard the men fanned out into the room and began to search for Gwenyfar.

'She can't be in many places,' he said in hushed tones. 'This fort is ancient in origin so most of the rooms are above ground. But sometime in the past the men of Rome expanded it and dug vaults beneath the earth to house the gold from the mountain,' he pointed to a locked door, 'through there.'

Lionides, eager to start looking, spoke up. 'Let's split up into twos and that way we can cover more ground.' The group nodded agreement and set off to find the captive.

Emrys was to go with Lionides and Alcaeus but as they set off, he pulled them to one side. 'I can't go with you. I have a path of my own to travel this day.'

Lionides studied the old man's face and saw a deep sadness.

'If anything happens to you, Arthur will string me up, old man!' he warned.

'If anything happens to me,' Emrys replied, 'it's my own stupid fault!' He smiled fondly. 'God go with you.'

'And with you.'

Emrys slipped off into the dark hall.

As the other men searched the chambers above ground, Lionides and his friend broke their way into the undercroft.

'I guess Arthur's distraction plan is working!' Alcaeus piped up. 'I haven't seen a soul yet!'

Lionides crossed himself. 'Don't speak too soon. We haven't found Gwenyfar yet, or got out!'

'Fair enough,' his friend said with a wink.

In the darkness below the two men were forced to light a torch to see their way down the passage. The smell of damp earth and must filled their nostrils as they crept along, opening any doors they came to. Lionides entered a large space as his friend carried on searching. Barrels and sacks lined the walls, and on inspection he found they contained a vast fortune in gold. 'Alcaeus!' he called softly, but his friend was obviously too far down the tunnel to hear.

Alcaeus, meanwhile, had reached the far end and stood before a smaller door than the rest. Bending down, he looked through the small window lined with an iron grate and from inside he heard sobbing.

'Gwenyfar,' he whispered. The crying stopped and then small, delicate fingers slipped through the window, brushing against his heavy calloused hands. 'Alcaeus?' a soft, timid voice spoke from the darkness.

'Gwenyfar. Thank God I've found you.' He opened the bolt and swung the door open. Lady Gwenyfar fell into his arms, her dirt-streaked face buried in his shoulder.

'Thank the Gods you found me!' she cried. 'They were going to burn me alive with their chief's body!' She sobbed again, hugging the big man tighter.

Alcaeus wrapped his muscular arms about her and made soothing noises to comfort her. He couldn't imagine what she'd been through, held down here in the dark.

'It's alright, girl,' he soothed.

'It is now!' she said, and she swiftly sliced across his throat with a long, narrow blade. Stepping back, he clutched the gaping wound as the blood sheeted down his chest, the torch lying discarded on the floor as he sank noiselessly to the ground. Dead.

Lionides searched the gold chamber but found no sign of Gwenyfar, so he went in search of his friend who was further along the passage. As he walked, he called out softly. Rounding a bend, he saw up ahead the flickering flame of a torch. As he got closer he saw a mounded shadow.

'No!' he shouted and ran over to where his friend lay in a pool of blood. Cradling his head on his lap, Lionides rocked, mumbling to himself, tears sliding down his face.

Laying his brother down gently, he stood. An ice-cold rage burned deep in his heart, and drawing his sword he searched the final chamber but found no sign of anyone.

Morgana slipped past the gold vault, a cruel smile upon her face. She would kill Arthur's men one by one and then destroy Emrys' hope of peace in the land once and for all.

Making her way back up the stairs she heard the keening cry of Lionides deep below and toyed with the idea of killing him now. But as she went to head back down Cadoc appeared with one of the mountain men.

'Lady Gwenyfar!' he cried in surprise. 'We've been searching for you!'

'Well, here I am,' she answered, and stepping close she stabbed him through the eye, ripping the blade free and swiping it across the face of the startled hillman, who staggered around mewling in pain, blinded. Morgana closed on him from behind and slit his throat. 'Oh, do shut up!' She giggled. Then stepping over them lightly, she went on the hunt for the rest.

Lionides entered the great hall only to find the bodies of Cadoc and Owain lying cold on the floor. The sky outside was flickering under the heavy outer door and he silently crept up and opened it a fraction. Out in the empty courtyard a great conflagration was burning. He could feel the heat on his face and shielding his eyes with an upthrown hand he saw the body of the chief on top, wisps of flame licking over him as he started to burn. Suddenly he heard a woman scream from the far side of the pyre and turning to look, he saw a stake with a desperately thrashing body tied to it. 'Gwenyfar!' he shouted.

'No need to shout, lover.' The soft, sinuous words came from behind, and whirling around, he saw his Gwenyfar.

'My love.' He reached for her sweet face, confused, but suddenly felt a stabbing, burning pain. Looking down, he saw the hilt of a dagger sticking out from his side. His legs suddenly buckled and he slipped to the floor.

Morgana stood above him, the glamour of Gwenyfar shimmering over her own form like light. She felt the power of her sacrifices infuse her body, giving her strength. She knelt before him as he fumbled the blood-slick knife and said, 'Gwenyfar is going to burn.' The illusion slipped away and Lionides gasped at the change that had overcome his love.

'What?' she cried. 'Do you no longer desire me? You wanted me before, up in the hills in that clearing.'

'No. You're not Gwenyfar, my Gwenyfar. You can't be!'

Morgana cackled, a crazed sound. 'Oh, but I was.' The illusion slipped back over her and she leant forward and kissed his mouth, biting his lip and drawing blood. He tried to turn away, but he couldn't; she still mesmerised him.

'Now watch. Watch as she burns!' And laughing, she threw open the door of the hall, forcing Lionides to watch as the pyre took hold, tears streaming down his blood-stained face.

Arthur and his army had ridden into the valley just before dawn, and were surprised when a mounted party carrying a flag of truce trotted out of the woods to the south and approached.

Kynan had waited hidden in the forest with what was left of the dragon host, for a chance to avenge their fallen lord. When scouts had reported the approach of Arthur and the size of his force a new path had opened for them, and once Kynan had discussed it with his captains they'd agreed.

'My lord.' The unarmed general rode up to Arthur with both hands raised. 'I come under a flag of truce to offer you my life and the lives of my men in your service, so that together we can drive these heathens from our lands. What say you?'

Idris sat on his pony and spat. 'He doesn't beat around the bush, does he, eh?!'

'Indeed not, friend, Idris,' Arthur answered. He leant forward, both hands resting on the saddle. 'How do we know we can trust you not to turn on us or leave even, if the battle goes badly?'

Kynan sighed heavily. 'I'm an old man, Arthur. My glory days are long behind me now. Most of these men,' and he pointed to the remnants lined up at the forest edge, 'are just farmers. They want to have a home to go back to after today.' The old general climbed down from his horse and approached Arthur. Throwing his cloak back over his shoulder, he knelt, with some effort, in the snow-damp grass. 'I pledge mine and my men's fealty to you, Arthur. From this day forwards let us go into battle as brothers.' He bowed his white-haired head.

Arthur dismounted and raised the old general to his feet. 'I accept your fealty and that of your men. Although I cannot promise victory today, I will lead you with a full heart knowing we fight together as brothers from this day on.' He embraced Kynan, and the men of both sides cheered.

'Now,' he said, 'let's chase these Hibernian bastards to their boats and send them back across the sea where they belong!'

'TO ARMS!' the cry went up. Aodh and his war band poured from the gates of Camelot, almost four hundred strong. Though many carried injuries, their losses were few compared to Uther's men.

In formation they made their way to the plain in front of the damaged fortress, shields slung over shoulders and spears carried tall, swaying like a forest of leafless trees caught in a breeze.

From where Arthur sat slightly south-east of the Hibernians' position, he estimated that they had a similar number of men, although the barbarians seemed to have no cavalry, relying instead on their shield wall. *So be it*, he thought as they formed a long rectangle of overlapping shields four deep. The heavy clash of spear on wood echoed over the field.

Arthur's own men were arrayed into three parts. The infantry took the centre, Kynan's archers and slingers bolstered by some of Idris' men formed a screen in front, and two blocks of cavalry to the left and right. The sounds of shields clashing came to a crescendo then stopped suddenly.

Arthur gave a signal and from a dozen lips battle horns were sounded as Aodh's men started their advance.

'Slingers and archers ready!' Kynan bellowed, leading from the front as was his duty. Dozens of bow strings were drawn taught as the whirring of slings filled the air. 'LOOSE!' came the cry, and the sky was darkened as the black shafts filled the air, thudding into shield and flesh as they struck the Hibernian line. There was an audible grunt as they felt the weight of the lead shot that whistled through gaps to break skin and shatter bone.

The Hibernian advance faltered, but Aodh exhorted the men, clashing his shield and pushing his way to the front. He pointed his sword at the Cambrian line. 'If you bastards want to go home, you'll have to cut your way through those whoresons.' He roared his war cry and stepped forward. The line hesitated for a heartbeat but then joined him. Inwardly, he sighed in relief. A relief short-lived as the arrows came again and again, causing the men to hunker down behind their shields. 'Fuck this!' he shouted. 'CHARGE!' And waving his sword overhead, he started to run at the enemy.

'Archers, slingers, to the rear,' Kynan commanded. The men obeyed, smoothly slipping through the shield line. 'Shields up, eyes forward. Keep an eye on the man on your left and right. Brace!'

Arthur signalled the cavalry to charge and they raced across the field heading for the enemy flanks, but as they got close, the edges of the Hibernian line curled back on themselves like a pulled bow, bristling with spears. His men threw their light javelins but had little impact against the heavy shield wall before them. Suddenly spears were thrown back at them, causing the horsemen to peel out, away from the attack.

'Back to the line!' Arthur bellowed, and the horsemen turned back, galloping across the cold earth, sending clods flying into the crisp air.

The two lines were only a few dozen feet apart. The Hibernian advance slowed now that they were too close for archers. He noted the cavalry charge had failed, and smiled a grim death's head grin. Battles were won shield to shield, in the blood and split bowels of your enemies. Here there was honour.

The two armies smashed together in a grunt of shoving and stabbing. Shields were punched forward as axes swung up and over to pull down the rim of the shield in front, allowing a spear thrust or short stab to the face. Blood sprayed as necks and torsos were sliced open, churning the mud to an iron-red paste. The smell of fear and ruptured guts filled the air, as high above carrion birds gathered for the coming feast.

In Camelot, Lionides found himself alone as Morgana had slipped away, leaving him to die. The blood steadily pulsing out of him filled him with fear as he lay looking at the burning pyre. 'Gwenyfar...' His voice a whisper. He started to drag himself out into the courtyard towards the blaze, determined to save the life of the woman he loved more than his own life, and drawing strength from that love, he raised himself to his feet and staggered forward. As he drew closer, he could see that the fire hadn't quite reached the stake she was tied to, although the choking smoke was thick in the air and the heat was almost unbearable. Reaching her, he saw that she was slumped against the ropes binding her to the post. His blood-wet hand touched her face and she stirred, moaning softly. He reached for his sword to free her but found he didn't have the strength to draw it. Fumbling for anything to cut the ropes, his hand touched the dagger in his ribs, his gasping breaths bringing him closer to collapse. He leant against Gwenyfar and gritting his teeth, pulled at the blade buried in his side. It came free with a gout of blood that made his knees tremble. Gripping the hilt firmly, he sliced away at the bonds holding her to the stake. The flames had at last reached the bundles of faggots that were stacked about her and with a whoosh they exploded into flames, just as the last rope parted and Gwenyfar slumped into his arms, knocking him backwards onto the floor where he lay gasping.

Her eyelids fluttered open and she saw her rescuer unmoving beneath her. 'Lionides?' Her gasping breath caught in her throat as she was wracked with a fit of coughing. Gwenyfar rolled off the body of her saviour and lay beside him, looking at that handsome face so pale and drawn now.

Without warning his eyes opened and he smiled as he saw her alive. 'Gwenyfar.' His voice was so quiet she had to put her ear to his lips to hear him. 'Gwenyfar, I'm sorry. It wasn't you. It wasn't you.'

Tears slid down his cheeks as she cupped his face in her hands. 'I don't understand. What wasn't me?'

Her puzzled expression brought a faint smile to his pale lips. 'But my love was real!' His last words were said with the force of death, and he gripped her hand fiercely. 'I love you,' he said so faintly she almost didn't hear him, and then Lionides' eyes closed with grim finality. And Gwenyfar felt love for the first time.

Morgana stalked the darkened hallways like a spectre of death, her bloody footprints testament to her insanity. All of Arthur's men were dead. Well, almost all. She laughed at the thought. 'Emrys,' she called out, 'Where are you, dear brother?'

'Right behind you, Morgana,' he said, stepping forward from the shadows.

'Ahh.' She whirled around to face him, shifting her appearance as she did, so that now Eilonwy looked into those ancient eyes that registered a long-forgotten memory.

'Eilonwy,' he choked, and took an involuntary step towards a face that he hadn't seen in years.

Quick as a snake Morgana lashed out, slicing deeply across the old man's chest, causing him to cry out in pain. 'You always were susceptible to beauty, you old fool,' she crooned, madness glowing in her eyes.

Emrys felt the wetness of blood running down his chest. How dare she use that face? He brought his staff down in a flash of blue light, and Morgana flew back across the room, striking the wall with a crack and slumping to the floor. Emrys hobbled over, bloody footprints painting his path.

'Not her,' he shouted. 'Never her!'

Morgana looked up into the blazing anger flaring in his eyes, and smiled.

'I knew you loved her. All those years ago, I knew, even though you tried to keep it secret from your teachers.'

Emrys pinned her with his staff, holding her to the ground. 'You knew nothing of her. She was pure and true, and she loved me, and I her.' Memories stirred and his mind reeled back to a time long ago, of a red-haired girl with flowers in her hair. Of blue eyes and a bright smile. Tears came unbidden to his cheeks as he remembered what he'd lost, sacrificed, for the land he was sworn to protect.

His senses returned when Morgana said, 'Pure? I know how the two of you used to meet in the grain barn in secret for your little trysts.'

Emery's eyes widened. 'You couldn't know!'

She smiled her cruel, taunting smile. 'Dear brother, you were so naïve. Your precious Eilonwy didn't always meet you in the barn!' She watched his face for the moment of understanding. There. There it was. She laughed again. 'Yes, my brother.'

'No, you're lying. It can't be true. It can't be!' The horror of what had happened rocked him to the core of his being. He staggered back, his staff slipping from his hands.

Morgana stood and dusted herself down, smoothing creases and picking imaginary lint from her dress. She looked into his ashen face knowing she'd scored a mortal wound to his soul.

'But it is true, brother,' she sneered. Now for the final blow. She walked slowly around him as he just stood, arms hanging loosely at his side. Seeing how weak he'd become, she couldn't see how she'd ever envied him. He was pathetic. Morgana stepped up behind Emrys and leant in to whisper in his ear. 'Do you remember that last meeting in the grain barn, where you told your precious Eilonwy that you were leaving? That night you lay with her for the last time?'

Emrys nodded dumbly.

'Well,' Morgana leant closer, her lips brushing his ear as tears washed his cheeks, 'that was me. Your beautiful maiden was already cold in the ground.' She laughed her mad laugh and spun away into the darkness. As she vanished, Emrys heard her whisper, 'A child was made that night!'

He spun around, shouting into the shadows, but she was gone.

In the madness of battle Arthur cut and slashed his way through the enemy. The sword, Caliburn, an unstoppable force that shattered shields and broke iron as if they were made of brittle ice. Idris stood next to him, a feral grin on his face as his wicked-looking long knife darted from behind his shield to bury itself deep in the enemies' bellies. The fight had descended into a melee of bodies crushed together in a claustrophobic press, screams of fear and death rising high above into the mist that swirled from the mass of men. Swords and spears became useless as men clawed and scratched with hands or pulled daggers from sheathes to stab into any unprotected flesh. The fear of slipping over in the churned mud and being crushed by hundreds of feet drove the insanity.

Aodh, at the front of his men, bled from countless cuts, his mail coat rent in several places as he battered the Cambrian man in front of him. The broad snarling face covered in grime belonged to a large man with golden arm rings, wrapped around bulging muscles that he was using to push Aodh's shield back, threatening to trap his arms. Throwing back his head, Aodh brought it forward in a crushing headbutt, the iron rim of his helm shattering the giant's nose in a spray of blood, causing him to stagger back. The pressure now gone Aodh brought his knife up and stabbed it into the man's neck before ripping it across and nearly severing the head. The now lifeless body dropped to the ground, adding more blood to the morass beneath the feet of the living.

The battle had ceased all forward movement and was slowly turning as men pushed and shoved to gain advantage. At the centre of the swirling melee Arthur couldn't tell how the battle was going. He'd lost sight of Idris, and the old general Kynan had been injured early on and was dragged out by some of his men. A short dagger sliced across his vision and by instinct he raised his shield, feeling the rim breaking the wrist of his assailant. Thrusting with Caliburn, he felt the sword cut through leather and flesh, and the man fell away.

Sweat running down his face from under his helmet stung his eyes as he momentarily rested, drawing in great lungfuls of air before the next man came forward, hacking at him with a short axe that split his shield. Dropping the now useless wooden disc he grabbed the wrist of the axe man as he swung again, pulling him forward onto the blade of his sword and tearing it upwards, cutting him in half from belly to crown before stepping forward again.

Seeing this, the men now facing him backed off, frightened of this giant of a man who split men in half with ease. A space was created and Arthur stood alone, brandishing Caliburn as men fought around him like water flowing around a river rock. 'FIGHT ME!' he challenged.

Aodh punched his shield forward, knocking his enemy off balance. Pushing once more, the man fell down to be trampled by his own warriors as his pitiful cries went unheard. He jabbed at another, feeling his knife bite deep, the taste of blood in his mouth and the smell of spilled guts filling his nostrils. He took a moment to look around but could see only helms and shields as men fought blindly, hacking at anyone in front of their blades. As he moved forward the pressure in front lessened until he stood in a calm space, like the eye of a storm, and there in front of him was Arthur.

The two men faced off against each other. Aodh grimaced. 'Arthur, we meet at last.' He put away his knife and drew his sword, resting it atop his shield, ready.

'I don't know who you are,' Arthur growled, raising Caliburn.

'My name is Aodh MacDuid. You killed my kinsman, Feargal. My chieftain. My friend!' He lunged forward shield first, forcing Arthur to fall back, sword snaking out and aimed at Arthur's face. Caliburn flashed, catching Aodh's blade and knocking it up and away. Swiftly turning, Arthur brought his weapon back around and shattered Aodh's shield with a mighty blow that numbed his arm. Tossing the now useless shield at Arthur, he pulled his dagger and dropped into a crouch, circling around his opponent, looking for a way under his guard. Spotting his moment, he quickly darted in and slashed at Arthur's leg just above the knee. The big man grunted as he felt the knife bite and the skin tear as he dodged away from a sword swing that would have disembowelled him.

Taking a firm grip on Caliburn's hilt, he drove Aodh back with the intensity of his attack.

Staggering as Arthur's fury sent vibrations up his arm, Aodh tried to disengage to gain some breathing space from this bear of a man. His blade, already badly notched was in danger of being sheared in half as the star steel blade cut deeply into the softer iron of his own sword. Suddenly, Arthur stepped on a half-buried helm and his foot turned sending him crashing to the ground. Seeing his opening, Aodh lashed out with a mighty blow, intent on taking his head only to be thwarted at the last second by Bedwyr, who'd seen Arthur trip and fall and raced to his side in time to prevent him being killed. Barging into the Hibernian, he sent Aodh reeling back into the melee where he was swallowed in an instant.

Helping Arthur to his feet, he winked at his leader and ducked as an axe sliced the air where his head had been a second before, then lunged with his tattered shield, smashing his attacker's teeth in a frothy spray of blood before stabbing him with his sword. Pulling it free, he glanced at Arthur and shouted, 'Try to stay on your feet next time, eh!' Then he too was gone, back into the mass of fighting.

Aodh cursed as he punched and stabbed his way through the throng, desperately trying to reach his hated enemy. *I had him!* he silently raged inside. Reaching the small space where he'd last seen him, he was surprised to find Arthur still there, engaged with two of his men. While his attention was elsewhere Aodh slipped around the side and came at him from behind.

Arthur turned an enemy blade and cut the man's sword hand at the wrist, sending the blade spinning. The man fell back, grasping his bloody stump. The second man, less sure, took measured steps as Arthur swung Caliburn in a circle, beckoning him with his other hand. 'Come, man,' he taunted, and with a snarl the second man leapt forward with an overhead cut that would have split Arthur's head down to his navel had he not dodged to one side. The man's face widened in surprise as Arthur swung his sword horizontally, slicing through his armour to lodge in his spine. Blood gushed from the wound, and as the man toppled over he pulled Caliburn from his hand. Aodh struck as Arthur lost his sword, but only a glancing blow as the force of his weapon being ripped from his hand tugged him off balance, causing the blow to cut across his back, slicing through damaged mail and deep into the tissue of his shoulder.

Bellowing like an injured bull, Arthur reared up in pain, feeling the cut to his back like a line of fire and turning, saw the Hibernian leader raising his weapon to strike again. Diving forward, he tackled Aodh to the ground, knocking knife and sword from his hands, punching and gouging as the pair of them rolled in the churned-up mix of blood and gore. Forcing his thumb into Arthur's mouth Aodh tried to rip open his cheek, but nearly lost a finger as the large man bit down hard, crushing bone. Crying out in pain, he felt Arthur's thick fingers claw at his face as his thumbs sought his eyes in an attempt to gouge them out. Rolling off, desperate to free himself from this demon, Aodh tried to scramble away, looking for a weapon to finish this fight quickly. As he slipped and slid across the muddy ground, fingers searching, he felt Arthur grapple him from behind. Trunk-like legs wrapped around his torso as the large man locked his hands under his chin and started to pull.

Seeing his enemy trying to escape, Arthur, groaning in agony, set off in pursuit. The slick ground caused him to stumble and fall as he tried to keep up. He watched as Aodh searched on all fours for a weapon as the melee continued its mad dance around them. Seizing the moment, he launched himself at the back of the clan chief, managing to wrap his legs around his waist and lock his blood-slippery hands under his chin. Tensing himself, Arthur arched his tormented back and pulled with all his might as his enemy struggled against his grip, fingernails scratching and tearing at the skin of his thick wrists.

With his legs kicking into the mud, Aodh felt his neck muscles and bones being stretched beyond breaking point until, suddenly, with a wet tearing sound, Arthur tore his head from his shoulders. Blood and steam pulsed from the ragged neck stump as his lifeblood pumped over Arthur, who lay spent on the ground.

Dragging himself to his feet Arthur raised the rent head of the clan chief over his head and roared in victory.

Niall had witnessed his chieftain's death, horrified that one man could pull the head from another with just his hands. As he looked at his dead leader's face he saw to his disbelief the eyes looking about as if in confusion. 'Dear Gods,' he whispered. 'He's still alive. He sees his own death!' This realisation unmanned him and turning from the enemy, he ran for his life. His men, watching in confusion, also saw their chieftain's head, and realising all was lost followed their captain from the field.

A great cry went up as the men of Cambria saw the Hibernians' spirit break and turn to a rout as men ran.

Emrys heard the cheer of victory from where he sat slumped against the wall in Uther's great hall. With a grunt of effort, feeling his wounds pull, he got to his feet and slowly staggered to the door and out into the courtyard. The pyre had burned down to flaming ash and he saw the lifeless body of Lionides wrapped in the arms of a sobbing Gwenyfar. He pondered what cruel tricks Morgana had played with the hearts of these two as he slipped through the open gates of the fortress. Looking out across the valley, he saw the army of Arthur cheering victoriously, spears and swords thrust into the sky as exhaustion melted away in the face of the primal joy of surviving. To the west he saw the remnants of the barbarian force disappearing into the trees. It was over. The old man sighed in relief then toppled forward onto the frozen ground.

Several days after the battle was won, Arthur sat stiffly on Uther's old throne. His wound, though significant, was healing well thanks to Idris' wife Bronwyn, whose knowledge of herb lore and medicine had saved more than a few men who teetered on the brink between life and death.

'What was the final butcher's bill?' Arthur asked. He looked about the hall, seeing too many missing faces. Lionides and Alcaeus. The loss tore at his heart. Cadoc, an honourable man in the end. Kynan had succumbed to his injury despite best efforts. Kai and Bedwyr. Bedwyr! Who'd saved him from Aodh's blade. And so many others whose names he didn't know. His head hung and he openly wept for their loss.

There was a gentle cough, and he looked up. Gavain stood there, a soft smile on his gentle face. 'Sorry, Arthur, but you asked a question.'

Arthur waved a hand for him to continue.

'The final number is one hundred and seven dead, with another sixty injured but healing well.'

'Good. Thank you, Gavain. And how is your leg?'

Gavain smiled and looked at the bandage around his thigh. 'Not so bad, thanks. At least I can walk!'

Idris rose from the stool he'd been sitting on. 'God above!' he declared. 'Are we going to mope all day? Look, Arthur, you've just won a major battle for our people. Uther, that festering turd, is dead. And you've driven those hairy-arsed Hibernians back across the sea. It's a bloody victory, that's what it is. You should be celebrating, not sat in the dark brooding like a bear in its winter cave!' The mountain chieftain sat down with a thump and dared any to question him.

Arthur smiled and turned to his friend. 'You said God above. Have you become converted since the battle?'

Idris blushed and chewed his moustache. 'Well,' he said, 'it seems to me there's far too many Gods here in Cambria. So I thought I'd settle for just one, and it looks like he listens, so where's the harm, eh?'

Arthur laughed. The first genuine laugh in days. 'Well, my friend,' he wiped a tear from his eye, 'it's a start, I'll give you that!' He stood and embraced Idris, chief of the wolf clan.

Gwenyfar sat in her old chamber staring out of the window at nothing. The face of a handsome blond warrior was the only thing she saw, and the sadness she felt formed a knot in her belly that she felt would never fade. Once more, unbidden tears welled in her eyes and she wiped them away with her sleeve as a soft knock sounded at her door. Rising, she crossed and opened it to see Arthur standing there, his sad smile a mirror of her own.

'May I enter?' he asked in his deep voice. She pulled the door wider, inviting him in. Gwenyfar returned to her seat at the window as Arthur lowered himself gingerly to the bed. 'Are you alright after your ordeal?' he asked.

Her lungs had finally cleared of the smoke and soot but she still had nightmares about the fire. 'I'm getting better.' She continued to stare out the window. 'I've asked some of your men about Lionides. What he was like.'

'And what did they say?'

'The same thing, actually. They said he was a loyal friend, and a great warrior. The best swordsman in your company, and that he loved many women. Is that true?'

Arthur smiled at the memory of his friend. 'Yes, that's true. Why do you ask?'

'Because his last words to me were of love, and because I think I loved him.' She turned back to the window and cried.

Arthur got up and rested his hand on her shoulder. 'I'm sure he did. He was different after he met you.'

'Really?' She turned back to him, a weak smile on her face. Arthur just nodded. Gwenyfar rose and hugged him, causing him to wince as she brushed against his dressing. 'I'm sorry,' she said, stepping back.

'It's fine,' he shrugged, 'just a little sore.'

'Ahh. There you both are!' Emrys stood in the doorway, his features pale and drawn as leaning on his staff, he hobbled in and sat on Gwenyfar's bed.

'How are you today, old man?' Arthur sat beside him, placing a hand on his shoulder.

'I've been better,' he muttered, 'but all things considered everything worked out, just not exactly as I'd hoped.' Leaning his weathered staff on one shoulder, he grasped his hands between his knees and looked down in thought. 'Morgana was cleverer than I gave her credit for. But thankfully her plans were foiled. Also she's completely insane, but I'd guessed that already.'

'Just what happened between you two during the battle?' asked Arthur.

A flicker of something dark crossed Emrys' face, then was gone. 'It's difficult to talk about,' he said. 'She tried to kill me, and then told me some things I can't share with you.' He looked away, clearly troubled. 'But you should know that she has gone. I can no longer feel her presence, and that is something we should all be thankful for. But I fear she'll return at some time in the future.' He brightened up, rubbing his hands together. 'Anyway, have you made a decision yet?'

Gwenyfar looked at the two of them. 'What decision?' She arched an eyebrow.

Emrys chuckled. 'I bet you've not asked anyone's opinion, have you?' He fixed a twinkling eye on Arthur who looked decidedly uncomfortable.

'Decision about what?' Gwenyfar placed both hands on her knees and stared at the two men, her frustration growing.

'Whether I wish to be King or not.' Arthur looked embarrassed.

'Of course you must!' She leapt up and took Arthur's hands. 'Didn't Emrys say you carry the blood of the Kings of old? And of course you have the sword as well.'

'Well, yes...' He rubbed the back of his neck, easing a tension that had formed a knot. 'But I've just never seen myself in a role like that. I don't know if I'm suitable.'

'And that's the very reason you must be King,' said Emrys, all mirth gone. 'One who desires power is always unsuitable to wield it. Like Uther. But those rare few, like yourself, who desire it not, well, that's a different story.'

Arthur rubbed his chin, feeling the weight of destiny pushing down on his weary shoulders.

'Fine!' he said at last. 'I'll do it. I'll become the King if that means you'll stop badgering me!'

Emrys smiled and Gwenyfar hugged them both in a warm embrace. A peaceful future, she felt, was a certainty.

'Now we just need a crown!' Emrys said.

Epilogue

Gaius Flavins Silvanus, wrapped in his winter cloak, walked the narrow step behind the palisade of his command as a chill wind swirled flakes of snow from a leaden sky around his head. He wiped his dripping nose on the hem of his cloak as he stared out at the white-shrouded forest beyond the fort.

'It's been nearly five months,' he said to no one in particular.

'Sorry, sir?' A young auxiliary guard looked to his prefect.

Gaius fixed his wine-clouded gaze on his wind-burned face. *Was I ever that keen?* he thought to himself. 'I said, not that it's any of your business,' the guard shrank visibly at the prospect of a dressing down, 'that it's been five months since Artos went to rescue a lost patrol. I was wondering if he was dead by now. He must be, I guess. A shame, I could've been rich,' he sighed.

'Rich, sir?'

Gaius looked at the young guard. 'What's your name, soldier?'

The guard snapped to attention. 'Lucius, sir.' He saluted smartly.

'Well, Lucius, don't listen to the ramblings of your prefect; he's a little drunk,' he tapped the side of his nose, 'and a little melancholic today. Go on, go about your duties.' He waved Lucius away and continued to watch the trees moving slowly in the wind.

'SIR!' Gaius turned to the guard who was pointing to the west. 'Something's coming.'

'Where, soldier?' Gaius leant over the palisade, stiffening as a shadow moved amongst the swaying trunks.

A lone horseman trotted out from the cover of the woods. A large man carrying a banner with a strange device emblazoned on it. As he came closer, Gaius clapped his hands in delight.

'Artos! Is that really you?' He laughed at the sight of the single rider. 'Have you come crawling back to my fort looking for your old command, after, I'm guessing, losing all your men to some band of savages in the wilds? Oh, ho!' He slapped the side of his fort. 'I'll take your surrender, and have you hanged as a traitor!' he yelled. 'GUARDS, GUARDS!' Men started to fill the walls.

Arthur sat his horse patiently as his old prefect shouted insults and insinuations at him. *Nothing changes*, he thought, smiling.

'Have you quite finished, Gaius? I have something for you!' he shouted back, beckoning behind him.

Gaius watched as his former decurion called a wagon from the depths of the forest. He counted a half-dozen sacks on the bed. 'What's that then?' he asked. 'The remains of your men?' He grinned at his own humour.

'No,' Arthur called back, 'it's the gold you wanted.'

Gaius Falvius Silvanus' jaw dropped at that. 'Gold. My gold?'

'Yes. As you requested and I promised as part of our deal.' Arthur didn't move. He watched as the prefect disappeared behind his walls, to reappear seconds later accompanied by a dozen men at the gates. Stepping out swiftly across the snow-crusted grass, he reached Arthur and walking past, examined the sacks. 'Jupiter's eyes!' he swore. 'Is there more of this?' He patted the sacks.

Arthur levelled his gaze. 'Yes, there is. But this is all you're getting. It's a fortune for a man like you, Gaius. You could go back to Rome and buy half the Capitoline Hill with that!'

'More, eh?' Gaius looked slyly at Arthur and the lone wagon driver. 'Seize them!' he commanded. The dozen soldiers ran forward, spears at the ready.

'I thought you might try something like that, Prefect.' Arthur gave a sharp whistle and suddenly the forest was alive with warriors, hundreds of them. Drawing his sword, he walked his horse to where Gaius stood shivering with fear. The dozen Romans bunched together had lost all interest in arresting this bear of a man.

Arthur leant from his saddle, placing the tip of his sword at Gaius' bobbing Adam's apple.

'Things have changed here, Prefect,' he said calmly. 'I'm a King now, and these people follow me, not Rome.'

'You. A King? Ridiculous!'

Arthur held up Caliburn. 'See this?' The bright blade flashed in front of Gaius' wide eyes. 'This is Caliburn, Sword of Kings, and it belongs to me, as do all these lands. Now.' He leant across and cut through a sack, spilling gold dust onto the ground. 'I'll tell you this just once. Take the fucking gold and leave. Leave and never come back. Or...' He pointed to the forest bristling with armed warriors, leaving the threat hanging.

Gaius watched as the gold dust fell to the ground forming a small glittering heap. His greed finally got the better of him. 'Yes. Yes. I'll take the gold and leave this backwater shithole, and I'll be glad to do so!' He dropped to his knees, scooping the gold back into his folded cloak. He turned to the waiting guards. 'Don't just stand there scratching your arses. Give me a hand!'

Arthur turned his horse and waited while the wagon driver jumped down and then mounted behind him. Without another word to the prefect, he trotted back into the forest.

'Do you think he'll tell anyone about the mine?' Idris asked from behind Arthur.

'Unlikely,' he replied. 'Did you see the faces on those guards? I doubt he'll make it to morning without his throat cut!'

'Ooh. You're a hard bastard and no mistake.' Idris smiled behind his beard. 'Come on then. Let's go home!'

The black-hulled ship ground up onto the gravel beach amidst a spray of rushing water. Morgana jumped into the shallow surf, feeling the cold water bite through her leather shoes. *Damn but it's cold this far north*, she thought. A group of heavily armed men dressed in black leather stood waiting, stony-faced, their long flaxen hair and beards blowing in the harsh wind. Climbing up the shingle beach, her feet slipping as the stones shifted under her weight, she eventually reached the group and looked them over. One man in particular caught her attention. He was smaller than the others, and his dark hair made him stand out as different. But it was his face that stood out most. His square jaw jutted a bit too much to call him handsome and his mouth had a cruel slant that was almost a sneer. She looked into his glittering eyes; a hardness touched by madness stared back.

'Welcome to Scania, Mother,' he said, embracing her.

'Well met, Mordred, my son. We have much to discuss and plans to make!'

THE END.

ABOUT THE AUTHOR

Hi, my name is Jason and I was born and bred on the Isle of Wight. I still live here with my wife Lisa in a village on the outskirts of the town of Ryde. I trained as a dental technician, a job I still do to this day. I find working with my hands allows my mind to wander and dream up ideas for books, which I am now starting to write down. Surrounded by stunning countryside and the sea, I find lots of inspiration right at my front door. So, let's see where my ideas take me.

Printed in Great Britain
by Amazon